BLACK RIFLE

ALEX DAVIDSON

Follow the gun. Find the killer…

A Novel

PROLOGUE

I t took 5.4 seconds for Arianna to die.

But when you're bleeding from bullet wounds, it's like someone switched the outside world into slow-mo and hit fast-forward on your brain. A story can have a hundred different beginnings and she wondered which one had led her to this end.

She could start at the very first one. The beginning of her life at 5:37 AM on October 16 at McAllen Medical Center. After all, aren't we all born to die?

Or maybe she should start with her earliest memory. The way her father pronounced her name.

"Are"-ianna. So guttural and authoritative. It reminded her of a deep, dread-inducing organ chord. The sound hell might make.

She preferred the front-vowel a. "Air"-ianna. Saying it that way felt like floating on a cloud.

Dad's diction was as tough as he was. How else could he have swum in the swamp of crocodile smiles and tears that was Washington, D.C. for all of those years, while Arianna's mother raised her (if you could call it that) back in a poor border town near Edinburg, Texas? That was where her mother and her father were both from. She and her mother had moved back there from

D.C. after the divorce. Her father swore he'd never step foot in that hopeless place again, and he never did.

That was where she first met the church.

One Mississippi.

Her father didn't get to where he was by playing nice. "Airy"-anna, on the other hand, didn't have a mean bone in her body. Whether that was a flaw or a virtue, she could not say. In theory, it seemed swell to love everything and everyone, but part of her was sure it was a cop-out.

She was the one her friends would call to talk about their problems, and there she would be, dishing out sage advice, which was usually just a regurgitation of some sermon she'd heard that she herself wasn't even sure she completely understood.

In her darker, more private moments, she wondered, *Is it not the weaker person who loves their enemy? Is it not the stronger one who stands firm against them? Does not forgiveness (at least sometimes) amount to cowardice?*

But then she would remember the church. And she would repress these thoughts. Feel airy. And float away.

Two Mississippi.

She remembered how her mother used to call her a "mostly-Mexican beauty." Mom had told her that there was some *gringo* in there somewhere, but she couldn't say exactly what kind. Both of her parents were fluent in Spanish, but they never taught her, so they could, as her mother would say, "talk about you without you knowing." Arianna would snicker and snort at this.

She was a nerd and she knew it. Thick prescription glasses. Faint freckles peppering the coffee skin around her nose and cheeks. In her free time, she read, preferring fantasy novels. Tolkien was her favorite. Most people assumed, given her appearance and hobbies, that she was a straight-A student. In fact, her grades were abysmal.

She didn't blame anyone, but she knew she didn't have the stability other kids had growing up. Her mother was a loving but negligent alcoholic and her father was absent. Affection was a foreign language to him. She remembered smoking weed for the first time when she was ten. Her first taste of alcohol came in sixth grade. By fifteen, she was completely sober. Most other kids raised the way she was would have been lucky to have made it to twenty without a police record, drug addiction or death certificate.

But those kids never met the church.

Three Mississippi.

That's why she'd moved to Los Angeles. For the church. She'd found a shitty hostess job at a trendy burger spot downtown, earning minimum wage plus tips. She moved into the only place she could afford—some dump in South Central—and divided her time 70/30 between her church and hostessing duties.

Initially, the move to L.A. was nerve-racking. She wasn't sure she'd belong. Fortunately, hipsterism was the in thing and what were hipsters but wannabe geeks with a dismissive streak? She knew she already had the geek thing down. A few trips to Urban Outfitters with her church friends, mix in a couple Bible-verse tattoos and instant hipster missionary. She fit right in.

But for someone who grew up so fast, she worried she was naïve. Believing the answer to every problem, no matter how complex or multifaceted, to be "love." A notion as simple as it was abstract.

Four Mississippi.

She thought of Sean from Tipperary, who she'd met last month when he helped her at the Central and 7th bus stop after she'd been mugged and had her phone stolen. He'd moved to L.A. with dreams of becoming a cinematographer.

After they'd reported the mugging to the cops, he'd invited her for a drink. She'd declined, then invited him to church. She'd told herself it was so he could be saved. Definitely not because she thought he was cute.

She'd been texting him only moments earlier. When she'd still had her whole life ahead of her. She was in her small ground floor studio apartment.

Did you go to church?

Nah.

Por k?

In hindsight, she should have looked twice at the large black vehicle looming on the street outside her barred window.

I thought you didn't speak Spanish?

Lol. Why do you think I spelled it por k? Why didn't you go?

She should have been paying attention.

Ask me in Spanish.

Punk. I'll ask you in Irish. Po-Ta-Toes. Boil 'em. Mash 'em! Stick 'em in a stew!

Maybe she would have heard her killer in the hallway.

Are you quoting Lord of the Rings? You do know Irish people and hobbits aren't the same thing, right?

Could've fooled me.

She might have heard the footsteps getting closer.

I'm about to walk into the movies.

Geez. What is it with you and the movies? Don't you have Netflix? Streaming will be the death of cinema! Good night!

Arianna grinned and began to type "goodnight," but she only made it to the letter "n" before the gunfire cut her off.

Her message was left unfinished. It would never be sent nor received.

Five Mississippi.

And as she lay on her apartment floor, her heart pumping precious blood through dark bullet wounds, she wondered, *Where are the angels? The bright light?* Why did she feel so fucking cold?

She'd never thought it would be like this. She'd never imagined she would feel so alone. And in her final moments, she was terrified that God was a crock of shit and that she had lived her life as a coward.

PART I

GOT YOURSELF A GUN

1

He went by Cal for short, though no one knew what it was short for.

He was putting on black Everlast hand wraps. He hadn't boxed since it happened. A single event that he couldn't even remember, which was nevertheless responsible for the last four miserable years of his life. Years that he would never forget. They say war is hell. Well, so is prison.

Cal looped the hand wraps over his knuckles.

That was the first thing the police did, he remembered. When they brought him in that night four fucking years ago. They photographed his knuckles. They told him the bouncer he punched had been struck with so much force that it was like the poor bastard fell from a third-story window. They could've told him anything. He had no idea what the hell they were talking about. He didn't remember a thing.

He Velcroed the hand wrap around his wrist and slid on his sixteen-ounce sparring gloves.

No, it wasn't taking pictures of his knuckles, he remembered now. The first thing the cops did that night was breathalyze him. He blew a .3.

This one guy he did time with was named Vinny. He'd wake

up every morning craving a hamburger, but it couldn't be just any burger. Back when he was on the outside, Vinny'd drive across town past a dozen or so other fast food joints just to get to this specific Wendy's restaurant because he swore on his mother that there was something different about the burgers there. Nothing like any other burger on the fucking planet. Not even like other Wendy's. They were the greatest fucking hamburgers in the world and he just had to have one.

Every day.

The thing about this Wendy's was it happened to be in the red-light district.

Vinny was a sex addict.

He didn't wake up thinking I'm going to have sex today. In fact, a lot of days, he woke up swearing he wouldn't. But he just couldn't go without that fucking hamburger. From that fucking Wendy's. He really believed it tasted different.

Like how alcoholics say cigarettes taste fresher at liquor stores.

Addicts are masters of self-deceit.

Cal didn't smoke. In fact, he hardly ever drank. But when he did, it was at 100 miles per hour, just like everything else in his life. It wasn't on purpose and he didn't blame anyone else for his problems. His brake lines weren't cut, he was born without brakes.

Cal stepped into the ring. It was like coming home from college.

His opponent had about thirty pounds on him, but punching wasn't about size. You don't strike with your fist, you hit with your whole body. That was how Bruce Lee could throw a one-inch punch and little Russian girls on YouTube could strike through tree trunks.

In order to throw a real punch, he had to be in absolute control of himself. Everything had to be in perfect harmony. There was only the present and the ring was the universe. Cal was completely aware and in control.

Like God.

Cal was an addict. But his drug was not tobacco, or booze, or pussy.

His opponent launched a jab and Cal slipped left, turned on the ball of his foot and drove his power up through his body like a pressure vessel. Flicking his wrist forward, he drove his front two knuckles through his opponent's face.

As his opponent fell backward onto the mat, Cal's brain released a flood of dopamine and he felt euphoric.

Addiction is like Russian Roulette. You spin the chamber. You get the high. You spin it again. You keep playing, sooner or later, you catch a bullet. Every addict does.

Miranda and Camilla were lying in bed, passing a joint. Both were unclothed or, rather, "naked in beautiful vulgarity," as Miranda would sometimes say. That was how Camilla gauged how high Miranda was. By the floweriness of her language. Miranda was not a flowery person.

"I had a dream last night," Miranda said, the roach glowing between her fingers. "It was awful. And weird. I woke up crying. I was on a roller coaster with my dog from childhood. My dog jumped out of my arms. I saw him skinned along the tracks."

Miranda took a toke. Held the warm, musky marijuana smoke in her lungs.

"I looked it up and it's supposed to signify the loss of someone close to me." She exhaled.

"You don't have anyone close to you," Camilla said.

Miranda grinned. "Only my enemies." She kissed Camilla on the cheek.

If you'd have told Miranda when she was a kid that one day, she'd be in law enforcement, she'd have asked you what you were smoking. She grew up in East Los Angeles with her mom and four sisters. She liked to say that the only time the cops were around was to arrest or deport brown people.

She'd watched her mother work her ass off day and night making tamales she and some other people from the neighborhood sold at unlicensed street stands. Miranda saw education as a path out of poverty. She studied hard, got into Cal State LA, where she majored in PoliSci. She saw politics as the best way to change the system. So imagine her surprise when the system came knocking. The ATF recruited her directly out of college. They said they needed people like her.

Miranda lay in bed watching Camilla put on a dark pantsuit and wrap her hijab around her head.

Camilla could feel Miranda's eyes on her. "Don't," Camilla said.

"I was only going to ask, why hide that beautiful hair? Especially in the name of people who think we should be stoned to death?"

"That's what you don't get, Miranda. It's not in the name of *people*." Camilla moved to the door.

"Have a good night. Love you!" Miranda shouted after her. The slamming door was the only response she received.

Camilla's work had her coming and going at all hours. Such was the life of an orthopedic surgeon. She was born in Nigeria. After her father earned his medical degree from the University of Ibadan, he'd moved the family to the United States to continue his studies at the University of Southern California.

Miranda and Camilla had met four years ago, when Miranda visited Cedars-Sinai for a hand injury. She had just finished a stint on a joint FBI/ATF terrorism task force attempting to link gunrunning on the Mexican border to Islamic terrorism. The operation did not bear fruit. Frustrated at the powers that be for exerting their energies in all of the wrong places, Miranda had punched a wall. Rather, Miranda had punched *through* a wall, receiving fractures to her second and third metacarpals, as well as three weeks in finger splints and, finally, a date with her orthopedic specialist.

Camilla couldn't understand. "What did you hope to accomplish by striking an inanimate object?" she'd asked. Miranda told her to think of it as a metaphor for law enforcement. Pointless at best; maladaptive at worst.

Miranda used to joke that after 9/11, federal law enforcement agencies rushed to hire more black and brown people, even though most mass shootings and acts of domestic terrorism were perpetrated by angry, baby-dicked white males. Camilla didn't like it when Miranda made comments like this. She believed that law enforcement professionals should not engage in identity politics.

The two lived in Miranda's loft in Downtown Los Angeles in an unofficial capacity. Camilla still kept her own place in Santa Monica for appearances. Or at least, that's what she told herself. She couldn't ignore the fact that although they had been living together for nearly two years, the loft felt like it had never been moved into. The walls were bare. The furniture sparse. There was not a single photograph. Everything about the place was transient.

Camilla fixed broken things. It was her job. Her passion in life. Sometimes she wondered if that was what she really saw when she looked at Miranda. Something broken. A life to fix. Her father had always taught her that if a body can be healed, then so can a soul. Miranda, on the other hand, always saw the worst in people. Even herself.

Hours after Camilla left for work, Miranda was still lying in bed, trying to figure out what to do with the rest of her night. She was tired, but not sleepy. She could work, but by now, she was too high. She could smoke more, but she felt she was already high enough. She thought about Camilla. Why did she always antagonize her? She had to admit she found it hot when her girlfriend, usually so imperturbable, got ruffled. It was lust, she knew.

What is the difference between lust and love? she wondered. How could she ever be truly emotionally attached to someone she so disagreed with?

When her cell phone rang, it was a relief. Although—and likely because—they never show it, the toughest people often feel the deepest loneliness. "Agent Lopez."

"Miranda. It's Bob Greco." Bob was a Special Agent at the FBI's Los Angeles office. They'd worked together on the Mexico gunrunning operation and he was just as bitter about the whole thing as she was. They both agreed that her SAC, Mark Scarpelli, was a political hack more concerned with jerking off his bosses than fucking the bad guys.

"What's up?"

"There's been a shooting."

"There are shootings every day, Bob. Why does the ATF care about this one?"

"You'd better get down here."

Miranda thought about it. She was still pretty stoned.

"Gimme twenty." She hung up the phone, went to the bathroom and washed her face with cold water. After she patted it dry, she put Visine in her eyes and rinsed with mouthwash.

She arrived at Arianna's apartment building nineteen minutes later in her ATF jacket, feeling fresh as a fucking daisy. The area was cordoned off with police tape and red and blue lights danced.

Greco was waiting outside. "Thirteen dead. Someone cleaned out the whole building."

"Okay." Miranda popped a piece of Dentyne into her mouth.

"I haven't spoken with your SAC yet. Wanted you to see it first."

Miranda nodded, sauntered into the building and entered the first door on the right.

Bullet holes defiled the room. The dead girl was by the sofa. Miranda gnawed her gum, slapped on some nitrile gloves and approached.

Arianna's vacant dark eyes stared up at the ceiling.

"Her name is Arianna Barros," Greco said. "Her father is Marco Barros."

Miranda stopped chewing. Her eyes darted to Greco.

"Yeah," Greco said.

Miranda's gaze returned to the dead girl. She noticed a small crucifix tattoo on her wrist.

"This needs to be handled right," Greco said. "When powerful people are involved, investigations can get messy. Given the nature of the crime, the ATF should be involved, but I don't trust that shit-sack of an SAC you've got over there. I'll only work with you on this."

"If you didn't have a dick, I'd fuck you," Miranda said. Greco was probably the only cop she actually liked. "Let's get to work," she said.

By the time Miranda returned to her loft, the sun was rising and Camilla had just managed to drift off to sleep after a long, caffeine-fueled night shift.

"I've just been assigned Senator Barros's daughter," Miranda said as she burst into the room.

Camilla got her bearings and sat up. "What?"

"Shooting in South L.A. Senator Barros's daughter was among the victims."

"How terrible," Camilla said.

Miranda set her box of files on the kitchen table. "This girl," she said, shaking her head. "Moved out here with a Pentecostal church. You know how these Jesus freaks are. Anti-gay. Anti-woman's rights. They stand for an America where you and I don't exist."

Camilla glimpsed a crime scene photograph. A pretty, sort of nerdy-looking young Latin woman, sullied by blood splatter. "How old was she?"

Miranda was too outraged to hear Camilla's question. "And don't get me started on Marco Barros," she said. "No politician has accepted more money from the NRA. He's one of the main reasons why the ATF is one of the least funded law enforcement agencies in the country. Now I'm supposed to give his rightwing church kid special treatment?"

Camilla looked back down at the photo of Arianna. A human face staring back at her.

"I need to be in D.C. by noon, their time," Miranda said as she finished throwing clothes into a suitcase. "I don't know when I'll be back." She pecked Camilla on the mouth and rushed out the door.

2

C al always hated offing fat guys. You could unload a fucking clip into them and they still didn't go down.

But that was what Pat Roti wanted.

The first time Cal met Pat, Cal had only been working in the private sector for a few years. He'd just done a job for some Mexican cartel boss that pissed off the wrong people in Washington. See, the CIA does black ops, but Pat's the guy the CIA calls to do the dirt that even they won't touch. "Beyond Black," they call it. Pat's got friends in all the darkest corners of the world.

The way Cal remembers it, it went down like this. He goes to bed one night, sleeping like a baby. Next thing, he wakes up in the trunk of something foreign. His hands were bound and he had a bag over his head, no fucking idea how he'd gotten there. They must have somehow drugged him, and he was a careful motherfucker. These were serious people.

These serious people drove him to some black site and sat him in a foam-lined room. When they took the bag off his head, he saw this old guinea in an impeccable blue suit and piercing blue eyes sitting across from him. Late sixties. A cannoli or two heavy, but otherwise fit.

That was how he met Pat Roti.

Cal would later learn that Pat grew up in Chicago in a place called the Patch. It's not really around anymore, but back before the Seventies, it was an Italian enclave. This was a time when Mob guys were running Cuba and whacking presidents. But Pat was too smart to join the Outfit. With his skill set, he could have easily been a godfather, but Mafiosi are motivated by money. Pat had always been driven by something greater.

Back in the soundproof room, Pat gave his spiel. To this day, Cal still smiles whenever he thinks about it.

"When I was a kid, I had this puppy named O'Connor. I loved that puppy, with his wet nose and bushy tail always wagging. He did this thing where when you'd pet his head, one ear'd flop forward, and the other'd bend back." Pat chuckled with unsettling warmth.

"O'Connor. Hell of a pooch. Loyal to no end. But he was also wild. Started with him chasing cats or pigeons or bitches in heat, then he graduated to bitin' the milkman. Before I knew it, he was stealing chickens and steaks from the Fulton Street Market. I used to tie O'Connor up when I'd leave for the day, you know, to keep him outta trouble. This mutt'd chew through the fuckin' leash! Finally, the neighborhood'd had enough. So, the coppers, they tell me, they can't help me anymore. Next time they pinch O'Connor, they're putting him down. Whacking my fuckin' dog! You believe that?

"What could I do? I gave O'Connor a little kiss and a nice, warm bath. I brushed his fur and I fed him a delicious little game hen. And then I walked O'Connor out back behind my house to the alley and with a pellet gun, I shot his fuckin' eyes out.

"O'Connor yelped and cried bloody murder, but after that, you know what? No more chasing pigeons or cats or bitches in heat. No more assaulting the milkman or sticking up street vendors. He once was blind, but then he saw. He fell in line. And I was always happy that I could do him that favor."

Pat leaned back in his chair. Crossed his legs and folded his hands on his lap.

"I look at you, I'm reminded of O'Connor. And I ask myself: what favor can I do for a wild dog running outta control in the neighborhood?"

Cal would never forget how Pat's eyes saw into him. Crystal blue, yet somehow black as coal.

"Pablo Escobar used to tell people *plato o plomo*," Pat said. "Silver or lead. You can work for me..." Pat shrugged. "Or you can take the other option. Your choice." He rose and calmly walked out of the room.

Cal immediately loved the fucking guy and hadn't worked for anyone else since.

Of course, that was all before the night four years ago when Cal got drunk and cracked a bouncer's head open. Guy like Pat could've easily put in the fix, gotten him off the hook, but Cal wouldn't have it. He *wanted* to do his time. To this day, he couldn't really say why.

There were no ghosts. That much, he knew. Cal felt no guilt over the lives he took. A soldier followed orders and that was what he was: a soldier. What he did wasn't murder; it was assassination.

It was sanctioned and, therefore, legitimate.

He certainly never decided the people he killed should die. He wasn't the Man, or even the finger. He was just the trigger to be pulled. But some poor prick making fifteen bucks an hour to babysit a bunch of lushes getting his head knocked off? That was on him. That much, he knew.

Maybe Cal wanted to see if prison would change him. Help him cure his addiction. Maybe, just maybe, he could be rehabilitated.

After he got out, he tried to get a day job. His options boiled down to either welding or fast food. He knew which one he wanted, but the welder felt too much like a gun in his hand, so he took the fast food gig. The burgers made him think of Vinny, the sex fiend.

And he could've almost gotten by. Miserable and anesthetized. But he missed the boxing ring. It was a pebble in his shoe. An itch in the center of his back that neither of his arms could quite reach.

He didn't feel like himself without it. Couldn't focus. Didn't recognize himself in the mirror.

But he stayed away. He worried it could be a trigger. Until he finally convinced himself, *One time. What's the harm?*

I can control it. The beast. I can kill it.

He Velcroed the final hand wrap around his wrist and slid on his gloves. He stepped into the ring. It was like coming home from college.

His mind went clear. His anxieties whooshed away. For the first time in four years, he was comfortable in the world. He was Cal again.

His brain released cocaine-levels of dopamine as his fist crushed through his opponent's head.

That same night, Pat called, and Cal took the job.

The target's name was Victor "Kilo" Cortes. Cal didn't know who he was or why he had to die, just the specs. 5'10" and just south of three hundred pounds. He'd vanished three weeks ago and the trail had gone cold. He had a brother named Hector in San Diego, who also happened to be his criminal attorney.

Cal was authorized to offer Hector fifty thousand dollars for the location of his brother. If Hector refused, Cal was authorized to do the other thing.

Hector lived in a four-million-dollar Spanish hacienda in La Jolla. Cal rang the doorbell and asked for Hector. He came to the door. He was short, chubby and well-dressed.

"*Plata o plomo,*" Cal said. Hector's brow wrinkled.

Sometimes they chose *plata*. Sometimes they chose *plomo*. But he never asked twice.

Cal learned that Kilo was hiding out in the Sonoran Desert near Slab City. "The last free place on earth." A community of snowbirds, squatters and drug addicts living on a decommissioned military base.

Cal drove through the dusty desert settlement of lost souls. Junkies, freaks, bohemians, artists. His Range Rover stood out among the rusted trailers, dilapidated trippy murals and ragged tie-dyed everything. He wouldn't be there long. Hector had given him the number of the burner phone Kilo was using and he'd been able to get a GPS lock. He passed the last of the outcasts and misfits and drove onward into the desert.

Cal knew that it took a special type of psychology to do what he did, and he was worried he didn't have it anymore. He'd been away for a while. He'd made a conscious effort to change. And he wasn't getting any younger. But whatever the fuck. When your number's up, your number's up, was the way he saw it. He sure as fuck wasn't spending the rest of his life flipping burgers.

These were the thoughts running through his head (aside from what a pain in the ass it was to clip fat guys) as he sat in the Range Rover with his headlights off in the middle of the dark desert. He observed Kilo's travel trailer with night-vision binoculars. He lowered them and screwed a suppressor into the barrel of his Heckler and Koch Mark 23.

He was always very particular about his hardware. He treated each job like a marriage and chose his firearm as a man might choose a wife. For this piece of work, he'd chosen the HK. It was a military gun. He could rely on it.

Power and silence were necessities for this mission. The HK was chambered in .45 ACP, one of the most powerful calibers available for use in a suppressed weapon. Accuracy was not an issue because he would be able to get close to his target, although the HK was a very accurate handgun, too, in case Shamu tried to leg it.

Finally, it was a large and heavy handgun, weighing in at 39.36 ounces. If pouring two dozen bullets into the fat man didn't get the job done, he could still bludgeon the guy with it. It was unlikely to come to that, but he'd learned early on to remove the word "unlikely" from his vocabulary.

He was the Stoic Archer. He had no past and no future. There was only the present moment. He knew that no matter how true he might fire his arrow, the wind could change or his target could move. Some things would always be out of his control.

Nonetheless, it should be an easy job. A single target in a remote location with no security. Pat never would have sent Cal on something like this before he went to prison. He knew the old man was testing the waters. He was just as worried about Cal's ability to perform as Cal was.

Cal pulled on a pair of nitrile gloves, stepped out of the Range Rover and crept toward the trailer. He peeked in the window. An LED TV was the sole source of light inside. It revealed Kilo, sitting in a recliner like a mound of clay. He was asleep. He had been watching *Inception*.

There's something ironic about sleeping through Inception, Cal thought. Was that the right word? Ironic? Maybe just funny. Cal wondered what Kilo was dreaming.

He picked the trailer door's lock with ease, entered and circled behind the sleeping fat man. Then he raised the suppressed HK to the back of Kilo's head and pulled the trigger.

The gun pinged and a chunk of hairy scalp blew off of Kilo's head like a piece of roadkill.

Cal lowered his gun and there was terrible silence and stillness for a moment.

Then Kilo grunted and came to life. Startled at having half his head blown off, he sprang to his feet, turned, saw Cal, hollered and charged. The trailer shook as Kilo toppled furniture and pounded forward. Cal raised his handgun and unloaded into Kilo's massive body, but all that luxurious fat cushioned the volleys.

Kilo tackled Cal, wrapped his hands around his neck and squealed as he squeezed his throat.

It's funny the things one notices when they're having their life choked away.

For Cal, it was a tattoo on Kilo's right forearm of a piece of broccoli. Would this be his final thought? Wondering why a fat man would get a tattoo of broccoli? The one food he probably never ate? The fuck?

Cal struggled to raise the barrel of his HK to Kilo's Adam's apple. He squeezed the trigger. Blood spilled from Kilo's gargling throat and his body went limp. It took everything Cal had to heave the massive mass off of him.

He pointed the HK back down at Kilo's body and pulled the trigger. *Click. Click.*

He was out. So he reloaded. And he fired twelve more rounds into Kilo, just to make absolutely sure he was out of lives.

Easy work.

Cal left Kilo's body in the ransacked trailer. Pat would send cleaners. Cal was only a small cog in a big wheel.

Ultimately, he was not responsible.

But he couldn't deny he liked it. Killing. There was catharsis in wrath.

He thought maybe it would feel different this time. Maybe that it'd be harder for him. As if a soul were something you could take to the body shop or grow like a chia pet. That's why he'd taken the job to begin with, he reminded himself. To see if he'd changed in prison. Been "rehabilitated."

Addicts are masters of self-deceit.

On the drive back to L.A., he stopped at a Wendy's and ordered a hamburger and thought about Vinny, because why the fuck not?

3

Miranda believed all politicians were sociopaths and, in her opinion, none were more sociopathic than Jimmy McClean.

Jimmy McClean was the junior senator from Texas. He had won his first seat thanks in no small part to Senator Marco Barros's influence. He was a close personal friend of the Barros family and he had known Arianna. It was said that if Marco Barros had a son, it would be Jimmy McClean.

McClean was raised in a Catholic orphanage in Galveston, Texas. At eighteen, he enlisted in the Marines. He did two tours and was awarded the Navy Cross for valor.

He returned home, got a degree in economics from the University of Texas at Austin on the military's dime and when he turned thirty, he began campaigning.

He was the little guy. Some unknown kid no one had ever heard of. No money, no influence. None of his opponents took him seriously. But McClean knew all about guerilla warfare.

He built his Twitter following. Posted his speeches and campaign rallies on his YouTube channel. Created an online social network for his supporters to connect with one another, organize and donate.

He engaged support at all levels. His message got out. People donated something more valuable than money. They donated their time. They organized rallies for him across the state.

It was a strange thing. McClean was somehow making it cool for young people to vote Republican.

He was moderate and progressive. He had a reputation as a uniter. Democrats could work with him and a lot even liked him.

He was also young, handsome and charismatic. The camera loved him and he loved the camera.

Jimmy McClean. War hero. Heartthrob. The future.

It was all too fucking perfect for Miranda. The "pulled himself up by his bootstraps" American lie. Like he had been grown in a Republican lab somewhere.

His record was unblemished. But Miranda had also heard the whispers. Rumor was Jimmy was quite the playboy. More JFK than Ronald Reagan than anyone in the party would like to admit.

Miranda fucking hated hypocrites.

But most of all, it was that fucking smile. That's what she probably hated the most. That fake-ass, pandering movie-star smile always plastered on his stupid, handsome face.

But when Miranda met Jimmy McClean for the first time in the corridor outside of Marco Barros's office, he wasn't smiling. He was seething, and his outrage seemed authentic. He wanted blood and he didn't care what it would cost. He told Miranda and Greco that he was willing to follow the investigation wherever it might lead. He didn't give a shit whose toes he had to step on or how it might hurt him politically.

He would even go against the NRA, if that's what it came to.

It made Miranda dislike him a little less. Maybe he wasn't just all smoke and mirrors. She disagreed with his politics, but it was always refreshing to meet a politician that actually believed in *something*. She appreciated honesty and passion in a person.

The difference between a psychopath and a sociopath is that

a sociopath has a conscience, although it's about the size of a grain of sand. Maybe Arianna was McClean's grain of sand.

McClean escorted Miranda and Greco into Barros's office. The blinds were drawn and the air was thick with the expensive, woody aromas of mahogany and aged Scotch.

Marco Barros didn't rise from his desk when they entered. Didn't offer his hand. Didn't even make eye contact. He was unkempt in his disheveled Brooks Brothers suit. Like a crumpled hundred-dollar bill.

It had been fourteen hours since his daughter was murdered.

Miranda and Greco took seats across from him. There was a glass case showcasing an antique Colt Peacemaker on the bookshelf behind him. *Like a dick on display*, Miranda thought.

McClean made the introductions. Marco listened to it all. Not speaking. A lifeless, faraway look in his eyes. Miranda and Greco began with the boilerplate questions. How did Arianna seem in the days leading up to her death? Anything suspicious? Any reason why someone might want to hurt her?

"Aside from her being the daughter of a powerful senator?" McClean interjected with a grimace. He took a deep breath and composed himself. "She'd been mugged a few weeks before. Thrown to the ground at a bus stop for her iPhone."

Miranda was only half-listening. She was studying Marco. Why did he let her live in that neighborhood?

"Did they catch the mugger?" Greco asked.

"Yes. But Ari didn't want to press charges," McClean said.

Miranda's eyes remained on Marco. This man could give speeches. *Great* speeches. He could sell a glass of water to a drowning man. That was how a poor Latino kid from Edinburg grew up to become the senior Senator from Texas. So why hadn't he said a word?

What was he afraid he might say?

"Why didn't she want to press charges?" Greco asked.

"That's just how she was. She always saw the world through rose-colored glasses," McClean said.

"'Angel Eyes,'" Marco blurted out.

McClean and Greco turned to him.

"That's what Jimmy used to call her. 'Angel Eyes.'"

Marco began to weep. McClean stepped in. "Why don't we finish the interview in my office?" he said. He told Marco he would report back.

As she moved to the door, Miranda looked back at Marco. He was known for his ability to adjust reality to his views. Facts were never absolute. Truth was always relative. But this was not something he could adjust or distort. His daughter was gone and she was never coming back.

McClean's pretty young secretary escorted Miranda and Greco into his office and shut the door behind them. Upon seeing McClean's office, Miranda remembered why she couldn't stand him. The room was dominated by a large American flag and an even larger rosewood desk. Everywhere, there were framed photographs of McClean posing with various politicians, dignitaries, world leaders and celebrities. The sheer quantity was overwhelming. *This is a man who is completely obsessed with his image,* Miranda thought.

They sat across from McClean. He looked ridiculous behind his desk, surrounded by the photographs. Like a high priest in a temple to himself.

"There were a total of thirteen fatalities," Greco said. "One of which was a known drug dealer."

"So Arianna was what? Collateral damage?" McClean asked with more than a hint of outrage.

"We don't know yet," Greco said.

"She moved to L.A. to work for a church. Is that correct?" Miranda asked.

McClean scowled. "You think that cult had something to do with her death?"

Miranda noted the word "cult" and the contempt in his voice when he said it.

"Do you have any eyewitnesses?" McClean asked.

"Not as of now," Greco said.

"Do you have any leads at all? DNA?"

"It is still very early in the investigation," Greco said.

"So, what *do* you have?"

"We have a gun," Miranda said.

McClean perked up in his chair.

"You have the gun?"

"No. We have a *type* of gun," Miranda said. "Arianna was killed by an AR-15 style rifle. 5.56x45 millimeter, magazine-fed, air-cooled—"

"—semi-automatic, gas-operated, civilian version of the M16," McClean said.

"Through a process called rifling, we can match the shooter's bullets to the gun," Greco said. "So we are ordering that any AR-15 used in the commission of a crime nationwide be rifled."

"The problem is that the AR-15 is the most common rifle in the United States," Miranda said.

"That's it? That's all you've got?" McClean said.

Miranda's eyes landed on a photograph of McClean and four other soldiers, posing with their M27s in some Iraqi village. Smiling like idiots. *Talk about a dick pic,* she thought.

She shrugged. "Three hundred million guns in the United States with little to no regulation, Senator. And you want us to find just one."

McClean's face was red. Miranda couldn't tell if he wanted to hit her, but she hoped he did.

After Miranda and Greco left, McClean returned to Marco to give his report. He didn't mention the antagonistic ATF Agent, who struck him as far less apolitical than any law enforcement official should be.

He told Marco that the two had struck him as dedicated individuals, who were determined to bring Arianna's killer or killers to justice. He told him he had no doubt in their capabilities. He told Marco he was in good hands.

It was a lie and Marco knew it. He knew McClean was trying to protect him. That he didn't want him to suffer any more than he already was.

McClean wanted to stay and drink with Marco, but Marco told him to go home.

4

B randan hated working Friday nights to begin with, but this one was shaping up to be worse than usual.

Who the fuck orders a hundred hamburgers to go? Brandan was supposed to get off at eight, but now he had to stay late to organize and bag up the order, which was a real pain in the ass because he had to get to the gym.

On top of that, the burger prick arrived fifteen minutes late. Brandan sized him up. Five-nine, late-thirties, couldn't have weighed more than 170 pounds soaking wet.

Brandan was twenty-four years old and 200 pounds of pure muscle beneath a veneer of tattoos. He worked his ass off to get his bodybuilder's physique. Not to mention the cost of the steroids. He *looked* tough. People were scared of him and he liked that.

But not this guy. Didn't give him a second look. Acted like Brandan was just like anybody else. And that bugged the shit out of him.

What the fuck did this regular-looking dude have to feel so cool about? Didn't he see how dangerous Brandan looked?

It was the same feeling he got from his parents. They didn't take him seriously either. They wanted him to move out, but how did they expect him to afford rent on a burger waiter's salary?

Besides, he was saving up for a gun. He wanted the Kimber 1911 .45 ACP that the Bowery King gave John Wick in *John Wick: Chapter 2*. Thing looked like a fucking Rolex.

Then they'd take him seriously.

And John Wick can't even squat three plates, Brandan thought.

"Pick-up for Cal," the prick said.

Brandan carried the aluminum catering trays outside and put them in the back of Cal's Range Rover. He watched Cal drive away. *Don't know who you're fucking with,* Brandan thought, as he walked back inside.

The tented streets painted a tableau of despair and human misery. Vials, used syringes and trash littered the pavement like toxic autumn leaves. Cal parked his Range Rover in the usual spot: a vacant lot, surrounded by jagged and rusted chain-link webbed between leaning fence posts.

His regulars were waiting. Cal opened the back of the Range Rover and handed out the hamburgers. Most accepted with gratitude. Others rudely snatched their meal. Some tried to steal second helpings and cursed and spat at him when he wouldn't allow it. Cal took no offense and made no judgments. He understood demons.

After serving his regulars, Cal took the remainder of the burger trays and hiked through Skid Row, distributing meals to anyone who wanted one.

Cal did this almost every week. Sometimes it was pizza, or fried chicken, or burritos. He always saved the last meal.

He found the Marine outside of his tent, sitting on an overturned milk crate. The USMC tattoo on his gaunt arm was blurred by weight loss. His beard was filthy. So was his wild hair. He was no more listless than usual as he sat there in a daze, literally watching the world pass him by.

Cal knew that one day, he'd come and the Marine wouldn't

be there. That the opioids would kill him. Probably soon. But Cal didn't preach.

Cal wasn't here to save souls. Only to stand on the frontlines of the battlefield with his brothers and sisters in arms.

He handed the Marine the last hamburger and sat with him. The two had never exchanged a single word.

Cal's training in interrogation techniques had taught him that fifty-five percent of a person's language was in their body. Thirty-eight percent was in the tone and inflection of their voice. Only seven percent was in the actual words themselves.

Cal and the Marine didn't need to use words. They understood one another. So they sat in silence.

Cal was a kid in Boston. Sixteen. He spent every second he could at the local boxing gym. Why he liked it was, it wasn't really about fighting your opponent. The real battle was against yourself. You fought pain. You fought exhaustion. You fought to breathe. You fought to stay conscious. You fought to stay in the fight.

It was just before noon. Cal didn't remember where he was going. There was a man. Wiry and wound-up. He was stabbing street signs and tree branches with a pencil. People crossed the street to avoid him. Cal wasn't going to cross the street.

The man saw Cal and threatened him. Told him he'd killed a lot of people— with his No. 2 pencil.

The man was the aggressor. The man was in the wrong. But he was obviously mentally ill or an addict high out of his mind, or both.

"Do you really want to do this?" the man asked.

Cal could have taken the high road. Instead, he said, "Yes."

The man took a swipe at him with the pencil.

Then Cal beat him. Even after the man begged him to stop.

This was before Cal knew about the war. Cal regretted very few things he had done in his life. But he regretted that.

.   .   .

Cal nodded farewell to the Marine and rose from the milk crate. He walked through Skid Row. The people that lived here were all veterans. They might not have ever served in the military, but they had been to war. Mental illness, addiction, trauma, abuse.

They were veterans of their own wars.

They were his people.

When Cal got back to his Range Rover, he thought about the burger place. There was a reason why he'd chosen to give out burgers this week. It had to do with a phone call he'd received from Pat Roti hours earlier.

"I've got a job for you," Pat had said. "It's the Barros girl."

5

Miranda perused Sean's file outside of the interrogation room. He was an Irish citizen here on a six-month visa. No criminal record. At least, not in the States.

He sat hunched forward over the battered table. Miranda entered and sat across from him.

"Sean McGuire, I'm Special Agent Miranda Lopez with the ATF. I'd like to ask you a few questions about Arianna Barros."

Sean nodded.

"You're aware of what happened to Miss Barros?"

He nodded again.

"I understand you were texting with her on the night she was killed?"

"Yeah."

"What was your relationship to her?"

Sean shrugged. "Don't really know what I'd call it."

"Were you friends?"

"We were friend-*ly*."

"What does that mean?"

"It means I wouldn't say we were friends."

"Why not?"

He shrugged again. "I was an outsider."

"An outsider? Are you talking about the church? Valorous?"

"She wanted me to come to service. I went once. Didn't go back."

"Why not?"

"Wasn't for me."

"Not religious?"

"I wouldn't say that."

"You're very good at saying what you wouldn't say."

Sean lowered his eyes. "It's not a church."

"How do you mean?"

"They take advantage. Young people that come to L.A. with big dreams, they end up there, filling the pastors' pockets. Like they're brainwashed or something."

"You got all that from one visit?"

"You don't believe me, go check it out for yourself. I'm telling you, there's something not right about it."

"And Arianna? Why do you think she ended up there?"

"I don't know." Sean shook his head. "I liked her. I knew that it would never work. She was too deep in that church or whatever. But I didn't want to think about that. She was funny, sweet, smart. She made me want to be better. That fucking church. That fucking ex..."

Miranda looked up from her notes. "What ex?"

Sean stared at her with wide eyes.

Esau Gonzalez sat across from Miranda in the interview room with a dead stare. He wore black gauge earrings and a nose ring. Miranda noted the tattoos that lined his arms. Images of archangels slaying demons. Judith beheading Holofernes. Jephthah sacrificing his daughter. A tortured and particularly bloodied Christ on the crucifix.

"You dated Arianna?" Miranda asked.

"Yes," Esau said, his eyes blank.

"How long?"

"A few months. But we had been friends before that."

"You don't seem that upset that she's dead."

"Ari, like me, is part of a fearless church of men and women after God's own heart. Our vision is to infiltrate *Lost* Angeles, destroying the chains by which it is bound and rebuilding it from the ground up, all for the Glory of God. This, we would die for.

"Pastor Zach is our general. He is leading us, his army, against the devil and, in the name of Jesus, we will bring down Hell's gates."

"We're here to talk about Arianna," Miranda said.

"Ari was the kindest, most beautiful person I ever met. I love her. But God's will is real. And it is never wrong."

He stared at her with burning black eyes.

Miranda noticed a tattoo on the back of his hand. A sword and shining light with the words: "THE BATTLE HAS ALREADY BEGUN."

A black banner draped the entrance to the nightclub on Spring Street in Downtown Los Angeles. The word "VALOROUS" in red letters like a war flag.

It was Sunday morning and the sinners were off in one another's beds, sleeping off their MDMA hangovers. For the next two hours, this den of debauchery belonged to the Righteous.

Miranda took a pamphlet from one of the smiling greeters at the door. They wore black shirts with the Valorous church's trademark V branded on the chest.

A band of twentysomethings performed Christian rock on the nightclub stage as LED lasers danced over the congregation.

At the center of the stage was a big, wooden crucifix with the Valorous symbol glowing in color-changing neon.

The audience skewed young. Piercings and tattoos and the latest street wear. They raised their arms in worship, moshed, danced. They were on an older drug. A more ancient form of ecstasy.

Then the concert ended and somewhere between the strobe lights and fog machines, Pastor Zach materialized on stage. "Where my cheerful givers at?" he called out. The crowd roared.

Pastor Zach was a slight guy. Couldn't have been taller than 5'5". He had a movie star's face. He was L.A. mid-forties, which meant he looked like he was in his mid-thirties. He modeled a hundred-dollar, slicked-back skin fade and sported a drop cut t-shirt, faded skinny jeans and vintage Adidas high tops.

Everything about the guy screamed poser, but these kids worshipped him.

"2 Corinthians 9," said Pastor Kelly as she joined her husband on stage. Her California girl, bleach-blonde hair wasn't colored anywhere cheap. She wore skin-tight jeans, three-inch Converse Chuck Taylor wedges and a cropped T. *A total babe*, Miranda thought. "You must each decide in your heart how much to give. And don't give reluctantly or in response to pressure. For God loves a person who gives cheerfully."

It was immediately obvious that they were a couple. They were too similar not to be. Pastors Zach and Kelly both struck Miranda as narcissists, and what more does a narcissist want than to fuck themselves?

"Cheerful givers, let me hear you one more time!" Pastor Zach said.

The audience hollered in adoration.

"Where's David Smith?" Pastor Zach asked. A hand went up in the audience. "When David first came to Valorous, he was making minimum wage, trying to launch a tech startup. But still, he gave generously and now I am pleased to say David's company has become a phenomenal success!"

Cheers and shouts of worship.

"And what about Cynthia Ramirez? Her daughter was ill," said Pastor Kelly. "The doctors said she wasn't going to make it.

But Cynthia gave to Valorous and now her daughter is healed. 'For God loves a person who gives cheerfully!'"

More ecstatic cheering. Some weeping.

"I know you have been through a lot," Pastor Zach said. "Hopelessness. Depression. Thoughts of suicide. But Jesus can heal you."

"There are now two ways to give," Pastor Kelly said. "By filling out the envelope beneath your seat and handing your offering to one of our Valorous workers. They're the smiling, nice people in the black shirts."

A spotlight landed on the Valorous workers. Friendly smiles and thousand-yard stares.

"Or you can text your tithe to this number."

A telephone number appeared on the screen behind her.

Miranda looked at the guy operating the projector. It was Esau.

Unflinching eyes.

Two black holes.

After the service, the congregation had coffee and cupcakes. Miranda cornered the Pastors and explained that she was a federal agent investigating Arianna Barros's murder and they said they were both more than happy to answer any questions she might have. They sat with her at one the nightclub's VIP booths.

"Were you able to catch our service?" Pastor Zach asked.

"I was."

"We're sorry it is under such terrible circumstances," Pastor Kelly said.

"Can we get you some coffee or a cupcake?" Pastor Zach said.

"I'd like to get started."

"Of course."

"What was Arianna's role at your church?" Miranda asked.

"She worked in the day care, teaching two and three-year-olds about Jesus.

She was a dedicated member of our congregation. We saw her almost every day," Pastor Kelly said.

"And how long was she with your church?"

"About three years."

"Why did she join?"

The pastors exchanged cautious glances.

"She was saved," Pastor Zach said, as if that explained it all.

"I'm going to need a better answer than that."

"She accepted Jesus Christ as her personal lord and savior," Pastor Kelly said.

Miranda was annoyed. "Did she have any enemies? Anyone that might want to hurt her?"

"No one that we know of," Pastor Zach said.

"I'd like to review your church's records."

The Pastors paused. Pastor Zach cleared his throat. "I'm sure that would be very disruptive. After all, we have a church to run. The Lord never rests." He paused again. "Do you have a warrant?"

"I was hoping you'd just cooperate."

"We are cooperating," Pastor Kelly said.

"Then you won't need me to go get a warrant."

"What does any of this have to do with our finances?" Pastor Kelly asked.

Miranda tilted her head. "I didn't say finances. I said records."

"Records, finances. Whatever!" Pastor Kelly said, with more than an edge.

Pastor Zach rested a calming hand on her lap, then looked at Miranda. "It belongs to God. Not you."

"He did, though," Miranda said.

The pastor looked confused. "What?"

"You said, 'The Lord never rests.' He did. On the seventh day."

Pastor Zach scowled. "Well, *we* never rest."

"How much did you pay her?" Miranda asked. "She worked in your daycare, right? I understand she also did photography for your Christian clothing line?"

"We are a nonprofit. She was a volunteer," Pastor Zach said.

"In fact, she paid *you*. A tithe of 15% of her earnings, every month. Is that correct?"

"I'm sorry. What does this have to do with the investigation?" Pastor Zach asked.

"Here's what. When Arianna was younger, she was rebellious. Drinking, a little marijuana. Then suddenly, just like that, everything changes. She joins your church, moves to L.A. and gives everything she has to you."

"She gave it to Jesus."

"There's something missing. I think you know what it is and I think you don't want to tell me."

"I'm beginning to feel persecuted," Pastor Zach said.

"I'm not out to persecute anyone. The IRS, on the other hand, might wonder about your vacations to Hawaii and your mansion in Huntington Beach. It all depends on how much you're willing to cooperate."

Pastor Zach sneered at her. "We loved Arianna. Frankly, I'm getting the impression that you couldn't care less about her. I think you should go now. Feel free to take a cupcake for the road."

The couple rose from the booth and rejoined their flock.

If Miranda came off as hard-bitten, it was because she grew up among the voiceless. She knew what it was to be powerless and her opinions gave her strength. She learned the hard lesson at a young age that the weak—those who compromised in their beliefs—got rolled right over.

It was a recipe for survival, but also loneliness.

People didn't understand why she couldn't just go with the

program. Why did she always have to make everything so fucking difficult? Just shut up and be agreeable.

She dreaded the day that Camilla would inevitably leave her, just like all of the rest had. She'd gotten over them, but she wasn't sure she'd survive losing Camilla.

Camilla always cooked on Sundays. It was the one night she insisted that Miranda sit down and have a meal with her. Miranda was allowed to be absent the rest of the week. But not on Sundays.

"Where are you?" Camilla asked from across the dinner table.

Miranda was zoning out, thinking about the pastors. She sighed. "I'm under a lot of pressure."

"Okay." Camilla lowered her head and frowned.

Miranda ate a piece of chicken off one of the *suya* skewers. She'd left it sitting so long that it had become cold and chewy.

"How's the investigation going?" Camilla asked.

"The only lead is the rifle. I feel like I'm looking for a needle in a haystack in the middle of a minefield. If this doesn't go right, it could ruin my career."

"How is the senator handling it?"

"Not well."

"I can't imagine. Losing a child like that."

"True. But it's also kind of his own fault."

"What?"

"Marco Barros and people like him oppose any form of gun regulation. I hate to say it, but, I mean, we kind of reap what we sow, right?"

Camilla shook her head. She dropped her fork on her plate and rose from her chair.

"What?" Miranda said.

Camilla walked over to one of Miranda's file boxes, slid out the crime scene photograph of Arianna and placed it on the dinner table.

"Look at this picture. I know that it's easier to feel nothing. It's safer. But that's a human being. You may not agree with her politics, or those of her family and friends, but doesn't she deserve justice?"

"Don't do that."

"Do what?"

"Make it about her. When this is about you."

"Me?"

"I'm sorry if you feel like you're not getting enough attention lately, Camilla, but I've been busy."

Camilla shook her head and crossed the room.

"Where are you going?"

"I don't think I should come around for a while."

Miranda watched helplessly as Camilla gathered her things. She wanted to tell her to wait. She wanted to say, *I love you*. But what was the point? Would she even believe her? What were words without action?

Camilla left Miranda alone in the loft, staring at the photograph of a dead girl, with the knowledge that if she was ever going to get Camilla back, she had to first get justice for Arianna.

6

M arco Barros was a powerful man. Cal couldn't fuck this job up. He was in South Central, outside Arianna's apartment building. It was two in the morning. It had been two weeks since the shooting, and the place was boarded up. He didn't see the point in breaking in. He doubted he'd find anything that the Feds with their forensic teams had missed.

What he needed was a witness. Of course, the Feds had found none. But Cal had one advantage that they didn't.

He wasn't a Fed.

This neighborhood was what police called a "High Intensity Drug Trafficking Area." No one talked to cops because the cops weren't the ones who policed this neighborhood. The streets had eyes.

A civilian like Arianna wouldn't have known about them, but they would have known her. They knew everyone on their turf—civilians, soldiers, junkies, business owners to extort— so if an outsider came around, they would have noticed.

Cal just had to find them.

It didn't take long for him to spot the kid on the corner. He couldn't have been older than sixteen. He was built long and wiry like a kickboxer, with a square jaw and stone eyes. He wore a blue Dodgers cap, baggy jeans and no shirt. The letters "M" and "S" were tattooed in large letters across his upper back. Below them, the numbers "1" and "3" were equally prominent on his lumbar region, and in the middle of it all, there was a bright blue and white Salvadoran flag.

Not exactly subliminal advertising.

"Sup?" the corner boy said, as Cal approached.

"I need to talk to your shot caller." Cal knew it was no use questioning the corner boy about the shooting. The only person in a position to give him information was the guy who ran this block.

The corner boy mad-dogged him.

"I just want to talk." Cal held out a hundred-dollar bill. After a moment, the corner boy snatched the hundred and nodded for Cal to follow him.

He led Cal down the block and even though the neighborhood seemed to be asleep, he knew he was being watched. They stopped outside a vacant. The board on the door had been loosened. The boy peeled it back and held it for Cal.

Cal entered into a maze of dilapidation and decay. Dark and unholy. Walked through stench. Damp and shit. Vials and syringes littered the filthy floor. They cracked beneath his feet like a layer of ice.

The kid was behind him and Cal knew that he was reaching for his gun. He knew this was a possibility. The young ones always have something to prove.

Cal was about to turn around and break the kid's arm in three places, when something held him back. Some invisible force. It stayed his hand. He let the kid pull his gun.

He thought of how blue the sky was on 9/11.

The randomness of it.

The randomness of this.

Out of a clear blue sky.

It seemed fitting.

A killer of killers, of kings and dictators.

Done in by a baby banger with a cheap pistol.

He was tired of waiting for fate.

Let it be this, let it be this. This single random, violent action. A microcosm for existence.

The boy raised the gun to the back of Cal's head.

Was this it? Was this what it had all been about? Was his war finally over?

Should he cry?

A cry sounds the same in any language.

So does a laugh.

So does a bullet.

The kid pulled the trigger.

PART II

GLORY AND GODHOOD

7

R yan was on top of the world.
High on weed, cans of beer in the cup holders. Radio blasting John Cougar Mellencamp. Gotta love the fuckin' classics. His best buddy Jeff was in the passenger seat. They sped down the crumbling Arizona backroads in his '96 Ford Bronco.

There was a secluded spot where the high school kids went to drink and smoke. Out in a field near a cow pasture. Ryan parked the Bronco and got ready.

Tonight was the night. At long fucking last.

Ryan was eighteen and he had been trying to lose his virginity to anything with a heartbeat and a hole since the seventh grade. But tonight, he had a couple cases of beer and a bag of weed he'd traded for with a client (Ryan was also something of a small business owner) and Corey and Kyle wanted to party.

Corey and Kyle were chicks, even though they had boys' names. They did things that the other girls didn't.

He'd heard that Nick Nunez partied with them and they put a blindfold on his head and took turns blowing him. They wanted him to tell them who gave better head, like it was a competition or something.

When Kenny Carpenter was home from college, he banged Corey or Kyle, Ryan forgot which, on top of his white Honda Accord. He showed off the smeared make-up stain on the car's hood for weeks.

These girls were a sure thing, Ryan thought, as he watched the cattle graze in the afternoon sun. If he couldn't lose his V-card to one of them, he'd might as well go fuck one of the cows.

While Ryan and Jeff waited for Corey and Kyle to arrive, they discussed who got which one and if it really mattered and if they should try switching after and doing them both. They bitched about how they needed to get fake IDs, so they could get into bars because chicks in bars were always drunk and then they could get laid all the time.

Ryan told Jeff to slow down on the beers because they were for the girls.

After about an hour, Ryan texted Kyle to ask where they were at, but he didn't get a response.

When the sun started to go down, Ryan realized they'd been stood up.

Fuck 'em. Women are only good for one thing anyway.

They pounded the beers and got drunker and drunker.

They pegged rocks at the cows.

When they were each about ten beers deep, Jeff picked up a cow pie and chucked it at Ryan, giggling like an idiot. Ryan reciprocated. Soon they were having a drunken manure fight like it was cowshit Christmas.

After the beers were gone, they took off their shirts and slap-boxed in the darkness. Spanking the soft spots on each other's bodies. Once their energy was spent, they collapsed on the ground, sore, filthy and drunk.

"Fucking bitches," Ryan said.

"Yeah, man. I'm horny as hell," Jeff said.

"You can always fuck a cow."

. . .

The next morning, Lance was at the kitchen stove making bacon and eggs when his grandson stumbled down the stairs and into the kitchen, stinking of beer and cow shit.

Lance didn't mention Ryan's bloodshot eyes or the stench of alcohol seeping from his pores. He ignored the red hand-shaped welts on his arms and face.

"Mornin'," Lance said. "Breakfast?"

"No, thanks," Ryan said as he walked out the door. Lance watched him through the kitchen window. *Probably going to that damn barn again*, Lance thought.

Lance didn't understand his grandson. He thought he was very strange. But then again, relationships were not Lance's strong suit.

Lance's father had fought in World War II and then drank his life away trying to forget what he had experienced. Ryan played World War II video games and hooted and hollered as he blew away Nazis, or Allies, depending which side he was playing on. Lance found it all so incredibly perverse.

Lance never blamed his father for being absent or held it against him, but he swore he'd be better to his own son. The problem was he didn't know how. He'd never been nurtured, so how could he be nurturing? They had a good relationship, he and his son, Ryan's father, but there was a barrier. A distance he could never close. He raised him the best he could and now he was trying to do the same for Ryan, but ultimately, Sheehan men had to find their own way.

Ryan would have to find his own way.

Ryan and Lance lived together on a defunct hundred-acre Arizona ranch. The family had once grazed cattle, but when other ranches started using undocumented workers, they couldn't compete and refused to adapt. The place fell into disrepair. Today, it felt like a sprawling ghost town. Wood structures, once bright and colorful, had faded and darkened. They sagged and stooped over like wrinkled old men. Their exteriors rotting away, revealing the bones of their frames.

Ryan passed through metal gates chewed with rust and splintered fence posts clawing up from the earth at jagged angles.

He had been told all about the glory days when the ranch was still thriving. "Sheehans used to run this town," his father had told him. "We could walk into any bar and never pay for a drink."

If the Sheehan name was respected like it used to be, I'd have gotten my nut by now, Ryan thought.

Behind a dusty cattle corral reclaimed by cottontop grass stood a sleepy old barn. Its rusted hinges creaked and groaned like something shaken from hibernation as Ryan heaved open the large, wooden door.

Inside was a wonderland of weaponry. Rifles, shotguns and handguns meticulously organized and stockpiled in the old cattle stalls. So oiled and polished, they seemed to glow in the sunlight that streamed through the open barn door.

Metallic and resilient. Smelling of gun oil and metal alloy. This whole godforsaken ranch could come crashing down, but the guns would remain. They were made of tougher stuff.

Ryan's black Ford Bronco was parked in the center of the barn. Last night, he'd noticed that the vehicle vibrated whenever he pressed the brake.

He used a jack to lift the Bronco and removed each wheel one at a time. He examined the brake pads, rotors and calipers. Everything looked fine. Might be the engine, which meant he'd have to bring it out to ol' Arturo's. It was the only auto shop in town anymore.

Ryan had only just bought the Bronco from a seller off Armslist. They'd met so Ryan could buy some firearms and the guy threw the Bronco into the deal for only a thousand bucks.

Ryan couldn't believe his luck. It was like the guy was giving it away.

All said and done, he spent just under three grand for the '96 Bronco, an AK TR3 rifle, a Beretta 92FS, a Desert Eagle .44 Magnum, a Ruger .380 revolver.

And an AR-15 rifle.

8

W hen Russ first met D'Andre, he knew how easy it would have been to make a meal out of him.

D'Andre's father taught eighth grade calculus in Chicago's West Lawn neighborhood. When a brain aneurysm unexpectedly killed him, D'Andre was fourteen years old and he and his mother were not left with much. They had already been barely scraping by. His father's meager teacher's paychecks and the money his mother made as a social worker should have been enough to live a somewhat comfortable life in West Lawn, but D'Andre's parents were saving for his college education. This meant that everything was rationed.

After D'Andre's father died, his mother was faced with a choice: use the college fund to continue on in the mode of life they were accustomed to or relocate to a more affordable neighborhood. So D'Andre and his mother moved from the relative safety of West Lawn to Englewood on Chicago's South Side. It was one of the most dangerous neighborhoods in the city.

D'Andre's father had taught him to always do the right thing. He was a kind man and he taught D'Andre to be a kind man.

But kind men don't survive in Englewood. In Englewood, "the right thing" can get you killed.

Russ always believed that if he had been born somewhere else, he might have had a chance. But this was Englewood. Russ never knew his parents. He was raised in the system. It was at Miss Simmons's foster home, at the age of twelve, that he met Tyreek. Tyreek was five years Russ's senior. He took Russ under his wing. He taught him everything he needed to know about the drug game.

It was Tyreek who introduced Russ to AK.

Russ remembered one of the last things Tyreek told him before he died. They were walking down the street. Tyreek was bouncing his trusty marble bouncy ball. It was an idiosyncrasy he often engaged in.

"Everyone's afraid out here," Tyreek said. "That's why they act the way they do. Beefing with they neighbors. But they got it all twisted. Your neighbor ain't your enemy. It's the po-po. You gotta look out for you and yours 'cause ain't nobody else gonna do it. That's why niggas be shootin' each other.

"Police worse than the gangs. Only time they around is to set up, beat down, arrest or shoot a nigga. I want you to promise me, man, that if the trigger-happy po-po ever come around starting trouble, you gonna do one thing. Run. Just run."

Russ made the promise.

A few months later, Tyreek was shot in the back as he ran from the police. The cops said they mistook the burner phone in his hand for a weapon.

D'Andre moved to Englewood freshman year. He was chum in the water.

By this time, Russ was working for AK fulltime. He had honed a Machiavellian mind. He studied how and why gangstas got shot or put away. That wasn't going to be him. He knew D'Andre wasn't cliqued-up, and that was a death sentence around here. He also knew the kid was introverted and studious.

Russ understood that loudmouths got got. You had to choose your words carefully in this game. And it wasn't about rap videos and busting caps. It was about running a business. Shit, even AK took business classes at City College of Chicago. The more he thought about it, the more he decided he and D'Andre could really build something. D'Andre was smart. He could use that. All Russ had to do was teach him. So Russ took D'Andre under his wing.

He taught D'Andre the same way Tyreek taught him.

Russ introduced D'Andre to AK.

Before D'Andre knew it, he was cliqued-up.

On the front lawn of the home, they posted a sign showing a picture of a smiling Asian man and the words "VOTE CHARLIE YU FOR ALDERMAN."

"Say it again," Russ said.

"Megalodon," D'Andre replied.

"You tellin' me there's a shark out there the size of the Goodyear blimp?"

"Was. It ain't around no more."

"That's what these streets is. All a nigga can do is drown."

D'Andre laughed. "You ain't ever seen the ocean."

They approached the front door of the home and knocked. A black man in his fifties answered. He wore gym shorts and a white tank top with a brown stain on the breast. He sized the two boys up.

"What'chu want?"

Russ handed the man a clipboard. "We here to sign you up to vote."

"Fuck you talking?"

"By order of AK," Russ said.

Stained Tank Top's eyes widened. "You with AK?"

"We speak his word," Russ said.

"Spooky's niggas been around," Stained Tank Top said.

Russ glared daggers. Stained Tank Top nearly shit. "Just keeping y'all informed. Y'all know I'm with AK. Fuck Spooky. Gimme that."

Stained Tank Top took the clipboard and filled out his information.

"Election day is next Monday," Russ said. "You're going to vote Charlie Yu for Alderman. We don't see you there, we're coming back. Only this time, we won't have no clipboards."

Stained Tank Top's head nodded rapidly.

As Russ and D'Andre walked away, Stained Tank Top called after them, "Make sure AK see my name!"

D'Andre and Russ moved to the next house and planted another sign in the front lawn. "VOTE CHARLIE YU FOR ALDERMAN."

"So how you become Mega?" Russ asked.

D'Andre shrugged. "Gotta be strapped, I guess. The power be in the gun."

"You wrong."

"You ever heard of the Ku Klux Klan?" D'Andre said. "You know why those crackers started that shit? It was to disarm free blacks after the Civil War. They didn't want niggas owning rifles."

Russ laughed. "My nigga's always reading. Guns, homie. That be street shit. What you think AK's got us doing out here?"

D'Andre shrugged. "Tryin' to get this Chinaman elected."

"Tryin' to get a friend in City Hall," Russ said. "Take this shit off the street, make it a mafia. Guns ain't nothin'. The power, my nigga, be in the vote."

They finished posting the sign. Russ indicated the house and told D'Andre, "You do this one."

D'Andre knocked on the front door. Miss Evelyn answered. She was seventy-five years old and used a walker. She wore a turban to cover her balding head and a sweat suit out of necessity, not choice. Her health was declining and her movement was limited.

"Can I help you?" she said.

D'Andre shifted his weight. "Uhm... We're here to sign you up to vote."

A terrier puppy curiously peeked its head out behind Miss Evelyn.

"I'm already registered," Miss Evelyn replied.

D'Andre stuttered. "No... We're here to sign you up..."

"I've already registered."

"No. *We* sign you up," D'Andre said. "You vote for who *we* tell you to."

"Young man, do you understand how voting works?"

"This come straight from AK," D'Andre said.

"You can't go in the voting booth with me," Miss Evelyn said. "You have no control over whom I vote for."

Both boys looked stumped. D'Andre looked to Russ.

Not knowing what else to do, Russ lurched forward and grabbed the puppy.

"What are you doing?!" Miss Evelyn cried.

"Bitch. Charlie Yu don't win Alderman, I'ma kill your fuckin' dog!" Russ said.

"Give him back!" Miss Evelyn reached forward. D'Andre lifted his shirt, revealing the .38 in his waistband and Miss Evelyn stepped back.

"Let's go," Russ said to D'Andre. He turned and walked away, the puppy crying in his arms.

"What the hell? Man, you hurting it," D'Andre said.

"It's just a damn dog."

"Give it here." D'Andre took the puppy from Russ and stroked its head until it stopped crying.

Russ laughed at him. "Yo' new shorty!"

9

A rturo's brothers ran drugs.

They were born dirt poor in Santa Cruz County, Arizona. Their parents were illegal and got deported when Arturo was thirteen. He and his two older brothers dodged Social Services and lived on the streets. It was during this time that the brothers met *La Federación*.

The oldest, Rogelio, worked construction by day. He was hard-working and professional and was eventually promoted to foreman. His hard hat hid the spiderweb tattoo spread over his scalp. His button-down shirt concealed the topless, big-titted woman inked on his upper arm.

The middle brother, Eugenio, worked for his brother on the construction site and in the drug trade. Eugenio used to get high on his own supply. Arturo remembered wondering why Eugenio grew his one pinky fingernail so long, like a girl's. He understood now that it was so that Eugenio would never be without the means to do a bump of cocaine. Any other boss would have cut Eugenio loose, but not Rogelio. He was family.

The brothers made decent money. The tradeoff was their freedom. *La Federación* owned them and they demanded absolute loyalty. Once you were in, you had no other family but *La*

Federación. They expected you to kill your own mother, if so ordered. But Arturo never believed his brothers capable of doing something like that.

All his young life, Rogelio and Eugenio looked out for Arturo. He knew that one day he would have to start working for *La Federación*. He didn't feel one way or another about it. It was just the way it was. And when that day came, he understood that he would be theirs for life. *La Federación*. The only way out was death.

The funny thing was, Rogelio's gunfight with the police had nothing at all to do with the drug trade. Rogelio had divorced a good woman only to go through one toxic relationship after another. Smoke enough cigarettes, you get cancer.

Arturo didn't like the woman Rogelio murdered. He thought she was a very bad person. But he didn't think she deserved to be beaten to death like that. Her body thrown in a canal like common trash.

Rogelio was making a break for the border when the police caught up with him. He had an Uzi and a .44 Magnum in the front passenger seat, as well as his Remington 742 Woodmaster rifle in the back.

It wasn't a high-speed chase by any means. Rogelio was going below the speed limit through most of it. Every couple of miles, he'd pull over and take a couple potshots at the lit-up police cruisers that were tailing him at a safe distance. He caused a few thousand dollars' worth of damage and shot one cop in the head. But then his car ran out of gas and the cops put fifty-eight bullets in him.

Rule number one when fleeing across the border: Fill 'er up first.

Eugenio didn't know what to do with himself without his big brother. He was like a dog without a master. His drug problem got worse, he lost his job and, more seriously, *La Federación* began to see him as a liability. Two weeks after Rogelio's death, Eugenio hung himself in his bedroom closet.

With the demise of his brothers, so too died the prospect of Arturo ever working in the drug trade. His brothers were his only connection to that world and even if he could establish the link, why would *La Federación* want to work with someone whose brothers had proven so unreliable?

Which was fine with Arturo. He didn't want to work for them. And he didn't need to. Because his brothers had written wills, leaving him everything they had.

After reimbursing the town for the damage Rogelio's rampage had caused and paying out the family of the cop he shot in the head, it wasn't a lot of money, but it was enough for Arturo to open a small auto repair shop. An honest business. The work was hard and relentless. Eighteen-hour days, six days a week. Church on Sunday.

He met a woman named Valery and they had a daughter. He was a good and loyal husband and a doting father. When his daughter turned eighteen, he sent her to the American Academy of Dramatic Arts in New York City to pursue her dream of becoming an actor. When he was a boy, he never in a million years could have imagined something like that.

Every time he thought about it, it made him tear up.

And he thanked his brothers and prayed for their souls.

They were victims of circumstance. Forgive them.

Every single day, Arturo thanked God for the life that had been gifted to him.

Money may not be able to buy happiness, he thought, *but it can buy hope and hope can change a person.*

A little bit of money can change everything.

Arturo opened at five AM. When he arrived at work, migrants were already sifting through the recycling bins and dumpsters around the side of the garage. Other local business owners would call the cops or, worse, *la migra*, but Arturo left them alone. He only wished he could do more for them. But there were just too many. Buy one person a meal and you'd soon be feeding a small town.

Three and a half hours later, Ryan pulled up in the Bronco. Arturo always tried not to judge people, but if he was being honest, he didn't like Ryan. Rich *gringo* who never had to work for anything. Born on third and thought he hit a triple.

But Arturo knew that such thinking was toxic. He believed in always seeing the best in people. He believed that people could change, that we were all, to one degree or another, victims of circumstance.

So, he greeted Ryan with a smile. "Hola, Señor Sheehan!"

"Hey, Arturo."

"New vehicle?"

Ryan nodded. "Whole damn thing shakes whenever I press on the brake. Think it's the engine."

"Well, let's have a look."

Arturo lifted the hood and took out his flashlight. It took him less than five minutes to diagnose the problem.

"You need a new carburetor," he said. "I have the part here. I can fix it right now, if you want."

"How much?"

"A hundred."

"How long'll that take?"

"Oh, maybe an hour."

"Alright, then."

Ryan watched the illegals scavenge through the recycling bins and dumpsters. *Like rats*, he thought.

"Can I borrow your dirt bike? Somewhere I need to be."

"Of course, amigo."

The Marine Recruitment center was located in a desert strip mall. A thin veneer of sand coated everything. Ryan parked Arturo's dirt bike outside.

His meeting was with Marine Corps Sergeant Edwin Gutiérrez. They had done a preliminary telephone interview and now they were meeting in person to discuss the next steps.

The sergeant rose from his desk as Ryan entered and firmly shook his hand. Ryan was immediately impressed by the man. His beige uniform was perfectly pressed, with seven meticulous creases. Three on the back, two down the chest, one on each sleeve. His high-and-tight haircut was flawless. He looked like the action figures Ryan grew up playing with.

Fucking G.I. Jose, Ryan thought.

Ryan believed that you could judge a book by its cover. The way a person presented themselves to the world was a choice, which revealed character. Sergeant Gutiérrez's appearance portrayed core values that Ryan admired: discipline, honor and respect.

Ryan was eager to pass his physical fitness test and follow in this man's footsteps and he told the sergeant as much.

"Passing your PFT is not the issue," the sergeant said.

Ryan looked confused. "Issue?"

"Your medical records indicate you spent a few weeks in the hospital a couple years ago. Drug rehabilitation, as well as psych."

Ryan's face dropped. "My parents passed."

"I understand. Unfortunately, the Marines are restricted from accepting anyone with a history of mental illness."

"Mental illness? My parents died. It was sudden and I—"

"I do understand," the sergeant said sympathetically. "But these are the rules. They are ironclad."

Ryan's eyes became distant. He was suddenly hyperaware of the earth's gravity. He could feel its weight, stifling, suffocating him, and he could not suppress his body's natural response. The rage erupted from the pit of his stomach.

His eyes focused on the sergeant's name tag. "My family has fought in every major American conflict since the Revolutionary War," Ryan said. "We fought and we died for this country." He leaned forward, his eyes narrow, his face snarling. "Were you even born here?"

Before the sergeant had the chance to react, Ryan was storming out the door.

Lance remembered monsoon season in Vietnam. They couldn't always get food helicoptered in because of the weather, so they relied on homemade traps. He remembered the first time he caught a baboon. He was going to discard it, but the other guys in his squad told him not to. They ate it raw.

He remembered when Sergeant McCullough was rotated into his rifle squad. McCullough was twenty-one years old, had just graduated West Point. It was his first time on active duty. He wasn't too keen on eating monkey meat, so he used his extensive West Point survival education to brew a vegetable stew.

Lance and the guys warned him not to eat the vegetation in Vietnam, but he didn't listen.

There must've been something psychoactive in what he brewed up because after he ate it, he lost his mind.

Some of the guys just wanted to leave him in the jungle, but they were outvoted.

They bound and gagged McCullough and dragged him along with them.

At night, when they made camp, they'd tie him to a tree.

Lance's son and daughter-in-law, Ryan's mother and father, were killed in a car accident on Christmas Eve. They were drunk when they were hit by another drunk driver. Everybody died. After it happened, Ryan started to remind Lance a lot of Sergeant McCullough.

But Lance couldn't abandon Ryan in the jungle or tie him to a tree. He was Ryan's grandfather. His only living relative. So he sent the boy to a mental hospital.

Lance had spent some time in one himself after the war. He

knew it wasn't a cure. He still had the nightmares all these years later. He was still damaged. But he didn't know what else to do.

Ryan went in angry and hysterical and came out sedated and aloof. If he hadn't worked through his parents' sudden and unexpected deaths, he had at least been able to bury it. In Lance's experience, that was the most a person could hope for.

Ryan sped the dirt bike into Arturo's parking lot and screeched it to a halt. Arturo greeted him with a friendly smile.

"All ready, señor."

Without a word, Ryan shoved a wad of twenties forward and snatched the Bronco's keys out of Arturo's hand.

He turned and marched toward his vehicle, then he stopped, turned back to Arturo and nodded over at the immigrants picking through the recyclables.

"You shouldn't let them do that," Ryan said. "Only encourages them."

Ryan got into the Bronco, slammed the door behind him, turned the ignition and kicked up dirt as he sped out of the parking lot.

Arturo had heard about mental disorders. He'd read about children that the cartels used in Mexico. All fucked up from the things they'd seen and been forced to do. Bipolar, antisocial, schizophrenic, PTSD.

The kids in Mexico were given counseling. Maybe the gringo just needed counseling? Arturo always saw the good in people.

10

D'Andre was walking his tray of food through the crowded high school cafeteria when he noticed a pretty girl at one of the tables smiling at him. He looked back over his shoulder at her as he passed, then he took a seat at a table by himself. He always kept to himself when Russ wasn't around.

He took a bite out of the flavorless hamburger on his tray.

"You lookin' at my shorty?" Lamar said.

D'Andre glanced up from his burger at the husky eighteen-year-old standing over him.

"I ain't know she was your shorty," D'Andre said.

D'Andre calmly returned his attention to the rubbery meat patty.

"Punkass," Lamar said and strutted away.

D'Andre gnawed on the plastic meat. He'd be applying to colleges soon. He had done the math. Even with the money his mother had been saving, he knew he'd still need financial aid. He'd learned enough during his time in Englewood to know that he didn't ever want to be under anyone's thumb. And his mother could do a lot with that money for herself. All she ever did was work. She deserved a little happiness in her life. Besides, how could he ever get into a decent school coming from this place? Affirmative action? Fuck that. He wasn't about to be some college or university's nigga in the window. A fucking mascot for white people to pat themselves on the back about.

That's when Lamar chucked the can of soda across the cafeteria that struck D'Andre in the side of the head.

D'Andre didn't hesitate. He sprung from the table and tackled Lamar. The whole cafeteria went wild as D'Andre pummeled Lamar, venting his anger, whooping his fucking ass.

D'Andre would have gotten suspended, but Lamar refused to say a word to the principal. It wasn't out of any sense of honor, but for fear of being labeled a snitch, which was a fate worse than death in this neighborhood.

D'Andre finished out the school day and returned to the duplex that he lived in with his mother, Rosslyn.

Miss Evelyn's puppy always bounced and yelped joyously when he returned home from school. D'Andre hadn't named it. Didn't feel right. It wasn't his to name.

D'Andre's mother had left a note for him on the refrigerator. *"Picked up a night shift. Dinner is in the fridge. Love you. Mom."*

Rosslyn had been laid off from her social worker job due to budget cutbacks. Now she worked at an all-night diner, until she could find something better.

D'Andre opened the refrigerator, removed a plate of noodles smothered in red sauce and put it in the microwave for three minutes.

The doorbell rang.

"Yo, yo!" Russ said when D'Andre answered the door. "Muthafuckin' Ali!"

D'Andre looked confused.

"You ain't seen?" Russ asked.

Russ took out his phone and played a YouTube video of D'Andre beating the shit out of Lamar in the cafeteria. "Man. You blowin' up!"

The microwave beeped.

D'Andre split the meal into two bowls and he and Russ devoured small portions of steaming microwaved pasta.

After he ate, Russ said he had to go do some business for AK and bounced, leaving D'Andre alone with Miss Evelyn's puppy. D'Andre was used to being alone and never really thought it bothered him, but he had to admit, he was thankful for the puppy.

It was two AM when Rosslyn returned home from her shift. D'Andre was still up. He'd already finished his homework, but he couldn't sleep so he figured he'd get a head start on next week's. Not that it really mattered. Most kids in his class didn't bother doing their homework, so the teacher never really checked.

D'Andre hated seeing his mother in her waitress uniform. Rosslyn was in her forties, but she looked much older, especially after a night shift.

"Baby? What're you still doing up?" she said.

"Couldn't sleep."

"Did you eat?"

D'Andre nodded. Miss Evelyn's puppy was coiled in a ball at his feet. He had told his mother that the dog was a stray that he'd rescued.

"How was your day?" she said as she sat down at the kitchen table, took off her nonslip service shoes and massaged the sole of her right foot. "Anything exciting happen?"

"Nah."

She nodded at D'Andre's textbook. "What's that?"

"Algebra 2."

"It's Friday night."

D'Andre shrugged.

She smiled. "I'm proud of you."

D'Andre lowered his eyes.

She exhaled and rose to her feet. "Well, I'm off to bed. Gotta be up early tomorrow."

"You work too much."

"I'm sending you to college. You do your part, I'll do mine. Deal?"

D'Andre hesitated. "Yeah, Ma."

"Alright, then." She limped off to her bedroom.

The next morning Russ came by with some lo mein. His girl, Shanay, had recently gotten a job at a Chinese restaurant in the Loop, so Russ got the hookup. He and D'Andre sat in the living room with chopsticks and oyster pails. Miss Evelyn's puppy sat at their feet.

D'Andre scooped up some lo mein in his chopsticks and moved it around in the air. They watched the puppy's head follow. They chuckled as D'Andre pretended to throw the lo mein and the puppy turned and looked for it.

Finally, D'Andre dropped the lo mein at his feet and watched the puppy devour it.

"He a hungry muthafucka, ain't he?" Russ said.

D'Andre dropped more lo mein. He pet the puppy as it devoured the food. Then the puppy looked up at them and began to whine.

"I think it gotta shit, yo," Russ said.

They took the puppy out onto the front lawn. D'Andre dropped him on the grass.

"Aight. Do your business," D'Andre said.

The puppy sniffed around the lawn in circles.

"Come on, lil' nigga. Just shit, yo," Russ said.

Finally, the puppy copped a squat and D'Andre and Russ cheered.

"There you go, dawg—"

The gunshots interrupted them.

D'Andre counted six of them.

He dropped to the ground, looked up and saw Lamar on the sidewalk, holding a .38. They locked eyes, then Lamar turned and ran down the street.

D'Andre checked himself for bullet wounds. He was surprised when he couldn't find any.

Then he saw Russ, face down on the lawn, his body twitching, bleeding out next to Miss Evelyn's frightened puppy.

11

The sun was barely rising when Ryan walked to the barn and began loading the Bronco with guns and ammunition.

Though he hadn't been to church since his parents' funeral, he still considered himself a Christian. If not spiritually, at least socially. As he piled his guns into the back of the Bronco, he thought about the story of David and Goliath. What if David had been forced to give up his arms? Then where would we be? Even the Bible was pro-gun.

He was one of the first to arrive at the civic center. He had more merchandise to unload than most of the other sellers. He was known in gun show circles as the Kid because of his age. They got a kick out of his enthusiasm for all things guns and his entrepreneurial spirit. Love what you do and you'll never work a day in your life.

Ryan always said some of the best people he met were at gun shows.

The doors opened at nine AM and people were already waiting.

He sold a Ruger American Rifle to a man named Dan Peterson. It was a gift for the man's son. His first rifle, so they could go hunting together.

Wilbert Holland purchased an antique Mauser 1896. He was a collector of rare guns and was thrilled with the find.

Ryan recommended the Ruger LCRx .38 Special to Karla Lane, who was looking for something small enough to fit in her purse, but powerful enough to fend off an attacker when she getting out of her waitressing job at two in the morning.

He handed out his business card to browsers. Just his name, phone number and the innocuous words, "Private Sales."

His last sale of the day was a little after lunchtime to a chubby, baby-faced white dude in glasses and a "We the People" tattoo stamped across his fleshy forearm. He said his name was Jesse. "Like Jesse James."

After Jesse, Ryan closed down and spent the rest of the day checking out other booths, meeting people and handing out cards.

Everywhere else, Ryan felt overlooked and ignored. Treated like an outcast, a loser, a failure. After his parents' death, he couldn't feel God's presence anywhere. But here, among like-minded people, he felt a sense of community. This was where he was happy.

This was Ryan's church.

Jesse dollied his purchases through the civic center parking lot to his beat-up RV. He opened the door and heaved the boxes of ammunition in first.

The RV was already stocked floor-to-ceiling with firearms, but Jesse could always make room for more.

It was both business and pleasure. Every year, Jesse took a cross-country vacation, visiting gun shows and stocking up.

Jesse added his latest purchases to his inventory. A couple shotguns, a handful of pistols and a real pretty AR-15. He was so impressed by how well it had been cleaned and cared for that he decided to hang on to the seller's business card. Ryan Sheehan.

Jesse moved to the driver's seat and turned the ignition. The

RV grumbled to life and chugged out of the parking lot. Its dented and rusted Indiana license plate looked like it was hanging on by a thread.

Jesse figured he'd find a diner and grab some grub before heading north. There were still a few more gun shows he wanted to hit on his way home.

12

D'Andre ate cereal. Some Fruity Pebbles knockoff that smelled like medicine. It was six in the morning, and he hadn't slept since the shooting. It was going on two days now.

Russ was still in the hospital. He was in critical condition, but he was alive, so at least there was that. But that was the only good news.

D'Andre wished Lamar had known how to shoot. He wished Lamar had hit him instead of Russ, as he'd intended. That would have made things much simpler. But now, he knew, things were about to get very difficult.

Rosslyn entered in her waitress uniform. She looked at her son with sad eyes. "Did you sleep?" she asked.

"Yeah," D'Andre lied.

"You don't have to go to school today," she said. "I can stay home, too, if you want."

"Go to work, Ma. I'm aight."

"Are you sure?"

"Don't worry. I'ma go to school."

She gave him a kiss on the head. "Thank God it wasn't you."

D'Andre lowered his eyes.

After his mother left, D'Andre brushed his teeth and put on a sweatshirt. He slung his backpack over his shoulder, pulled his hood up and headed for school. He was halfway there when a Chevy Malibu pulled up beside him and Shanay called out from the driver's seat. "AK need to see you."

She wore chopsticks in her hair, black slacks and a Chinese red plum blossom blouse.

D'Andre pulled his backpack strap tight around his shoulder. "I got school."

Shanay reached back and opened the back door of the Malibu. "Get the fuck in the car."

D'Andre climbed into the back seat next to Shanay's infant, Russell Jr., in his car seat. Shanay drove to a rusted, old garage in an abandoned part of town. They got out of the car and Shanay told one of the guys hanging out front to keep an eye on RJ. D'Andre kept his head down and followed her inside.

Every morning, Alonso Karr shopped for oranges at the corner store. He carefully examined each one. Jimmy, the sixty-year-old store owner, had a reputation around the neighborhood for being surly, but never when AK came around. He always set the freshest oranges aside for him.

AK once asked Jimmy, "Hey, Jimmy. Why you don't sell organic up in here?"

Jimmy shrugged. "Who gonna cough up an extra fifty cents for the same damn orange? First rule of running a business: give the people what they want."

"I heard that," AK said.

He was a businessman himself. He didn't care what the product was, only that it sold.

AK would spend the next thirty minutes walking his turf. It was his habitat and he was the apex predator, yet he seemed to drift through the neighborhood like a sad observer. His patrol always ended at Miss Simmons's boy's home. She would light up when she saw AK. He'd hand her the fresh oranges.

"God bless you, Alonso."

After Miss Simmons's, AK would make his way past a series of vacant and nondescript row houses to the abandoned garage.

AK's employees were almost exclusively young, black males. Smurf would be supervising them as they packaged crack cocaine into vials. AK had known Smurf since they were kids at Miss Simmons's. His real name was Chris, but they called him Smurf because the Adderall he liked to snort turned his snot blue.

AK would spend a few minutes, hovering around the floor like a foreman. His employees would greet him as they worked. Once satisfied, he would go into the next room, take out his Kindle eReader and study whatever that week's assignment was from the City College of Chicago. He was halfway through a chapter on the IS-LM Model, learning how the market for economic goods interacts with the loanable funds market, when Smurf escorted Shanay and D'Andre into the room.

AK put away his Kindle and gestured for D'Andre to take a seat across from him at the table. "You know why you here?"

D'Andre nodded.

"What da' fuck happened?"

D'Andre's words failed him.

"Nigga, you need a translator?"

D'Andre flinched, then spit it out. "I got into it with this nigga Lamar at school. Wasn't no big beef, but he come to my crib, blasting."

"What you say to 5-0?"

"I ain't say nothing."

"You sure?"

"I swear, AK."

"This nigga Lamar, he run with Spooky."

"Disrespect, yo!" Smurf said. "AK, we need'a teach these niggas!"

"So what'chu waiting for?" Shanay said. "Hand homeboy that nine so he can handle his business."

Shanay reached for the 9mm Glock on the table, but AK moved it away.

"Russ was one of my best earners," AK said. "It ain't enough that one nigga get got over this." He turned to Smurf. "Barbeque be on this year?"

Smurf grinned. "I ain't heard otherwise."

"I think this be the year," AK said.

"Hell, yeah!" Smurf said.

Shanay looked confused. "What'chu mean, 'barbeque?'"

AK pulled out a wad of cash and started sliding out hundreds. "Ya'll two get down to Indy for gats. Talkin' the type of pieces where you shoot a nigga, he ain't gettin' back up. Them Glock 22s, them AR-15s." He handed the cash to Shanay.

"AK. What barbeque?" Shanay said.

AK nodded to Smurf.

"Every fourth, Spooky be havin' a barbecue over Jackson Park with his whole clique," Smurf said.

"We ain't just gon' get this Lamar muthafucka," AK said. "We gon' 1-8-7 the whole set, and then we gonna take they corners."

D'Andre shifted in his chair. AK's eyes darted to him. He could sniff out weakness like a bloodhound.

"Problem, nigga?" AK said.

"Nah," D'Andre said, trying to stay cool.

"You down?"

"I'm down."

"Then get steppin'."

D'Andre rose from the chair and headed for the door with Shanay.

"Yo, Nay-nay," AK said. "Hang back a minute."

Shanay stayed behind as D'Andre left the room.

"How Russ doin'?" AK said.

"He shot. What'chu think?" she said.

"How 'bout you?"

"How 'bout me what?"

"How you doin'?" He indicated her red plum blossom blouse. "Lookin' all fine-ass Geisha an' shit."

"Geisha's Japanese, stupid. This is my work uniform."

"You givin' massages or something?"

"I work at a restaurant."

"Why?"

Shanay shrugged. "Bitch gotta make a livin'."

"You know I could take care of you."

"We ain't having this conversation, AK."

AK reached out to cup Shanay's ass and Shanay smacked his hand away.

"Russ my man," she said.

"Russ my nigga," he said.

"No. He just yo' excuse to get at Spooky."

AK smirked. "Yeah. He dat, too."

Shanay scoffed.

"Even if he do pull through, he ain't never gonna be the same," AK said.

Shanay shook her head. "Russ gon' be just fine," she said and walked to the door.

D'Andre was waiting in the back of Shanay's Malibu with RJ. Even though he was just an infant, the kid already looked like Russ. D'Andre watched the baby nap and felt sad.

Shanay stormed out of the garage, got in the driver's seat, looked back at D'Andre and frowned.

"What the hell you doing in my car?" she said.

D'Andre shrugged. "I thought you'd gimme a ride to school."

"Nigga, I got work."

D'Andre sighed and got out of the car.

"Be ready tomorrow morning at nine," she said to him from the car window. "You and me taking a trip."

Shanay sped off.

. . .

Gary, Indiana, is approximately twenty-five miles from Englewood, Chicago and only about a thirty-minute drive, depending
on traffic. It's convenient because there are no gun shops in
Chicago.

When Sal opened Patriot Guns in a strip mall on the Indiana-
Illinois border, he caught a lot of flak from law enforcement,
particularly the jackbooted Nazis at the ATF. Especially when his
guns started showing up at Chicago-area crime scenes.

Sal's reasoning was, "I can't read minds." All of his
customers were of age and they passed their background checks.
He was in full compliance. What they did with their guns once
they left his shop had nothing to do with him.

What was he supposed to do? Turn down a customer because
they "looked" like a criminal or a gang member? What does a
gang member look like? Wasn't that getting dangerously close to
racial profiling?

Sal used to be a cop. He loathed the hypocrisy of liberals. So,
when the door chime sounded and Shanay and D'Andre entered
his shop, he made no judgments. As far as he was concerned,
these were two more customers just like anybody else and he
would sell them anything they wanted within the confines of
the law.

"Hello, folks," Sal said with his best salesman's smile. "How
can I help you today?"

The two stood by the door. Timid. "I wanna buy a few
things," Shanay said.

"Absolutely," Sal said, handing her a clipboard. "Fill this out,
please."

While Shanay filled out the form, D'Andre gazed at the rifles
that lined the walls of the shop and the various handguns
behind the glass counter case. The husky stockboy had his back
to him, stacking boxes of ammunition.

Shanay finished filling out the clipboard and handed it back
to Sal.

"And your ID, please."

Shanay handed Sal an Indiana driver's license.

"Great. Just give me a minute to cross my t's and dot my i's here," Sal said as he typed her information into the NICS Background Check database on his computer.

"And this is your current address?" Sal asked.

"Mm-hm."

After a moment, the background check came back clean.

"Great," Sal said, handing her back her ID. "You're all set. What were you interested in today?"

"I'ma just look myself," Shanay replied.

"By all means," Sal said with a smile.

Shanay pulled out the list AK had written for her and wandered off to browse the store's selection.

Sal glanced at D'Andre. "How about you, young man?"

"I'm aight," D'Andre said.

"Are you sure you don't want to at least take a look?" Sal indicated the glass case, showcasing various handguns. "You'd be surprised by how affordable some of these pieces are."

"I'm only eighteen," D'Andre said.

"I see," Sal said. "In that case, you're restricted to long guns."

"Long guns?"

"Shotguns. Rifles."

D'Andre looked surprised. "I can buy a rifle?"

"Or a shotgun. Yes, sir," Sal said, offering D'Andre a clipboard.

"I ain't have my ID."

Sal frowned, pulled the clipboard back. "Legally, I cannot help you if you do not have identification." Then he indicated his stockboy. "But Jesse can."

The chubby-cheeked stockboy turned around and looked at D'Andre through his glasses.

"Hey. I'm Jesse. Like Jesse James," he said with a smile.

D'Andre thought the "We the People" tattoo on his forearm looked out of place. Like a spiked dog collar on a puppy.

Jesse walked D'Andre across the strip mall parking lot toward his RV.

"See, Sal's a licensed dealer," Jesse said. "He's got to run background checks and follow all of these other rules. But I'm just a private citizen, so I can sell to you without any of those headaches."

They entered the RV. D'Andre was dizzied by the number of rifles and shotguns Jesse had stored in here.

"This ain't illegal?" D'Andre asked.

"You're telling the truth about being eighteen, right?"

"Yeah."

"Then this is all completely legal," Jesse said. "Let me know if you see anything you like."

D'Andre didn't know where to begin. Every gun looked the same to him. He couldn't tell the difference between a shotgun or a rifle. When Jesse talked about handguns, he used words like .22 LR, .38 Special, .45 ACP. He might as well have been speaking Chinese.

Then D'Andre saw the black rifle. He recognized the design from movies like *Scarface*, *Platoon*, *Heat*. It beckoned him like a light in the fog. And though he did not know its name, it seemed as familiar and American to him as apple pie.

D'Andre held the AR-15 in his hands.

D'Andre and Shanay loaded their newly-purchased weapons into the back of Shanay's Malibu. Shanay had bought a small arsenal. Five rifles, three shotguns, a dozen handguns and ammunition. D'Andre feared his AR-15 might get lost among the others, so he rode with it in the front seat.

About ten minutes later, they were on I-90 and Shanay pulled over to the shoulder.

"What'chu doing?" D'Andre asked.

Shanay grabbed a semi-auto AK-47-style rifle from the back seat. "Come on," she said as she got out of the car.

D'Andre reluctantly followed her into the woods off of the interstate.

He'd heard gunshots before, but he'd never actually fired a gun. He knew the movies got it wrong. It sounded more like a loud pop than a bang. Shanay fired three shots into a tree. The rushing cars on the nearby interstate masked the sound. Besides, there was no one else around to hear it.

Then it was D'Andre's turn. He raised the AR-15, not sure what to expect.

He pulled the trigger and the muzzle exploded. His pupils dilated. Oxygen rushed to his muscles. His hormones spiked and his brain flooded with cortisol and adrenaline, serotonin and dopamine. Aggression and ecstasy. The rifle kicked back into his shoulder and his bullet tore through the tree trunk.

He stood there trembling. Palms sweaty. Heart pounding. Gripping the rifle. Melding with it. The feeling... It was Godhood.

As the two drove the rest of the way back to Chicago, D'Andre couldn't remember the last time he'd felt so relaxed. He sat in the passenger seat and watched the setting sun cast a calming red-yellow pall over Wolf Lake and for a moment, seemed to forget the problems that lay on the road ahead of him.

Shanay glanced at him from behind the wheel. "You know, Russ always talks about you. How you always reading and shit. You ever read *The Inferno*?"

D'Andre looked at her, uncertain. "Nah."

"Read it last year in Miss Jackson's English class. It's about this nigga Dante from back in the day. He saw hell and he wrote it all down in a poem, so that others would know. Called it *The Inferno*. Only thing is, Dante was just visiting. He got to leave. Go see heaven and purgatory too."

D'Andre watched Shanay. Her edges seemed smoother in the soft, waning sunlight. He returned his eyes to the window and they drove for several minutes in silence.

"You ever shot anybody?" Shanay asked.

D'Andre didn't answer.

"You never even fired a gun 'til today, have you?"

D'Andre lowered his eyes.

Shanay shook her head. "I'ma talk to AK for you."

D'Andre knew better than to hope, but he did all the same.

13

R yan was a senior in high school and he had never had a girlfriend. All his life, he'd believed Becky Brock was the one. She lived down the street from the ranch and he'd known her since kindergarten. She and her mother and father used to come over for barbecues. Becky liked to see the cows and horses back when they had horses.

They used to pretend they were farm animals. Mooing and oinking on all fours in the grass and once when they were seven, she sort of oink-kissed him on the side of the mouth. Her mother saw it and after that, their playdates were supervised.

Becky grew into a beautiful young woman who didn't drink or smoke and he grew into an awkward teen who listened to Papa Roach and Hed PE. The visits to the ranch stopped and she became very involved with her local Baptist Church.

Ryan was raised Catholic, but he tried going to her church once, just so he could stay a part of her world. She seemed pleased to see him and greeted him warmly, but she did not sit with him and after the service ended, she seemed to forget he was there. He stood awkward and alone until he decided to leave. He never went back.

She always wore long skirts and sweaters that covered her

shoulders. Never the tiny cutoff jeans or barely-there halter tops that some of the other girls wore. He liked that about her. How she didn't let anybody in her pants.

After his parents died, he worked up the courage to ask her out. She let him down easy, but Ryan didn't give up. He was quietly saving himself for Becky.

A couple months later, he heard how she was caught making-out and dry-humping Chase Hunter in the back of his Ford Mustang behind the high school. Chase was the captain of the football team and he and Becky were in the same youth ministry together. Since there was a barrier of clothes between them, they hadn't technically broken their vows of chastity.

After Ryan heard about it, everything just became about getting laid. He didn't have any luck with that either. Resentment of the opposite sex grew inside him like a baneful tumor.

The only reason Fernanda and Lauren even came over to Ryan's ranch to hang out was because Jeff had scored some coke. Or at least, what he thought was coke. Jeff bought it from one of the Mexican cooks at the restaurant he worked at. It sparkled more than the coke he was used to. He'd heard that that meant it was purer.

He figured that explained why it hit so hard. Why it burned the nostrils the way it did.

Crystal meth produces three times the amount of dopamine in the brain than the equivalent amount of cocaine. After their second round of lines, the four of them were high as fuck.

Jeff and Lauren started making out on the sofa and within minutes, Jeff was on top of her, pants around his ankles.

Fernanda pulled down her jeans and lay across Ryan's lap. Ryan poured a line on her ass cheek and snorted it.

Fernanda flipped over, pressed her open lips against his and shoved her tongue into his mouth. Ryan moved his hands down inside her thong and pressed them into the first hole he could find.

Fernanda grunted and unzipped his fly. She took him in his hand and scoured him like a dirty shower rod, but it was no use.

She pulled her mouth away from his and looked at him.

"You okay?"

Ryan blushed. "It's the coke."

Fernanda tried again. Biting his ear. "Tell me what you like, baby," she whispered.

Fernanda had been in and out of anger management programs since she was thirteen when she'd ripped out a girl's nose ring for saying that the only reason she wasn't a hooker was because she didn't charge. She had learned different ways to manage her rage. Breathing exercises, meditation, yoga. She was thinking about those exercises now. She was high and horny and she wanted to fuck someone.

Instead, Ryan led her into an oak-paneled study with various glass display cases. He said it was the Sheehan family gun room, a small museum of the family's private collection of firearms from every era. Pictures of Sheehan patriarchs dating back to the 1800s lined the walls.

Ryan removed an old, wooden rifle from a display case. "American long rifle. Circa 1777." He held the rifle as gently as a newborn baby. "My ancestor used this rifle to pick off British Officers in the Revolutionary War. This gun helped give birth to this nation."

He carefully replaced the rifle, then moved on to another glass showcase. "Colt 1851 Navy Revolver." He gazed at the revolver behind the glass with reverence. "Same model Wild Bill Hicock used. Only his had an ivory handle."

Then he approached another display case. "And this here's the pride and joy of the collection." His voice quaked with excitement. Or maybe it was just the crystal.

Inside the display case was a Winchester rifle. The name "Sheehan" was engraved on the butt. "Winchester rifle. 'The gun that won the West.' Jesse James's gun of choice and my great-great-granddaddy's, who built this ranch in 1884. It's the rifle of cowboys, ranchers and homesteaders."

Ryan looked at the gun with pride.

"You sell these?" Fernanda asked.

"Not these. This is my family's personal collection. The ones I got stockpiled in the barn, I sell," Ryan said. "Oh, shit, I almost forgot."

Ryan heaved a massive M60 machine gun. "Same gun Rambo used. Cool, right?"

She looked at him flatly, unimpressed on so many levels. "I'm gonna go do another line," she said and she walked out of the room.

The next day at school, Fernanda wouldn't talk to him and by lunch he had heard about the rumor going around that he couldn't get it up. Ryan felt violated. He'd let that bitch into his family's gun room, and for a split second, and only a split second, he fantasized about shooting her.

14

D'Andre was on the corner. How it worked was the client
would pay down the street and D'Andre would get the
signal. The stash would be hidden nearby. D'Andre would
prepare the order. The client would approach him in their car or
on foot and D'Andre would hand them the product. Like
McDonald's drive-thru.

D'Andre always put in an hour or two after school while his
mom was working a shift at the diner. It wasn't for the money.
The job paid less than minimum wage. The truth was, he didn't
really have a choice. He had to stay cliqued-up. Loners didn't
last long on his block.

Afterwards, they'd walk the afternoon's take and what was
left of the stash back to the garage, where Smurf would make
sure they weren't light.

You didn't want to be light.

AK and Spooky had been rivals for years. Their turfs abutted
each other, so they couldn't help finding themselves competing
for business. Things had been relatively peaceful until last year,
when AK started making moves, running his shit like a CEO and
not a gangster.

That was the difference between AK and Spooky. Spooky was

only about the life; AK was about the business.

AK was always trying to better himself. He had a philosophy that everyone in this world was better than him at at least one thing. Whether it be the CEO of a Fortune 500 company or the janitor who cleaned his toilet. AK believed that he could learn at least one thing from every person he met. It was a twisted form of humility, but if it sounded at all altruistic, it was not. AK took whatever he could and he never gave anything back. At least, not unless there was something in it for him.

AK applied what he was learning in his degree program to sell a better product for a lower price. Soon, he was siphoning off Spooky's clientele left and right. Spooky tried to parley, but there was no deal to be made. Spooky didn't have anything to offer. AK was putting Spooky out of business and Spooky knew it. There was only one way Spooky could compete.

He had to make it known that AK's gang were a bunch of bitches. Spooky may have sold an inferior product, but he had to brand it as the only game in town. He had to make people too afraid to buy from AK.

His soldier Lamar had already put Russ in the hospital and AK had yet to do shit about it. That already had people talking. Who's gonna buy Coca-Cola if Pepsi'll put a bullet in you? This was Spooky's Hail Mary.

"It don't make no sense," Shanay said to AK. She knew Spooky was dying a slow death. Hitting him at the barbeque was an overreaction. It was a mistake. "You really want 5-0 looking at you right now when you so close to having it all? 'Cause that's what's gonna happen the second you start blasting in the middle of Jackson Park. Fourth of July, families all having picnics and shit. They gonna bring the FBI down on yo' ass."

The Spooky problem would take care of itself, she assured him. Spooky couldn't compete. All AK had to do was be patient.

"What about Russ?" AK asked.

"Russ would agree with me."

AK shook his head. "Spooky been talkin' shit."

"So let him talk. You the one makin' his paper."

"My niggas is ready for war."

"AK. You surround yo' self with men. Men only be thinkin' with they dicks and they guns. You need to listen to me. This here bullshit's gonna come back and fuck you. Call it off. You know I'm right."

AK considered her. *You can learn at least one thing from every-one.* She was right. He was thinking like a gangster, not a CEO. He decided he would call off the hit.

Smurf was going over D'Andre's count when Shanay exited AK's office. D'Andre tried not to stare as she approached. She whispered to him, "You good."

D'Andre felt his chest flutter. He wanted to wrap his arms around her and lift her in the air and say thank you a thousand times. Instead, he nodded and muttered, "Word."

The shooting started just as Smurf was finishing up the count. Even though it happened outside the garage, D'Andre ducked.

"Bitch. What'chu doin'?" Smurf shouted at him. "Grab a strap!" Smurf grabbed his Glock and ran to the door.

It was a drive-by. By the time Smurf rushed out of the garage, the shooters' vehicle was already at the end of the block, banking a sharp turn out of sight.

Three of AK's guys lay bleeding on the sidewalk.

Smurf wasn't able to catch the vehicle's make or model before it disappeared, but they all knew who was responsible.

AK marched out of the garage and saw the bodies. Now there'd be cops. AK would have to ditch the stash house.

Spooky had crossed a line. Fucking with his paper.

D'Andre and Shanay watched AK. They knew what he was thinking. They all knew why this had happened.

It was because they hadn't answered for Russ. It was because Spooky thought they were bitches.

Now AK was gonna show him. There was no talking him out of it now. The barbecue was back on.

Don't nobody escape the Inferno.

PART III

ROCKETS' RED GLARE

15

The rifling of AR-15s nationwide had turned up nothing and there were other leads to follow up on besides Arianna. Among the victims of the shooting were a drug dealer, a bunch of undocumented immigrants, a Muslim man, and a woman whose ex-boyfriend had multiple domestics against her. Miranda and Greco had to explore the possibility that the shooting may have had nothing to do with Arianna.

Miranda wasn't buying it. The evidence suggested, but did not prove that Arianna had been shot first. So either she was the target or it was just a random rampage.

They decided that Greco would do the legwork on the other leads, while Miranda went to Texas to question Arianna's mother. They figured the mother would feel more comfortable talking to another woman.

Arianna's mother lived in a single-floor, two-bedroom home with a cracked and discolored concrete driveway and a dirt yard. There were about a dozen Private Property signs hung around the small chain-link perimeter fence.

When Miranda arrived, the front door was ajar. She knocked and announced herself and waited. When no one answered, she entered. The door opened into the living room.

The shag rug was spotted with cigarette burns and butts. Black mold bruised the corner of the room like something Satanic. The stench of stale liquor rose from old cans and bottles that littered the floor and the whole place smelled vaguely of vomit.

Arianna's mother was passed-out on the sofa in her panties and a faded, oversized Disney World T-shirt. She hugged a half-empty bottle of tequila in her arms. She was a round woman in smeared days-old makeup.

Miranda searched the house. In the kitchen, dishes were piled high in the sink. The ceramic floor was dotted with marijuana roaches and, well, regular roaches. The master bedroom was a dump of dirty laundry and stank of body odor and urine.

Over the bed, there hung a version of the American flag where the stars were blue on a white background and the red-and-white stripes ran vertical instead of horizontal.

She tried to open the door of what she assumed would have been Arianna's bedroom, but it was locked. A dark red light shone through the door gap. The doorknob had a spring bolt lock.

"Anyone in there?"

When no one answered, she removed a credit card from her wallet and slid it between the door and the frame, unlatching the lock. She turned the knob and opened the door.

The darkroom had line after line of photographs hanging from clothespins like Sunday laundry. Women bound in leather straps or ropes. Wadded-up panties or ball gags stuffed in their mouths. Whipped or dragged on leashes like dogs.

Miranda returned to Arianna's passed-out mother.

"Are you Cecilia Hernandez?" she asked. "Formerly Cecilia Barros?"

Cecilia's eyes squinted opened and when she saw Miranda, she quickly sat up. "Who are you?"

Miranda showed her badge. "Special Agent Miranda Lopez. ATF."

She was suddenly wide awake. She seemed scared. "You can't be here."

"I'm investigating the murder of your daughter."

"You need to go. If he sees you..."

"Do you mean your boyfriend? Are you still living with Elián Killington?"

She looked terrified. "Please, just go."

Miranda gestured toward the darkroom.

"Is that his work? Not exactly Norman Rockwell."

"Oh, God."

A beat-up Honda parked beneath the latticed carport outside. It had a homemade license plate that read only "EXEMPT." No state identification or registration number.

Miranda met Killington in the front yard. He wasn't what she was expecting. He had a goatee, and wore round glasses and a knit beanie. He looked like any other wannabe artist.

Elián was the illegitimate son of a wealthy Texas businessman and a Mexican prostitute. Miranda had checked out his rap sheet before leaving for Texas. He had a string of arrests for drugs and domestic battery.

"Mr. Killington?"

Elián grimaced. "This is private property."

"I'm Special Agent Miranda Lopez with the ATF." She showed her badge.

His eyes darted to Cecilia and she flinched.

"I'm investigating what happened to Arianna."

At this, Elián softened some. He casually grabbed a .357 Magnum from the passenger seat of his Honda. Miranda tensed.

"Come inside," he said.

Once inside, Elián set the Magnum on a side table and sat in the living room with Miranda. He answered all of her questions. It was the same story. Arianna was wild when she was younger, than she got involved with that church and moved out to L.A.

Then Miranda got to what she really wanted to ask him.

"Mr. Killington. What do you do for a living?"

"I'm a photographer and a filmmaker."

"I saw some of your work."

"It's a new series I'm working on."

He leaned back in his chair and crossed his legs. "Do you know what the French call an orgasm?" he asked.

"I don't."

"*La petite mort*. It means, 'the little death.' The idea is that at the height of orgasm, a person feels this sensation of transcendence, of death." He stared into her eyes.

"Where were you the night Arianna was killed?"

"I was casting my next film."

"Where?"

"I rented a room at the Hampton Inn. I was there all night."

"Do you have anyone that can confirm that?"

"The desk clerk. And a parade of actresses that came to audition."

"You have a list of their names?"

"Yes." He uncrossed his legs and sat forward. "Have you ever thought about acting?"

Miranda gave him an *are-you-serious?* look.

"I believe pornography is the truest art form. What could be more primal? More honest? More naked? You know, *Deep Throat* was a landmark of pornographic cinema. I want my film to be an homage to that. It's called *Hole*. It's about a woman who can't orgasm, no matter how hard she tries, no matter how many dicks and pussies she fucks. So our heroine, she goes to the doctor and the doctor discovers this physiological anomaly. The woman's clit is in her asshole.

"You see, it's about America. The only way this little whore can get off is by doing anal, which she's never done before, which she's never wanted to do before. But now, if she wants any sort of fucking relief, see, she's gotta do it. Lots of it. Lots and lots of anal. She symbolizes America and how we're all taking it up the ass and what can we do?"

He paused and waited for her reaction and the longer he

waited, the more certain Miranda was that he wasn't fucking with her.

In her freshman year Modern Art class at Cal State LA, she remembered her professor asking the class, "Is there such a thing as bad art?" He'd meant the question rhetorically, but she knew now that the answer was, yes. Most definitely yes.

She let the moment pass.

"Did you ever take any photographs of Arianna?" she asked.

"Are you crazy?" he said, tilting his head. "Of course I did." He stood up, walked to a bookcase and pulled out an old photo album and handed it to her. "She was one of my favorite models."

Miranda got a sick feeling in her stomach. She opened the photo album slowly.

Inside were wholesome photos of Arianna and her mother at the beach, in the park, by a lake. There were other models, too. Brides and grooms. Weddings. All tasteful and professionally done.

"It's my portfolio for my family and wedding photography business. Hey, even Andy Warhol worked in commercial advertising before he made *Blow Job*."

After her meeting with Elián, Miranda drove to the Hampton Inn in McAllen to check out his alibi. The manager had a record of his stay and remembered him well, mostly because of all of the women coming and going.

Miranda called each of the women who auditioned and pieced together a timeline. Elián was at the hotel until five in the morning.

No wonder Arianna ran the hell away from Texas to join a cult. But he had an alibi. Elián Killington may have been a psycho pervert, but he was fifteen hundred miles away when Arianna was killed.

16

Ryan had been waiting months for the next gen Glock to be released and when the day finally arrived, he was one of the first in line. He was waiting outside the gun store when his cell phone rang.

"Hello?"

"I'm looking for Ryan Sheehan?" said a gravelly voice with a slight Texas twang.

"Speaking."

"My name's Chip. I got your card at the gun show last week. I was interested in making a purchase."

"Looking for anything in particular?"

The voice paused. "You could call this more of one of those know it when I see it type of deals."

"No problem. You can come by today, if you want." He gave the caller the address to the ranch and arranged to meet any time after noon.

Ryan had just begun target shooting with his new Glock when a red pickup pulled into the ranch at around 12:15 PM. The driver was black. He stepped out of the truck. He was short, but not diminutive. He had a trim build and chiseled features. Ryan could see how women might find him handsome.

He wore a cowboy hat, a Western shirt, tight dark jeans and cowboy boots. Ryan always thought it was funny to see black cowboys, mostly because he was so used to John Wayne and Clint Eastwood movies. He didn't have any problem with it. Hell, he loved Morgan Freeman in *Unforgiven*. He holstered his Glock as the man approached.

"Chip?" Ryan asked.

"Yessir."

"Ryan Sheehan."

"Pleased to meet ya'."

They shook hands.

"This way."

Ryan led Chip to the barn. Chip whistled when he saw Ryan's stockpile.

"It's all used, but I test and retest every piece. I take great pride in my stock. You won't find no lemons here."

Chip nodded.

"So, where do you want to start?" Ryan asked.

"How much would you reckon all of this is worth?"

Ryan shrugged. "Well, I got about thirty rifles, twenty-some shotguns and around thirty assorted handguns and revolvers, last I checked."

"I'll give you fifty thousand dollars."

Ryan wasn't sure he heard him correctly.

"Come again?"

"Fifty thousand dollars for the lot of it."

Chip backed his pickup into the barn and Ryan helped load the guns into the truck bed. He was fifty K richer and Chip had enough firepower to arm a small rebellion.

"How'd you get into this trade?" Chip asked.

"Well, I come from a family of soldiers, sir," Ryan said. "My forefathers have fought in every war since the American Revolution."

"What about you?" Chip asked.

"I'm a different type of soldier."

"How do you mean?"

"Right now, our country is engaged in multiple wars," Ryan said. "There are the obvious ones. The ones being fought overseas against the Muslims. Then, there is the war at home. The one being waged against the real America."

Chip thought about this for a moment, then said, "What're you doing with the rest of your afternoon?"

"Why?"

"I think there's someone you should meet."

Chip made Ryan wear a bag over his head. Ryan would have objected, but the guy had just paid him fifty thousand dollars, plus it gave the whole thing a real cool air of cloak and dagger. Besides, Ryan was dying to see what Chip had to show him.

He was sitting in the passenger seat of the pickup. Chip was behind the wheel. He could tell that they had turned onto a dirt road a few miles back. The pickup bumped and lurched along.

Soon, Ryan heard the distant crack of rifle fire. Getting closer. They finally stopped and Chip told Ryan he could take the bag off of his head.

They were in the remote, Arizona wilderness. Emory oaks and Arizona Cypress hugged a lakeside camp.

"Welcome to the Lord's Predators training compound, Arizona branch," Chip said.

As Ryan and Chip stepped out of the pickup, balaclava-clad men and women in camo fatigues began unloading the arms from the truck bed.

"This way," Chip said. Ryan followed him through the compound. The crack of gunfire filled the air like a sweet symphony. Men and women in camo fatigues were lined up by the lake, target shooting rifles and pistols.

In the weightlifting yard, militia members pumped iron, pummeled heavy bags or scuttled across monkey bars.

"Muscle Beach," Chip said with a smirk.

There was a plywood maze. Ryan watched a team of militia

members rehearse moving through the structure, clearing rooms, finding concealment and covering one another.

"This here's the 'kill house,'" Chip said. "We use it for urban warfare training."

Further along, Ryan saw a man in a gi teaching a martial arts class. "And we call this 'the dojo,'" Chip said.

At the heart of the camp, trailers were circled around an old hunting cabin, which seemed to be the group's headquarters. Militia members congregated there and Chip introduced Ryan around. They greeted him guardedly. Wary of taking off their scarves or balaclavas or of using their real names.

At five o'clock, all training ceased and the entire unit crowded around the hunting cabin. They fell completely silent.

John Wilcox was a white man in his fifties with salt and pepper hair. Despite the arid Arizona climate, he wore a flat cap, plaid hunting jacket, tweed shooting trousers and white New Balance sneakers. If he were a cocktail, he'd be a double Evan Williams with a splash of eighteen-year single-malt Highland scotch. He stepped onto the porch of the hunting cabin like he was General Patton.

"I believe in America," Wilcox said. "I also believe that a government left unchecked risks becoming a dictatorship. I am a Christian, and I believe America to be a Christian nation, governed by God's laws.

"The Federal Government tells us we can slaughter babes in the womb, that a man can lie with another man, yet they do nothing about the invasion our country is facing from the south and the Middle East. The enemy is all around us!"

There were whoops and shouts and angry applause.

"I do not believe in yielding to what is politically correct or the lowest common denominator of what the federal government deems acceptable. I believe in speaking truth to power. Terrorists are Muslim. Drug cartels are Mexican. And the Bible is the only true law. And I don't give a damn what the liberal zealots and the jackbooted government thugs have to say about it! Now who's with me?"

The crowd flared like books on a bonfire.

Ryan turned to Chip, his eyes gleaming. He only had one question.

"How do I join?"

17

Over the weeks leading up to the Fourth of July, D'Andre became closer with AK.

Or rather, AK kept him close. Making him feel like he was part of the inner circle. He wanted to make sure D'Andre wasn't going to pussy out on him.

In order for the crew to save face, it was important that D'Andre was the one that got Lamar. D'Andre had to avenge Russ for the bullets that were meant for him.

So, D'Andre spent most nights at the garage and AK did all he could to indoctrinate him.

He tried beer. He tried kush. He tried pussy. Hoodrat pussy, but pussy. But what really interested D'Andre were AK's studies.

AK would lecture him for hours about organizational behavior, marketing, accounting, finance, strategy, and operations management.

Fuck if AK wasn't starting to like the lil' g.

One night, Democratic Alderman Charlie Yu appeared on the local news.

"The second amendment reads: 'A well regulated Militia, being necessary to the security of a free State, the right of the people to keep and bear Arms, shall not be infringed.' I repeat:

'A well regulated militia,'" he said. "In the days of our Founding Fathers, citizens were guaranteed the right to bear arms for militia use only. Today, we have the National Guard, making the Second Amendment moot. The Second Amendment does not guarantee an individual right to bear arms, which is why all civilian firearms should be outlawed."

AK chuckled and shook his head at Yu on the television. "This nigga."

The very next night, Yu came to see AK and AK let D'Andre sit in on the meeting.

"I'm sick of going to Indy for civilian hardware. I need that military shit," AK said.

Yu simply nodded.

A week later, a delivery of crates arrived from Indonesia.

18

Ryan had heard the rumors about Arturo's brothers. How they imported drugs for the Sinaloa cartel. But Arturo was a respected member of the community. By all accounts, he was hard-working and honest.

That's what everyone said about Gus Fring on Breaking Bad, Ryan thought.

It was just after 10 PM and Ryan was staked out in his Bronco across from Arturo's garage, sipping from a bottle of Wild Turkey. He could see the figure of Arturo in the office window. He was finishing up with a customer. A wetback, probably.

Ryan could count on both hands the number of American-owned small businesses that he'd seen come and go over the years. Arturo might have been born in the United States, but that didn't mean he wasn't the enemy.

How the fuck did that little spic manage to beat the odds? He couldn't have. Not without cheating.

All those beaners always coming and going. Ryan was sure he used illegal labor, stealing American jobs, and every Mexican in three counties patronized him. He put every other nearby garage out of business, this little wetback.

It wasn't right.

It was un-American.

And that was before whatever work he was still doing for the Cartel. Arturo may have had everyone else fooled, but not Ryan.

Both the guy's brothers were members of the most violent and ruthless organized crime group on the planet, but he's somehow a choirboy? Get the fuck out of here. You believed that, Ryan had some sand in Sonora to sell you.

"The enemy is all around us." Ryan repeated it like a mantra as Arturo's last customer of the night fucked off.

Arturo began the work of closing up.

When Ryan entered, the door chime sounded and Arturo looked up from his work and was about to tell whomever it was he was closed when he recognized Ryan and smiled.

That was when Ryan shot him.

The bullet struck Arturo in the hip and Arturo yelped and fell to the ground.

Ryan looked just as shocked as Arturo did. It took them both a moment to process what had just happened.

Then Arturo began to crawl. Desperate. Terrified.

Ryan watched blood streak across the linoleum floor in his wake.

Arturo huddled in the corner of the room. Nowhere to go. He whimpered, "Please, señor. Do not kill me. I have a daughter. Do not kill me. I want to see my daughter again. Please."

Ryan didn't like what he was saying. In order to do this, Ryan needed Arturo to be the one thing. Not a father. Not a victim. Not a *person*. He needed him to be the one thing, the enemy, and nothing else.

Because this was war.

"Shut-the-fuck-up."

"Please. This was just an accident. I will not tell. I won't say nothing."

Then Arturo began to cry and that was too much.

"My daught—"

Ryan fired into Arturo's body until he was quiet. And then everything was terribly still.

Nitroglycerin incense and the metallic scent of blood hung in the air. Death's cologne. He let it waft over him, *into* him.

He had killed for his country. He was a soldier now.

This is who I am, and this who I've always been, he thought.

He was eerily calm. Disassociated.

Ryan returned to John Wilcox and was formally inducted into the Lord's Predators militia.

19

W ilcox was proud of Ryan and that made Ryan happy. They walked together by the lake. Ryan was no longer required to wear a bag over his head when he came to the compound.

It had been three weeks since Arturo's murder. The investigation continued, but police could find little reason why anyone would have wanted to kill him. Everyone loved Arturo. They didn't know where to even begin.

Ryan spent every minute he could at the militia compound. He would often disappear from the ranch for days at a time. Lance had no idea where his grandson was getting off to. He didn't understand Ryan; he didn't know how to communicate with him and it was futile to try to discipline him. So Ryan came and went as he pleased. He seemed happy and he didn't come home with strange welts, stinking of booze and cow shit anymore, so Lance took it as a win.

"Why do we celebrate King David?" Wilcox asked Ryan as they strolled along the lakeside. "Because he killed Goliath and delivered the Israelites from the tyrannous Philistines," Wilcox said. "My point is: there are man's laws and there are God's laws. God's laws are what rose these United States from the ashes of English tyranny. And it's man's laws that are raping her today."

Ryan nodded, rapt and reverent.

"Your ancestors fought for this country. They gave their lives. Is this what they fought for? It falls upon us to honor them. To carry on their legacy," Wilcox said. He put his hand on Ryan's shoulder and stared hard into his eyes. "Never forget the price of freedom."

Ryan got goosebumps.

Ryan had never been athletic, nor had he ever really had any interest in sports, besides hunting and competitive shooting, but after a few weeks with the militia, he felt like he could've played varsity football.

Every morning started with a high intensity warm-up. Fifteen minutes of high knees, fast jacks, butt-kickers, burpies, squat jumps, push-ups, pull-ups. Then they moved on to an hour of hand-to-hand combat training. Boxing, Muay Thai and judo.

The rest of the day was dedicated to tactical firearms training.

After six weeks, Ryan was certified and assigned to a border patrol unit. On the night he was certified, Ryan stood outside the cabin with the others, listening to another of Wilcox's sermons.

"'A well-regulated Militia, being necessary to the security of a free State, the right of the people to keep and bear Arms, shall not be infringed.' I repeat, 'the right of the people to keep and bear Arms, shall not be infringed.'

"Citizen militias are what won American independence from King George. And how did settlers survive Natives, wild animals and bandits on the wild frontier? This country was built by Americans and their guns.

"As Thomas Jefferson once said, 'The tree of liberty must be refreshed from time to time with the blood of patriots and tyrants.' Make no mistake, my brothers and sisters. We are coming due for another revolution."

Coming due? Shit. The revolution had already begun.

20

On the night of July 3, D'Andre came home from AK's and let the puppy out. He watched from the window with his AR-15. The gun made him feel safe.

After the puppy finished its business, D'Andre opened the door and called it back inside. He carried the dog up to his bedroom and placed the AR-15 under his bed. Then he lay down on his mattress, stroked the puppy's warm and furry little body and made peace with the fact that by this time tomorrow, he would be a killer or dead or both.

The next morning, D'Andre visited Russ in the hospital for the first time. It had been over two months since he had been shot. Various surgeries and medical complications had prolonged his stay. Russ lay in his bed in a web of IV tubes and monitoring wires.

"D'Andre?" Russ said. "What you doin' here? You should be out getting drunk!"

"Ain't thirsty," D'Andre said, unable to meet Russ's eyes.

Russ raised a weak fist. "Happy Fourth, homie."

D'Andre met him with a fist-bump. "Happy Fourth." He sat by Russ's bedside. "How you feeling?"

Russ shrugged. "I'm aight."

"You know when you be out?"

"Shit. Who knows?" Russ said. "Guess I'll be seeing the fireworks from my window."

D'Andre shook his head. "If only that nigga knew how to shoot."

"Then what?

"You wouldn't be here."

"No. Your ass would, or in the morgue. Bitch, you know I'm tougher than you," Russ said with a smirk.

D'Andre's eyes welled up.

"Lamar be wiling out," Russ said. "But I'ma handle him soon as I'm out this hospital bed. Believe that."

"I talked to AK," D'Andre said.

"What he say?"

D'Andre sat hunched over like he'd been punched in the stomach. Russ pretended not to notice.

"I'ma be out soon. I'll handle Lamar. You tell AK," Russ said.

D'Andre shook his head. "Fourth of July's the only time Spooky's whole clique is together out in the open. We ain't just clipping Lamar, we wiping out Spooky's whole crew."

Russ hardened.

"I'ma handle Lamar," he said. "You ain't doing shit, nigga."

A tear streaked down D'Andre's cheek and he was immediately embarrassed by his show of emotion. D'Andre rose.

"Hey, yo, D. Hold up," Russ said.

D'Andre retreated toward the door.

"Don't do it, D'Andre! That nigga mine!" Russ said as D'Andre rushed out the door.

It had been many weeks since Arianna's death and Marco Barros had been conspicuously mute, but on the morning of July 4, he released a statement condemning senseless gun violence, but reaffirming his stance on gun rights and his support for the NRA.

"Had my poor daughter been armed that night, she would probably still be alive today," he said.

Miranda was having breakfast at the Hilton in Houston, Texas when she read the story on CNN's website. She nearly choked on her coffee. How could he say this? What the hell was he playing at?

It's true that he'd been polling badly before Arianna's death. Texans felt he'd gotten too rich, too old and too moderate. It had remained to be seen how the death of his daughter would play to his base.

But this…

This was fucking sacrilegious.

Did power mean that much to him? Politicians. Fucking sociopaths. Every. Last. One of them.

Miranda paid her check and left before they brought the omelet she'd ordered. She'd lost her appetite.

She was in Houston for the annual NRA Meetings and Exhibits. She was meeting Jimmy McClean, who was going to introduce her to Paul Atkin. He was the Executive Director for the NRA's Institute for Legislative Action. She was hoping he might be able to help her turn up some leads.

She arrived at the convention, showed her credentials and was screened by security. She always thought it was funny that these events had a "No outside firearms allowed" policy.

She passed through the metal detectors and entered the exhibition hall. Representatives from gun manufacturers operated booths, showing off their wares.

She noted the different advertising strategies. Some manufacturers billed themselves as the latest thing. Their representatives spoke to their consumers like Steve Jobs at an Apple Conference. Professional and sleek.

Others ran their booths like live-action beer commercials. Large-breasted women in cropped, skintight tank tops and camo booty shorts modeled rifles and handguns. "Booth babes" was how she heard one man refer to them.

At one of the booths, she watched a young girl with her father. The girl couldn't have been older than ten. She perused the different brightly-colored pistols and the various prints. Zebra, cheetah, snake skin, croc. She gawked at a neon pink Glock 42 and begged her father to buy it for her. The miniature gun was the perfect size for her little hands.

Miranda met Jimmy McClean in a meeting room. "What the fuck is Marco thinking making statements like that?" she said.

"How do you think you got this meeting? This is how it works," McClean said.

While they waited for Paul Atkin, she gave McClean an update and he was less than enthusiastic.

"Has the investigation gone cold?" he asked.

"Cold? It was never warm."

McClean looked sick. Miranda actually felt sorry for him. "But this meeting could really help," she said.

Paul Atkin entered the room. He was tall and lean with thick dark hair that was just beginning to gray at the temples. He wore an expensive tailored suit and a million-dollar smile. "Sorry to keep you waiting," he said.

McClean shook his hand. "Paul, this is Special Agent Miranda Lopez of the ATF. Miranda, Paul Atkins, Executive Director for the NRA's Institute for Legislative Action."

Miranda shook his hand. "Nice to meet you."

"You, as well. Shall we?"

They sat around the meeting table.

"It goes without saying, we are all mortified by what happened to Senator Barros's daughter."

"And we really appreciate your help, Paul," McClean said.

"Absolutely. Anything we can do."

"The shooter had firepower," Miranda said. "He could be a member."

Paul shrugged. "It's possible."

"It's *probable,*" Miranda said.

Paul squinted at her. "Okay."

"The NRA receives thousands of letters and emails from its membership," Miranda said. "I need access across the board to anything that mentions Barros."

Paul snorted. "That's quite a request."

"Anything you can do to help, right?"

"You know I can't share our member information."

Miranda frowned. "Don't you want to help us catch this person?"

"Of course. But not by resorting to 'unreasonable search and seizures.'"

"This isn't political," Miranda said.

Paul tilted his head. "Everything is political."

After the meeting, Miranda was in a fury. "You told me you would do whatever it takes. You promised you would stand up to them."

"I will," McClean said. "But you can't cross a bridge by burning it. Let me work on him."

Miranda shook her head.

"Please. Don't lose heart." McClean said. His voice was choked with emotion. "This isn't about the NRA, or politics, or you, or even me. This is about Arianna. I'm begging you. Please, don't give up on her."

Miranda met his pained stare. The poor bastard. Jesus. Was she actually starting to like him?

Miranda went to the hotel bar. She had never been a big drinker, but after that meeting, she could do with a cocktail. Besides, it was the Fourth of July.

Jackson Park was packed. Chicago was a very cold city most of the year, so when it was warm out, residents took advantage.

Runners jogged, dogs fetched, people played baseball or

frisbee or soccer. Lamar was with his set, laughing and bullshitting. A forty in one hand, passing a blunt with the other. Spooky was the grill master, all three hundred pounds of him, cooking up dogs and burgers and chicken wings for his soldiers.

The element of surprise was everything.

Ryan glassed the illegals from about a hundred yards away. He could see them, but they couldn't see him. It was nearly a hundred degrees, even with the sun setting in the Arizona sky. They were distant black specks moving in a line under the blistering sun. *Like ants under a magnifying glass,* he thought.

Ryan's squad consisted of himself and two other militia members. A man with an overbite and a woman with a braid so tight it looked like it was about to peel off her scalp. The group worried their SUV might give away their approach. The migrants would see them coming and they would scurry like cockroaches. They wanted to catch the whole herd, so they proceeded on foot.

The heat was oppressive. Lance fanned his face with his embroidered Vietnam Veteran cap. He hadn't seen Ryan for a few days now. He figured he'd be alone for Independence Day, so he went to the rodeo, mostly just to be around other people.

He rose to his feet and put his cap over his heart as a chubby cowgirl sang the National Anthem.

If Lamar and his homies hadn't drank so much malt liquor or inhaled all that bud, they might have realized it was ninety-five degrees out and the young men on their periphery had no need for their baggy sweatshirts.

· · ·

They were penning them in. Ryan from the north. Underbite from east. Hair Braid from the south. The migrants marched on, unaware and exhausted, into the trap.

When everyone was in position, they struck.

AK's shooters pulled handguns and sawed-offs from their sweatshirts and let loose.

The migrants raised their hands as they stared down Ryan's rifle.

Fight or flight.

Lamar ran for his life, as bodies dropped all around him. He emerged onto the street.

Looking for a way out. Any way out. The will to live overpowering.

A migrant charged Ryan. He froze.

The van cut Lamar off and D'Andre stepped out and pointed the AR-15 at him.

The cowgirl reached the crescendo. "O'er the land of the free…"

• • •

"Kill that nigga," AK said from the van's driver's seat.

"...and the home of the braaaaave?"

The audience cheered. The stall gate rose and a cowboy rode a bucking bull. In the sky, fireworks exploded.

Ryan's rifle cracked. The migrant fell down dead.

Lamar tried to grab the rifle. D'Andre fired a .223 round into Lamar's chest.

The migrants swarmed like bees.

"Shit!" AK said, as a police cruiser hits its lights and sped toward them.

One fired. Then another. Before Ryan knew it, all three of them were.

AK floored it, leaving D'Andre behind.

Lance whistled and cheered, as the cowboy held on and more fireworks lit up the sky while, in the desert, Ryan and his brothers-in-arms gunned down the helpless migrants and in Chicago, D'Andre dropped the rifle, put his hands in the air and was cuffed by police. A dark shadow flashed across his soul.

• • •

Ryan, Overbite and Hair Braid returned to their SUV and Ryan guzzled water. They had left the bodies in the desert. No one would ever find them and even if they did, nobody would care.

21

M iranda gestured to the bartender for another glass of wine. She spotted McClean down the bar. He raised his glass, and she returned the gesture. Then he indicated the empty seat next to him.

They had a drink together, then moved to the outside patio for a better view of the fireworks.

"I was sure you hated me," McClean said.

"I just think you never left the frat house."

McClean smiled. "At least you're not a liar."

"We're all liars."

"It's not true, you know. What they say about me."

"Oh?"

McClean shrugged. "Plays better. Sex sells."

Miranda shook her head.

"Have you ever been in love?" McClean asked.

She thought about Camilla. Love or lust?

"I've been in love only once in my entire life," McClean said.

"What happened?"

"I went into politics, and I lost her."

The fireworks cracked above them in brilliant displays of light and color.

"Isn't this nice? Talking instead of yelling over each other?" Miranda said.

"It's alright."

"What if it was always like this?"

McClean shrugged. "War is not a quiet thing."

"No. And we all have our roles to play, I suppose," Miranda looked into her empty wine glass. "Nice drinking with you."

"We should do it again sometime."

She smiled. "Good night."

Back in her hotel room, Miranda called Camilla, but it went to voicemail. *She must be working*, Miranda thought.

Her phone chimed. A text from McClean. *Night cap?*

She hadn't been with a man since before Camilla. What was it? Four years?

Why was she tempted? Was it his vulnerability? Was it about having power over him? She ignored the text, took an Ambien and went to bed.

Her cell phone woke her at a quarter to four. The sun wasn't up yet.

"Yeah?" she said.

"Special Agent Miranda Lopez?" She could tell from his tone that he was some kind of cop.

"Speaking."

"This is Detective Morris of the Chicago Police Department. You're handling the Arianna Barros murder?"

"Yes."

"We had a shooting yesterday involving an AR-15. We had it rifled and it came back positive."

Miranda was still half-asleep. She wasn't sure she heard him right.

"Sorry? What?"

"We found your gun."

PART IV

AGAINST ALL ENEMIES, FOREIGN AND DOMESTIC

22

Within hours, Miranda was in a forensic firearms lab in Chicago, examining an AR-15. "The serial number. Can you salvage it?" she asked, noting the scraped patch near the trigger where the number had been removed.

"We tried, but whoever removed it knew what they were doing," the lab tech said.

Detective Morris was a balding bulldog with barbed blue eyes. "The shooter is waiting in interrogation," he said.

He sat in the interrogation room staring at the floor. He didn't look like a killer, but Miranda knew that looks could be deceiving.

"Where'd you get the rifle?"

He didn't respond.

"I can help you," she said. She leaned forward, trying to catch his gaze. "You wanna do twenty-five to life?"

Silence. D'Andre didn't say a word.

. . .

D'Andre's mother's red and puffy eyes suggested that she had been crying. She sat in the interrogation room, wringing her hands.

Miranda pitied her. One thing she loathed was seeing a mother in pain, having watched her own mother work her fingers to the bone for her children.

"Can you tell me about D'Andre's friends? People he hangs around with?" Miranda asked.

"I don't know. Kids from the neighborhood, I guess…"

"Do these kids have names?"

Rosslyn lowered her gaze. "I work a lot. I'm not home as much as I should be."

"I understand," Miranda said.

"No. You don't. You look at him, you see just another angry young black man with a gun. He's a good boy." She broke down in tears. "When can I see my son?"

Miranda handed her a Kleenex.

Miranda sat across from Shanay. "Can I get you anything? A soda? Coffee?"

Shanay looked right through her.

"You know you're not in any trouble, right?" Miranda said. "I'm bringing in all of D'Andre's friends. It's my hope that one of you might be able to help my investigation."

Shanay leaned back, pouted her lips and crossed her arms.

"Nothing to say?" Miranda said. "Okay. That's fine. If you don't know, you don't know. But it's my duty to warn you that if you withhold information, you can be charged with something called obstruction of justice. In this case, it would be a felony. I've seen people get five years for felony obstruction. That's what I will recommend for each person I find out is holding out on this. See, I'm not regular police. I'm ATF. We're federal. We have considerably more power."

"I don't know nothing," Shanay said.

"Five years. Your son would be, what, eight, by then?"

"Don't be talking about my son!"

"His childhood spent in the system. Would he even recognize you when you got out?"

Shanay's lip trembled. A mother's pain. "You just said I wasn't in any trouble."

"You're not. Because you don't know anything. You're telling me the truth, right? Because after you leave this room, there's no turning back."

"I already told you, I don't know nothing."

"Great. Then you have nothing to worry about. Thank you for your time, Shanay. You're free to go."

Shanay rose from the interview table. Her body was tense. She took a couple hesitant steps to the door, then stopped.

"I'm sorry, Shanay. I don't mean to rush you, but I have a lot of other people to interview." Miranda indicated for her to leave. "Please…"

"I may have heard something… I don't know… About this gun shop down in Indy…"

Miranda smiled.

Miranda called Bob Greco at the FBI and caught him up on the investigation. He managed to catch a flight and be in Chicago by that evening. The next morning, they drove down to Gary, Indiana.

The door chime sounded as they entered Patriot Guns. Sal looked up from behind the counter and immediately smelled a rat. Thirty years as a cop in Indianapolis had taught him that Feds carried themselves a certain way. Like they owned every building they walked into. He resisted the urge to spit.

"Welcome to Patriot Firearms," he said, sparing them his salesman smile.

They flashed their badges.

"We need to ask you some questions," Miranda said, as she

heaved a gun bag onto the counter, unzipped it and showed him the AR-15 rifle inside. "You sold this last week to two young people."

"No, ma'am. That was not sold in my store," Sal said.

"We have a witness that says otherwise," Greco said.

Sal jabbed his finger in the air. "That rifle was sold off-site."

"By whom?" Miranda asked.

"Me." Jesse entered from the stockroom.

"Where's the 4473?" Greco said.

"There isn't one," Jesse said. "It was a private sale. Like Sal said, sold off-site."

"Look. I run an honest business here," Sal said.

Miranda glared at him with flinty eyes. "Where'd you get the gun?" Miranda asked Jesse.

"I don't think I have to tell you that," Jesse said.

"Why wouldn't you?" Miranda asked.

"I haven't broken any laws. I have a right to privacy."

"The serial number was removed," Greco said.

"News to me," Jesse said. "Had one when I sold it."

Miranda had had enough fucking around. "Okay, shitbird," she said. "I assume you watch the news." She indicated the rifle. "Do you know what this is? This is the rifle that killed Senator Barros's daughter."

The blood drained from Jesse's face.

"So what are you doing with it?" Miranda said. "Maybe you're helping get rid of a murder weapon? That'd make you an accessory. Hell, maybe you killed her yourself?"

"None of that's true!" Jesse was sweating now.

Miranda took out her handcuffs. "Do I look like a give a fuck?"

"This isn't legal," Sal said.

Miranda looked at him and smiled. "Call it a loophole." She turned to Jesse. "Hands on your head."

"I got it at a gun show," Jesse said, digging in his pockets.

"Where?"

"Arizona."

"Did you get the seller's name?"

Jesse fished through his wallet. "Here." He handed her a card.

Ryan Sheehan. Private Sales. (520)458-0927.

The FIM-92 Stinger is a man-portable infrared homing surface-to-air missile launcher that can be shoulder-fired by a single operator. The missile is five feet long and three inches in diameter with four-inch fins. It has an outward targeting range of up to 15,000 feet, making it an ideal choice for shooting down low altitude UAVs, airplanes and helicopters.

In theory, a single man positioned within a few miles of an airport could easily shoot down a passenger jet.

They cost around thirty-eight thousand dollars each. Wilcox had a guy that was going to sell him four for three hundred thousand, which was a steal on the black market.

Not much was known about Wilcox or where he got all of his money. It was likely that he had served in some branch of the armed forces. He knew too much about military training and tactics not to have.

But Ryan also knew, or at least had a very strong suspicion, that Wilcox was not the top of the pyramid.

For one, the Stingers would only be staying in the compound for a night. In the morning, they'd be picked up and moved, presumably for use in operations in other parts of the country.

Which meant there were others. Branches, units, cells. Whatever you want to call them.

No, Wilcox wasn't a general. He was a colonel, at best.

Lance never slept through the night. He'd stir most mornings at around three or four, pop in his earbuds and watch Amazon Prime or Netflix on his worn iPad 3 until he was asleep again.

His son had gotten him the iPad for Christmas eight or so years ago. Lance never imagined he'd ever actually use it, and at first, he didn't, but he finally relented and brought it along to watch movies on a five-hour plane ride to an old army buddy's funeral. He found it therapeutic. Just the headphones and the screen and the story in front of him. His thoughts and memories often felt like an albatross and while nothing could ever free him from them, the stories streamed on his iPad at least let him forget for a while.

It was just after one o'clock in the afternoon and Lance was napping on his front porch. The iPad rested on his lap and one of the earbuds hung from his head, having slipped out of his ear. Miranda and Greco approached. When he was younger, it would have been impossible to sneak up on Lance. Age had dulled his senses and heightened his paranoia.

"Excuse me?" Miranda said.

Lance awoke with a start. "What do you want?" He had a scratch on the side of his face, like he had recently fallen.

"We're looking for Ryan Sheehan," Miranda said. They showed their badges. "Is he home?"

Lance squinted. "Feds?"

"He's not in any trouble. We just want to ask him a few questions," Greco said.

"About what?"

Miranda and Greco exchanged glances.

"Are you a relative?" she asked.

"I'm his grandfather."

"And your name is—"

"None of your business." Lance's nostrils flared.

Miranda paused, then said, "We're trying to trace a firearm that was used in a crime. We think your grandson may have possessed and sold this firearm. We do not believe your grandson broke any laws. We only want to know where he got the weapon."

Lance sized them up like cattle, then scoffed. "Good luck."

"Does Ryan live here?" Miranda asked.

"He pops in from time to time, never stays long," Lance said. "But even if you do find him, I doubt he'll be able to tell you anything. Just too many guns, coming and going."

"Thank you for your time," Miranda said, offering her card. He didn't take it, so she left it on the porch step, then she and Greco retreated back to their rented Toyota Camry.

The truth was Ryan was rarely home at all anymore. Lance was worried. A few days ago, Ryan came back in the middle of the night. He was only home for a half an hour, but it was long enough for Lance to hide his iPhone in Ryan's Bronco. He'd learned how to use the "Find my iPhone" app a couple years ago while messing around on his iPad.

Lance tracked Ryan's Bronco to the middle of nowhere. Worried about what he might find, Lance chose a stealthy approach.

He scanned the compound from a distance with his hunting binoculars. He saw the camo-clad fundamentalists training and playing at war.

Jesus. His grandson was hanging out with fucking terrorists.

Lance approached the compound and was stopped by a pair of armed guards.

"Halt!" They said, raising their rifles.

"I'm here to get my grandson."

"This is private property," one of them said, taking a step forward. "You need to turn around."

Lance swatted the rifle barrel away and cracked him in the nose. The other guard tackled Lance. The gravelly dirt scraped the side of his face. The militiaman with the broken nose pressed his gun to Lance's skull and moved his finger to the trigger.

"No!" the guard said to his enraged partner. "It's not time yet."

After a moment the militiaman lowered his rifle.

"Get the fuck out of here, old man."

After Miranda and Greco left, Lance was a mess. He couldn't stop thinking about Ryan. What if those militia nutjobs did something to Ryan because of him?

Not time yet. That's what the militiaman said. It meant that the time was coming. The time when they actually would pull the trigger.

They were making plans.

How much longer would the hidden iPhone's battery last?

Soon, he would lose Ryan forever. He couldn't. He couldn't lose another son. The clock was ticking and he was running out of options.

He didn't trust the Feds, but the devil you know...

He downed a quarter bottle of Irish whiskey, then went out to the porch and snatched Miranda's card off of the step. He picked up the landline and dialed.

Miranda and Greco weren't far. They had been staked-out all night just outside the ranch, hoping to catch Ryan returning. Miranda's cell phone rang.

"Special Agent Lopez."

"Sometimes I believe we're just a nation of extremists with no common ground, no room for understanding." Lance spoke slowly. The whiskey still warm in his stomach. "If I tell you where he is, give me your word you'll bring him home."

Miranda paused. "Mr. Sheehan. I give you my word."

Miranda and Greco used Lance's iCloud account to track the iPhone to the militia compound. This was going to be tricky. The place was private property and they didn't have a warrant. The militia was heavily armed, but did not appear to be breaking any laws. Miranda and Greco knew that their presence would only antagonize them. The whole thing had the potential to turn deadly fast.

So they waited. It was all they could do.

Wilcox decided that they would use the Bronco. Pickup trucks were too risky. The cargo would be visible. The last thing they needed were prying eyes. Ryan was more than happy to volunteer his vehicle.

Wilcox had also chosen a half dozen militia members to trail them in a trio of Jeeps. Just in case. Ryan knew these soldiers were whom Wilcox considered the cream of the crop. Ryan was thrilled to be counted among them.

Once everyone was clear on the operation, they loaded into their vehicles and the convoy snaked out of the compound.

Miranda was napping in the front passenger seat when Greco noticed activity on the "Find My iPhone" app. He shook her gently. "They're on the move."

The sun was beginning to set and Ryan couldn't see anything around them but an ocean of desert. He guessed that they were somewhere near the border.

Up ahead, he saw four vehicles, parked in the shape of a crescent moon. The convoy had no choice but to meet the sellers in the kill zone.

Miranda and Greco followed several miles behind, so as not to be spotted in the open desert. They did not have a visual on Ryan's Bronco and the GPS signal had died. But it was fine. They could follow the tire tracks.

• • •

The convoy pulled up to the rendezvous and Ryan disembarked with the other militia members. Each of them was armed with an AR-15. America's rifle.

"There they are," Miranda said, spotting lights in the distance. Greco parked the Camry out of view.

They got out and circled around to the trunk. Inside, there were a pair of tactical vests which read "ATF" and "FBI" in large white letters, respectively.

Time to suit up.

Miranda pulled the slide on her Glock, then slid the weapon into her vest's chest holster. Greco pumped a Remington 870 Express shotgun and slid extra rounds into the hook and loop shell panel on his breast.

They ascended to the top of a rocky ridge, crouched low and glassed the rendezvous with binoculars.

The place reminded her of a story she'd heard about how when old-time Las Vegas gangsters caught somebody cheating in their casino, they'd drive them eight miles out into the desert and put them six feet under. 86'ed.

Nothing good ever happened this far out in the desert.

Certainly nothing legal.

Ryan was excited. The whole thing seemed like something out of the movies. The sellers carried themselves like soldiers. Caps and sunglasses and neck gaiters. They held their rifles with the barrel down and the butt outside their arm.

The guy who seemed to be in charge approached Wilcox. He wore hiking boots, jeans, a black camp shirt and a cowboy hat. He was Chinese.

"All this necessary?" Wilcox said, indicating the armed coterie.

After all, the weapons had already been paid for. If anyone needed to worry about getting ripped off it was Wilcox.

"It looks like they're doing some kind of deal," Greco said, binoculars cupping his eyes. "We should call this in."

"How?" They were in a dead zone. No cell signal. No radio frequency. The Wild fuckin' West.

It was weird to see a Chinaman in a cowboy hat.

In *Breaking Bad*, you only ever saw white people or Mexicans at these types of deals.

The whole setup reminded Ryan of that scene when Walter White was in the desert and looked the bad guys dead in the eyes and said, "Say my name."

Ryan thought of what his nickname should be when he started getting a rep.

Wilcox told his men to hang back. He walked with the Chinaman to the back of one of his vans. Inside were four crates the size and shape of baby coffins. Wilcox opened one of the crates, rifled through the wood excelsior and heaved out a stinger missile launcher.

"Fuck!" Both of their stomachs churned.

When Miranda thought of rightwing militias, she usually pictured a dozen unemployed, white trash Army rejects hanging out with Walmart rifles talking about how they need to kick out all the Mexicans. This was definitely not that.

"What do we do?" Greco said. "We're not equipped for this."

"Back to the car," Miranda said.

They moved through the dark desert.

Nothing but the sound of an occasional gentle breeze.

Despite the stress of the situation, she found the environment soothing. If she ever became deaf, she'd move to the desert. It was one of the few places in the world that spoke louder without sound.

The buzzing interrupted her ruminations. It was strange to hear a honeybee at night. Unnatural. Then her face turned ashen. That was no honeybee.

The drone hovered about twenty feet from the ground, watching them with its night vision eye. The words "ATF" and "FBI" plastered across their vests like scarlet letters.

Wilcox's men were loading the crates into the Bronco, when the Chinaman received a phone call. He listened, smiled politely at Wilcox and walked a few steps away.

Then he shot Wilcox in the back of the head with a .357 Magnum.

Skull fragments and brain matter fell to the ground like ticker tape.

It sounded like kernels popping.

Miranda ran back to the ridge and glassed the horizon.

The militia had been aching for a gun battle and they'd found one. She lowered her binoculars, thought about Camilla, then charged toward the fight.

"Where are you going?" Greco said.

"If we lose Ryan Sheehan, we lose our only lead."

Ryan couldn't get his legs or lungs to work. He stood there frozen as rifles exploded all around him. It was different when the other guys could shoot back.

A militiaman ran to him and tried to snap him out of it. The militiaman caught a bullet in the jugular. His blood spritzed Ryan's face. That did the trick.

Ryan dropped his rifle and fled into the desert bramble.

Miranda could run a six-minute mile. She would make this one in five.

Ryan lay prone in the darkness. He watched his comrades get picked off one by one. Then the guns fell silent. His brothers and sisters in arms were dead in the dirt.

The slaughter was over. Now it was time for the hunt.

The enemy spread out and searched the area for any survivors.

"Got one," one of them said, as he took aim at a militiaman fleeing for his life into the dark desert. A single squeeze of the trigger put him down.

These guys weren't taking prisoners.

There was nowhere to go. And Ryan was unarmed.

Miranda crept up and took cover behind one of the Jeeps. She slipped underneath the vehicle as a mercenary patrolled past.

"On your fucking feet," she heard one of the gunmen say.

She watched Ryan rise to his feet. Tears streaked down his cheeks and snot bubbled in his nostrils.

"This one looks like a teenager," the gunman said. "You like playing G.I. Joe?"

From beneath the Jeep, Miranda weighed the pros and cons of her situation.

Con: She'd have to take out two other guys before she could get to the gunman that had Ryan. Con: The gunfire would undoubtedly attract the attention of the other gunmen in the surrounding area. Pro: As an ATF agent, Miranda received extensive firearms training. Con: She hadn't practiced shooting in over a year. Con: She had never shot a living person before. Pro: She had the element of surprise. All of her targets' backs were to her. Con: She would have to announce herself.

That made two pros to five cons. She probably wouldn't make it out of this.

Ryan pissed his pants.

The gunmen laughed.

Miranda thought of Camilla again and quietly rolled out from under the Jeep. "Federal agent."

The first target was the closest. He swung around with his rifle in his hands. She squeezed the trigger and hit her mark, splitting his temple. She had to adjust quickly to aim at the second mark. She fired a three-shot burst. The first two bullets passed over his right shoulder, and the third lodged just above his vest in his collar bone. It didn't kill him, but it was enough to render him no longer a threat.

This gave her primary target enough time to turn away from Ryan and level his rifle at her. Her training kicked in. She dropped to one knee and inhaled as bullets sailed over her head. She took careful aim, exhaled and pulled the trigger.

It was a beauty. Right between his eyes.

She didn't have time to appreciate it though. The others would be on their way. She ran to Ryan, grabbed him by the arm and sprinted back toward the ridge.

Greco was still jogging toward the scene when he saw Miranda sprinting back toward him with Ryan. Greco had quit smoking five years ago, but not before his pack-a-day habit fucked his lungs.

They heard the crack of rifles.

"With me," Miranda said. She zigzagged with Ryan across the open desert. Bullets exploded in plumes of sand at their feet or whizzed by their bodies, missing by inches.

They found cover in a shallow ravine. The Camry was just over the next rise.

"Go," Greco said, gripping his shotgun.

Miranda rose with Ryan and sprinted the last leg of their marathon.

When he heard the rifles crack, Greco rose from his cover and answered with shotgun volleys, keeping the pursuers at bay.

Miranda and Ryan pushed onward. Never looking back. Fifty yards. Forty.

Greco ducked down and reloaded.

The rifles went silent.

Greco waited in his hiding place.

Had they retreated?

He peeked over the edge and a high caliber bullet tore the left side of his face off.

Greco fell back into the ravine and gagged on blood.

Miranda reached the rise and looked over her shoulder long enough to see several murky figures standing over Greco's limp body.

Their muzzle flashes announced Greco's demise.

Their four-door Toyota mid-size salvation was parked just ahead. By the time she saw that the tires had been slashed, it was too late. The Chinaman and a contingent of gunmen had been lying in wait. They sprang their trap.

Miranda and Ryan were surrounded.

Cowboy Chinaman sized Miranda up, then gave the nod to his men.

The bullet struck him in the nape of the neck, snapping his head back and sending the cowboy hat flying through the air. The shot had been suppressed, but it came from somewhere above them, so the gunmen raised their rifles and scanned the ridgeline.

Miranda threw her body over Ryan as lead rained down from above. Little meteorites peppering the gunmen like pin cushion dolls.

The gunmen raised their arms and tried to surrender, but the onslaught continued.

When the desert dust had settled, Miranda was left crouching with Ryan in the center of a bullseye of dead bodies.

The man with the suppressed FN SCAR rifle descended from the ridge. He was average height and average build and had a calm, almost absent way about him. He did not look or seem nearly as threatening as he should have.

Miranda raised her Glock.

"Easy," the man said. "I work for Marco Barros."

Miranda held the gun on him, her arm trembling.

"Who the fuck are you?"

His voice was at once firm and comforting.

"Call me Cal."

23

A cry sounds the same in any language.
So does a laugh.
So does a bullet.

The kid pulled the trigger.

The kid's name was Rodrigo. He worked as a spotter for the local MS *clica*. It was volunteer work. He wasn't paid for it. He did it to earn respect.

Rodrigo didn't have a dollar to his name, so when Cal handed him the hundred, it was like winning the fucking lottery.

He'd never had enough to be able to afford a real piece and, besides, the *clica* didn't want anyone else packing on their turf.

For one, in the land of the blind, the one-eyed man is king, just like how in the 'hood where no one's packing, the men with the Glock 22s and MAC-10s wear the crown.

These gangstas were gun control all day.

But most of all, a gun charge was a lot of years and could

lead to people snitching about *clica* members' identities and criminal activities.

The 'hood had eyes.

But Rodrigo would never flip. He was hardcore. 'Least he wanted to be.

Sure, he had the MS13 ink, but ink didn't really mean shit. Everyone in the neighborhood was rocking MS tats. It was more about national identity than gang affiliation. The leadership didn't mind because it made it harder for law enforcement to tell the difference between the half-steppers and the real deals.

The truth was few people sporting MS tats were actually inducted members.

The hardcore members, the guys who ran the neighborhood, they were the *clica*, the clique. Each *clica* ran their territory and answered only to *la mesa*, or the table. The ruling council.

The local *clica* was only about ten guys.

Hardcore members.

Under them were the associates. The guys climbing the ladder. The next generation of hardcore.

And finally, there was the biggest group. The one Rodrigo belonged to. The uninitiated. The wannabes.

Rodrigo got his gun off a crack addict that tried to rob him. The guy was thin as a board and fiending so bad he couldn't see straight, so it was easy for Rodrigo to overpower him. He hit him in the head with a brick and left him bleeding on the side-walk. The next morning, he wasn't there, so Rodrigo assumed he lived. He didn't give a shit either way.

The piece looked like something you'd get at Toys R Us. It was small and he felt like if he tried hard enough, he could crush it in his hand like a Coke can.

He'd seen hardware like it before. People called it a *puta*'s gun. A Saturday Night Special. His original plan was to use it to stick up people until he had enough cash to buy a real piece.

Then Cal walked into his life.

An outsider, asking about the *clica*.

This was his chance to move up.

Cal would be his induction hit. He'd be in.

An associate.

The gun was chambered with a 22-caliber round, which was actually more dangerous at close range than higher caliber munitions because the bullet had only enough energy to penetrate the skull, but not enough to exit, so it would basically bounce around the inside of the head, turning the brain into guacamole.

Rodrigo'd say the guy came around looking to roll up on the *clica*, so he smoked him like kush.

That was the plan anyway, but then the *pinche* piece of shit gun jammed.

You can't force fate.

After the junk gun misfired, Cal sighed and turned around and did what he had to do. He went easy on the kid though. He only broke his wrist. The kid dropped the piece. Cal asked him about the Arianna Barros shooting, but even with a broken wrist, the kid was defiant.

"Fuck you. I don't fear death," he said. "I'm a man."

Cal smiled. "Do you know what happens to a man after you cut his balls off?"

The kid didn't flinch. He'd heard shit-talk before.

"The body stops producing testosterone," Cal said. "You gain weight, lose muscle, grow tits." Cal removed his K-BAR knife from his ankle holster. "You become a woman."

The kid swallowed hard.

"Are you still a virgin?" Cal asked, knowing full well that half the reason any of these kids joined the life was to get laid. "Do you have your eye on any particular female? Maybe a few? I bet you do. Like you said, you're a man. How could you not? Now, I want you to picture those young women, and I want you to imagine what it will be like when they see you walking down the street. Fat, bitch tits, voice like a little girl.

"I want you to imagine the homeboys running a train on your chubby bitch-ass, holding you down while you squeal like a drowning rat."

The kid started to lose color in his face.

Cal waved the knife. "Just a flick of my wrist. One clean slice. But I will not let you bleed out. Some gun powder and a lighter will cauterize the wound. It will not feel good, but you will survive. No. I'm not going to kill you, my young friend. Because life can be so much worse."

Yeah, the kid had heard shit-talk before. Enough to know that this wasn't shit-talk.

"He drove a black Bronco," the kid said. "Old school. Like from the '90s."

The '90s. Before the kid was even born.

"What did he look like?"

The kid shrugged. "I don't know. He was wearing a ski mask."

Cal's glare cut into him.

"The Bronco had Arizona plates," the kid said.

Cal left the kid without harming him any further and called Pat Roti. Pat ran the info through his intelligence network and within an hour, he came back with a black 1996 Ford Bronco, Arizona plates FNS-215, which was spotted at a Compton traffic cam immediately after the shooting.

The driver's face was obscured, but the vehicle was registered to John Irwin of Tuscon, Arizona. Using compiled data from John Irwin's social media, Roti forwarded Cal a profile. Irwin was an Antifa sympathizer and a self-dubbed "Revolutionary socialist."

Cal grabbed a coffee at a Burger King and began the drive to Arizona.

. . .

Irwin lived in a tract housing development that grew out of the unblemished Arizona desert like a patch of bacteria. Cal cruised his Range Rover through the endless rows of cookie cutter homes until he found number fifty-nine, and parked in the empty driveway.

Cal tried the doorbell and a dog barked somewhere inside. After a few moments, he slipped on a pair of nitrile gloves and picked the lock. When he opened the door, he was immediately assailed by a fog of canine shit.

The dog was still barking and Cal found her in the kitchen. A Boykin spaniel, locked in a crate. It looked like she had been left alone for days. Crap caked in her fur. Starving and filthy. There was absolutely no need for it. No utility. It was just cruelty for the sake of cruelty. What type of animal treated another living creature like that for no reason?

Cal let the spaniel out and filled a bowl with water. She drank and drank and drank. He opened the window over the sink to air the place out. Then he began his search.

There was a large bong on the living room table. The bookshelf had writings by or about Karl Marx, Lenin, Che Guevara, Ho Chi Minh and other communist and socialist revolutionaries, as well as multiple mason jars of marijuana.

In the bedroom closet, he found a rifle and a couple of handguns.

He opened Irwin's laptop. Password protected. He'd take it with him and crack it later.

Cal returned to the first floor. The place still reeked. He moved into the living room.

The pine-y smell of Christmas clashed with the smell of excrement in nauseating fashion. The adjacent wall appeared freshly plastered.

Cal went to the garage and got a hammer. He chipped away at the living room wall like an ice sculptor.

The body inside was shrink-wrapped. Pine-scented car air fresheners hung off it like ornaments.

Cal studied the bloodless face mashed against the plastic. It was Jon Irwin.

Merry fucking Christmas.

In the fridge, Cal found some ground beef that was only a few days past its sell by date. He cooked it up with some white rice and gave half to the spaniel.

After lunch, he took the dog outside, wished it luck and they went their separate ways.

Pat Roti called two days later. Cal was at the boxing gym. No one would agree to spar with him, so he had to settle for bag work.

Using traffic cams, Roti's people had tracked the Bronco from California back to Arizona.

"It's like the shooter wasn't even trying to hide," Pat Roti said. "The shooter used highways and toll roads the entire way. They stayed highly visible."

The trail ended at a Walmart outside of Tuscon. Pat Roti couldn't get access to the Walmart's closed-circuit camera feed and they couldn't get a warrant because theirs was a covert operation, which was just another word for illegal.

They couldn't exactly tell a judge that they learned about the Bronco by breaking a kid's wrist and then threatening to castrate him.

So they'd have to send an operator in to steal the security footage.

Covertly.

Hank wanted to be the black Bruce Willis. This was back in the early '90s when *Die Hard* movies were all the rage.

He'd rehearse in the mirror. "That punk pulled a Glock 7 on

me. You know what that is? It's a porcelain gun made in Germany. It doesn't show up on your airport X-ray machines, and it costs more than you make here in a month."

Willis delivered the line in *Die Hard 2* and it was total bullshit. There is no such thing as a Glock 7. Glock handguns are made of polymer, not porcelain. They do show up on X-rays. Glock is Austrian, not German. And finally, Glocks are relatively inexpensive firearms. But great actors made you believe what you knew was a lie.

Hank moved to Los Angeles in his early twenties. No money and no contacts. Just a dream. And an anaconda between his legs.

He hadn't realized when he walked into the room that the audition was for a softcore porno flick. It wasn't until they asked him to disrobe. By this point, Hank had been in L.A. for two months and become so used to rejection, he figured what did he have to lose?

They hired him on the spot.

He wasn't sure about taking the role. It didn't pay much. But then he read about how plenty of A-list action actors had gotten their start in adult films. Sylvester Stallone. Jackie Chan. Cameron Diaz. She may not be an action star, per se, but she did play one of Charlie's Angels.

After he did the scene, he couldn't believe he got paid at all. It was hardly work.

He did a few more porno gigs just to keep the money coming while he took "real" auditions. But so much of who you are in Hollywood is who you know. Hank had to go to the right parties, drive the right car, do the right drugs.

Money got tight. He started missing out on auditions. Then he was offered guy-on-guy. It was a lot of fucking money. He could pay off his debt and get his acting career back on track.

Only problem was he wasn't gay. But great actors made you believe what you knew was a lie. And there were no small parts, only small actors.

And Hank, well. There was nothing small about his part.

He went all in. Put his heart and soul into the role.

The fans loved him. Hung Hank. Hank Horsecock. He got famous. Too famous. He couldn't even get guy-on-girl gigs anymore. It was all gay, gay, gay. He was typecast. Homo Hank.

Mainstream audiences didn't want no cupcake action star. So he buried his dreams in Hollywood. 86'ed them.

That was thirty years ago. Back when he was about twenty-five pounds leaner and had hair on the crown of his head. He didn't get recognized anymore. Nowadays, he was just Hank the security guard.

He still had the anaconda though. He kept a string of middle-aged girlfriends. They all knew what it was. That Hank wasn't the settling-down type.

And none of them were looking to settle down with him. They were lonely. They were widowers, or divorcees or women trapped in bad marriages. They were just looking for a temporary release. Like how some people go to a yoga or boxing or spin class. Or get a massage. A deep, deep tissue massage.

Tonight, it was Wanda. She was a teacher at a school for disabled children and she loved her work. Hank thought she had a beautiful soul. He was amazed that at forty-three, she had never found anyone. Wanda always attributed her bad luck in romance to her weight. She was a larger woman, but Hank didn't believe that was why. Her weight was only a problem because she made it a problem. Her poor self-image restricted her from ever taking a chance on love.

He had told her all of this once, but he wasn't sure if she took any of it to heart.

It was Tuesday at midnight, and there she was, standing outside the locked automatic doors, right on time.

Hank killed the security cameras. No one ever looked at the night shift security footage anyway. Never had reason to.

This wasn't exactly the Louvre.

Who's going to rob a middle-of-nowhere Walmart on a Tuesday night?

Cal was staked-out in the Walmart parking lot when Wanda arrived. He watched Hank the security guard unlock the front door and let her inside.

Cal had come prepared. He was ready to pick the lock, hack the security system and incapacitate the guard. But that was all Plan B.

He found that in low-risk operations like this, things tended to take care of themselves. The fifteen-buck-an-hour rent-a-cop would inevitably take an extra-long cigarette break or a thirty-minute dump or a nap in the break room.

Cal always waited for an opening to present itself before resorting to Plan B.

It didn't make sense to hurt people when he didn't have to. It was cleaner all around if they never even knew he was there.

Hank's late-night booty call was Cal's opportunity. He snuck into the Walmart and immediately heard Wanda moaning. She and Hank were somewhere in the home décor section, getting down on a display sofa.

Cal crept into the security office and went to Hank's workstation. Hank had left himself logged in.

Wanda began to yelp.

Cal accessed the security surveillance log, chose the date and time and popped a flash drive into the machine.

Wanda was singing soprano now...

The download bar began to fill...

Wanda started screaming...

The download neared completion...

Wanda came and the file transferred.

Cal pocketed the flash drive.

Yippie-ki-yay, motherfucker.

• • •

The footage was from several weeks earlier. Marco Barros's delay in hiring Pat Roti had put them behind the eight-ball. The Bronco arrived at two forty-five in the afternoon and parked away from the camera. Three minutes after three, an Uber arrived and dropped off a high-school-aged white male in jeans and a black Punisher T-shirt. The teen approached the Bronco.

The driver met him. He was approximately 5'10" with a medium build. He wore jeans, threadbare tactical boots, a faded camo jacket, baseball cap and sunglasses. He never once turned his face toward the camera. Because of this, it was difficult to determine his age. He was most likely over thirty and under fifty.

They appeared to exchange a few words, then the kid in the Punisher T handed the man an envelope. The man opened the envelope and fingered through what looked like cash, then he nodded and turned toward the camera and led the kid toward the back of the Bronco, keeping his head down the whole way and avoiding any reflective surfaces.

It was ninety degrees out, but the man appeared to be wearing layers under his camo jacket to confound forensic video analysis of his body type. The cap and boots would also make it difficult to accurately determine his height.

The man opened the back of the Bronco. Inside, Cal could make out three handguns and a pair of rifles, one of which was an AR-15.

The two chatted for a few moments, then the man handed the kid the car keys. The kid closed the rear door, got in the driver's seat and pulled away in the Bronco, while the man disappeared on foot down the street.

The entire exchange occurred in less than two minutes. Cal watched the video over and over. Studied it, frame by frame.

When Pat Roti had put Cal on this job, part of him had wondered if they were all reading too much into the shooting. After all, the universe was arbitrary and violent. What if Arianna was just another casualty?

But Cal was sure now. The Arianna Barros murder was not random. It was a hit. The other people in the building were killed to cover it up. The man was just too good at avoiding cameras and hiding his face. It was tradecraft. He was a professional. But there was something else about him. Buddhists called it *sati*, or mindfulness. The focusing of one's awareness only on the present moment. It is considered part of the path to rebirth and the attainment of nirvana.

Japanese samurai had a similar tradition called *iaidō*. A state of total awareness, in which the samurai is prepared to quickly draw his sword in response to a sudden attack. *Iaidoka* would spend countless days and hours, drawing and resheathing their swords. Drawing and resheathing. Living only in the present.

Cal understood that at the end of the day, we are all just sacks of chemicals. Serotonin, dopamine, glutamate, norepinephrine. We are walking punch bowls of drugs. Pocketed in flesh and buttressed in bone. Slaves to our nervous systems. The sympathetic. The parasympathetic. The enteric. Dosing us.

But Cal had learned how to control his chemicals. How to self-prescribe. With mindfulness. And he had learned to spot it in others.

It was hard to explain. The man in the video exhibited microexpressions only someone like Cal could pick up on. A secret language.

The man floated. Like walking on water.

Cal understood. This man had no past. He had no future. He was only right now.

Cal felt as though he were chasing himself. And in a strange way, he felt less alone in the world.

Pat Roti ran facial rec on the kid in the footage. The intelligence apparatus kept an extensive database of facial records plucked from social media. Facebook, Instagram, Tinder, you name it.

Anyone who had ever had an account or even been tagged in a photo was in there.

Lambs not led, but rather offering themselves up to the slaughter.

Pat got a hit on the kid in the Punisher T-shirt. His name was Ryan Sheehan.

He forwarded the information to Cal.

Why didn't the man just destroy the Bronco?, Cal thought, as he drove south toward Sheehan Ranch. Why sell it and (presumably) the murder weapon? It was the only loose end. The only thing linking the man to the crime.

And why leave all these breadcrumbs? Taking highways and toll roads, leading them to the Walmart, but expertly hiding his identity from cameras?

If it were him, Cal knew why he would do it. It was Russian Roulette. The thrill. The man couldn't let it end.

He needed to keep the war going.

They both did.

It was July 5 and Lance was up before the sun rose. He needed to get his mind off of Ryan, so he grabbed his thirty-ought-six Springfield and went out hunting.

Hunting was what he called it, anyway. He didn't like to kill things. Not since the war. So, he'd shoot tree branches on distant ridges, cacti in deep valleys, stones atop high canyons.

He'd killed his first man on his second week of active duty. He was point man, clearing what he thought was an empty village, when he came face-to-face with a Viet Cong. Literally almost bumped into one another turning a corner. The poor bastard looked just as surprised as Lance did. Lance squeezed his eyes shut and reacted, pulling the trigger of his M16. The man's blood and brain tissue splattered all over him.

He got a little hysterical after that. It was a quiet hysteria that followed him through the war. And followed him home.

He watched a lot of people die. Why he survived, he didn't know.

Lance had to spend a lot of time in a hospital when he got back to the world. And all these years later, he still couldn't sleep through the night. So now he only shot things that didn't bleed.

Like restitching a wound that would never heal. Each trigger pull eased the power those terrible years had over him.

The gun was just a tool. Nothing more. He was the one in control, he assured himself.

Cal watched the old man leave the ranch with his thirty-ought-six and, seeing that there was no one else home at the ranch, decided to tail him. He followed his tracks out into the desert until he heard the rifle shots. Cal was not armed, but he was not worried.

He followed the sound until it fell silent. In a clearing, he found slugs lodged in tree trunks. Cactus arms blown off and stones chipped from ricocheting bullets.

The old man was either the world's worst hunter or a few fries short of a Happy Meal, Cal thought. He picked up the old man's trail and followed it into a boulder-strewn maze of cliffs and crags.

He stealthily followed him through the labyrinth of sandstone. All he could hear was the wind.

Then abruptly, the tracks disappeared.

Cal smiled to himself. He knew the old man was somewhere up ahead, waiting to ambush him.

Cal couldn't tell you why he did it. Maybe it was admiration. For the old man. For the fight still left in him. Or maybe it was the same reason he allowed the baby banger to pull his junk gun on him in South Central. Something he was still trying to figure out.

But for whatever reason, Cal didn't turn around. He walked forward until he heard the rifle cock behind him.

When Lance first noticed him, he didn't think the man was following him. Although, he had to admit something wasn't right about him. He didn't have a rifle or bow for hunting and he wasn't dressed for hiking. What the hell was he doing out here in the desert?

Lance had little reason to suspect the man had any interest in him because, well, he wasn't that interesting. He lived a quiet life and kept to himself. But there had been that incident recently with the militia. When he tried to go get Ryan. When he broke that fella's nose. Would they...?

No.

No way.

Either way, Lance didn't appreciate the interloper. He retreated to the solitude and privacy of the cliffs to wait for him to move on.

That's when Lance saw the man examining his marksmanship before following his tracks into the cliffs. Lance's "hunt" had just become a hunt.

Lance laid a trail that led to a confined gorge with steep rocky walls and multiple places to hide. Standing in the middle of the gorge, he leapt sideways onto a stone and backtracked. He concealed himself beneath the shadow of a small boulder.

Soon, he heard his pursuer's footfalls in the sand. Lance tracked the sound as the man followed the path that he had laid out for him, and when the time was right, Lance rose from his cover and trained his rifle on the intruder's back.

Lance didn't like killing things. But sometimes a man must do things he doesn't like.

Cal raised his arms slowly. "I'm not armed."

The old-timer held his gun on Cal. Quiet.

"I'm going to turn around, okay?" Cal said as he slowly turned and faced the old man. "I just want to talk."

"I bet you do."

"I'm looking for Ryan Sheehan. Do you know him?"

The old man's eyes narrowed.

"He's driving around in a stolen Ford Bronco," Cal said.

"Police didn't say anything about it being stolen."

"That's because it hasn't been reported yet."

"Why's that?"

"Because the owner was murdered."

The old man blinked. "Turn back around. Hands where I can see them."

Cal never got nervous in these types of situations. Staring down the barrel of a gun. Others might feel their hearts palpitating. Their palms sweating. But his body didn't react that way. It was the same reason he could pass a lie detector test. The average man or woman feels anxiety when they lie. Guilt. This feeling is recorded in a rise in blood pressure. A normal person's body will always betray them. But not Cal's.

Cal rarely felt guilt.

He knew he probably had what psychologists deemed an "antisocial personality." It was why he was so good at what he did. Guilt was a useless emotion. It was weakness.

He knew he could easily disarm the old man. He knew he could make him talk. He'd feel nothing about it. But it went against his principles.

He could tell. This man was one of the warriors.

Lance never went to college. In 1969, the country was desperate for soldiers and his number was up. He went in for a physical and never came out. He had to call his mother from the induction center and tell her he wouldn't be home for dinner. He didn't even have his toothbrush.

His first skirmish occurred less than a week into his tour. He was in a trench, manning an M60 heavy machine gun. Bullets whizzing over his head. The enemy was out there in the jungle. Invisible. Omnipresent.

Lance squeezed the trigger and fired blindly. Tears and snot streaming down his face. All of the veterans were laughing at him.

The enemy retreated and when Lance opened his eyes, he saw the smoldering pit of phosphorus a few feet in front of him, dug by tracer bullets. He had been shooting the ground.

After that, he learned to cry only on the inside. He carried his silent hysteria like a tumor that grew and grew. He was scared every second of every day.

But the man Lance was now holding his rifle on seemed incapable of fear. Lance had encountered men like him in Vietnam. It was like they were missing something. Not completely human.

They were involved in the blackest, most secretive operations. They were the men who didn't exist.

"Who sent you?" Lance asked the stranger.

"I'm investigating a murder."

"You're no cop."

"I'm a private investigator."

"What do you want?"

"To talk to Ryan Sheehan."

Lance paused. The man didn't seem like he was from the militia. He displayed little emotion, while militia members tended to have entirely too much of it. Hate, mostly.

Lance always thought it made no sense to be offended by racists or hate groups. In his view, people like that rode the short school bus. They deserved their own Olympics.

"I already told the Feds where they can find Ryan," Lance said.

"They're just cops."

"And you are?"

The stranger locked eyes with him. "You know what I am."

Lance saw the war in his eyes. "If I tell you where he is, you promise me you'll bring him home?"

"Yes."

"Bring him back alive or I swear to God—"

"I know," the stranger said softly. "I know."

Lance gave Cal his Apple ID and password, so Cal could track the phone in Ryan's Bronco. He was ten miles away when the signal died. All he had were the tracks in the desert.

It was dark when he heard the crack of gunfire. He parked his Range Rover and grabbed his suppressed HK and FN SCAR rifle from the back. He followed the sound on foot, ascending a rocky ridge.

The gunshots were closer now. He glassed the clearing below with his night-vision scope. He saw a group of armed men assembled around a Toyota Camry. An Asian man in a cowboy hat was bent over the vehicle with a knife, slashing its tires.

Then the group hid in various places, surrounding the car. An ambush.

The gunfire continued somewhere out in the darkness. Cal moved east across the ridge and scanned the dark horizon.

It was quiet now. A man in an FBI vest was crouched in a ravine, gripping a shotgun. Further south, silent gunmen lurked like tigers in tall grass, waiting for their prey.

"Don't do it," Cal whispered to the crouching man in his scope. "Stay hidden."

Fifty feet behind the crouching man, a woman in an ATF vest sprinted away with a young man by her side. Cal focused his scope on the young man's face and made the ID.

Ryan Sheehan.

A single gunshot cracked the night like a bone.

Cal returned his scope to the crouching man. He was now lying on his back. Shot in the face, but still alive. His executioners converged on him. Cal traced their figures with his scope.

He could take them out and save the man in the FBI vest, but he wasn't the priority.

Cal moved west to cut Ryan off.

He arrived back at the ridge overlooking the Toyota Camry. He glassed the Asian man and his goons waiting in ambush.

Now he watched the woman in the ATF vest emerge from the inky night with Ryan. They sprinted toward the Camry.

Cal flipped out his FN SCAR's bipod attachment and lay prone in the dirt. Through his scope, he watched the men surround Ryan and the woman.

He traced his crosshairs over the half-dozen armed men. Exposed and unsuspecting.

Each trigger pull was like a hit of cocaine. He shot the Asian man first and then worked from the outside in. After the first three kills, the other gunmen seemed to realize the futility of their situation, dropped their weapons and raised their arms. But an addict doesn't stop until the baggie is empty.

After the massacre, Cal slung his rifle over his shoulder and descended the ridge. The woman was frantic. She covered Ryan and leveled her Glock at Cal.

"Easy," Cal said. "I work for Marco Barros."

"Who the fuck are you?"

She was scared to death and it made Cal smile. He wasn't sure why. Maybe he thought it was cute. Her being so afraid of dying. He tried to make his easy grin come off as friendly, not cynical. "Call me Cal."

After Miranda took a few minutes to compose herself, she told Cal her name and that she was the ATF Agent in charge of the Arianna Barros investigation and to drop his weapon until she could get to somewhere with a cell phone signal and verify who he was.

"Call who you need to call," Cal said, handing her a sat phone. She took it and called McClean.

"He's only there to help," McClean said.

"I think you're confused. This is my investigation."

"And how's that going? Are you any closer to finding the killer?"

Miranda didn't answer.

"The Senator isn't taking any chances," McClean said. "That man is the best of the best. You will work with him, or we'll have someone assigned to this case who will."

McClean hung up. Miranda would have liked nothing more than to be reassigned. But there was Camilla. She couldn't go back empty-handed. She was stuck working with this mercenary. Her investigation now floated in the murky waters of legality where the rich and powerful live.

Cal reached out for his sat phone, but Miranda held on to it.

"I need to call this in," she said.

"Not yet," Cal said, grabbing the phone back from her. He walked off into the desert.

"Where are you going?" She followed with Ryan.

They found Greco's bullet-riddled body about two hundred yards east of them.

"The first shot wasn't fatal," Cal said. "Sad."

"How do you know that?"

"Because I watched it happen."

Miranda's eyes narrowed. "Could you have saved him?"

Cal didn't answer. He lifted Greco's body over his shoulder.

"What the hell are you doing?" Miranda said. "This is a crime scene."

Cal marched north with the body.

"Stop," Miranda said.

When Cal didn't respond, she stepped in his way and pulled her pistol. "I said stop." This time Cal complied. "Put him down," she said.

"The FBI doesn't have jurisdiction to operate in Mexico," Cal said.

"Mexico?"

Cal raised a Navstar GPS receiver. "You're about fifty yards over the border."

Shit, Miranda thought.

"You want to have to explain this? Why you and another Fed went on a shoot 'em up rampage on Mexican soil?" Cal asked. "He was killed in the States. And that's where they'll find his body." He went back to marching.

"What about all the other bodies? What about the people you massacred?"

Cal shrugged. "They're Mexico's problem." Cal checked his GPS receiver, then placed Greco's body down on what Miranda assumed was the US side of the border.

Cal turned to Ryan. "Come with me, kid."

"He's under arrest," Miranda said.

"I know he is. But I promised his grandfather I'd bring him home. You can have him after."

"That's not your call."

"Look. I just saved your fucking life. Now you can come with us to his grandfather's and then take custody from there or you can stay out here in the desert with your friend here."

The threat was hardly veiled.

Miranda was never one to be intimidated. Not by anybody.

Except maybe Cal.

Ryan rode with Cal in the Range Rover. Miranda followed in the Camry.

This is so completely fucked, she thought, as they pulled into Sheehan Ranch.

Lance heard them approaching. When he saw Ryan, his eyes gleamed. Then he saw the handcuffs.

"He can't stay," Cal said.

Lance opened his mouth to speak, then seemed to change his mind and simply nodded.

"You've got five minutes," Cal said.

"Stay within twenty feet and do not leave my sightline," Miranda said.

Lance and Ryan walked over by an old barn, leaving Miranda with Cal.

"Cal?" Miranda said. "Cal what?"

"Just Cal."

"I don't understand why Barros sent you."

"It never hurts to have another set of hands."

"Only I don't know who the fuck you are."

"I am someone who is very good at what they do."

She glared at him, unsure. "So what the hell do I say about Greco?" Miranda said.

"He was shot on US soil by narcos."

"And all the other bodies?"

"Dozen dead banditos in the Mexican desert. Won't even make the news."

"But we'll know. Those men were surrendering. You butchered them."

"Were they good men?"

Miranda paused. Of course, Cal didn't believe in such abstract concepts as good and evil, but he guessed that she did.

"Is the world better without them?" Cal asked.

"That's not the point," Miranda said.

"There once was a three-legged ass," Cal said.

"What?"

"He was the loneliest animal on the farm. You see an ass with three legs, you think, 'That bastard can't haul, what's he good for?' So, all this son of a bitch wanted to do was to haul. Al he wanted was his chance.

"Until one day, when the barnyard was terribly busy, our gimpy hero was recruited as a last resort to haul a shipment of milk. And he's doing great. All heart. You'd think he had five legs. That was, until he came upon a hill that even a seven-legged mule would have trouble mounting.

"Well, he climbed and he climbed, and the milk bottles in the back were wobbling. He sprained an ankle, but he didn't quit. Frightened, the driver ditched. For he had no faith. But the ass didn't bat an eye. The ass persisted. And as he reached the final stretch of his trial, all of the milk bottles shattered and were drunk up by the earth.

"And as he reached the top of the hill, the sun beamed down gloriously on him and, just then, all of the sudden, he had a heart attack, shat himself and died. Dead as dirt, on top of that great hill." Cal checked the time. "But he made it there."

Cal went to Lance and Ryan and escorted the prisoner back to Miranda's Camry. "He's all yours," he said.

"So what the fuck was the point of that story?" Miranda asked.

"The ass triumphed, but no one ever knew and he died all alone in his own shit, so was it really a triumph?"

Miranda didn't have an answer.

"Like those Mexicans baking out in the desert right now. Was it really a massacre if the knowledge of the event is buried with the dead?"

"But I know about it."

"And that bothers you?"

"Yes. Doesn't it bother you?"

"Should it?"

"Yes."

"Why?"

"Because that's what makes us human."

"That's what makes us human. And not gods."

PART V

TEAR DROPS

24

The sidewalks sparkled.

Russ looked up in the sky and he couldn't see one star. Not a single fucking star. Just the smoggy orange glow of street lights.

He looked at the ground and he saw chewing gum and all the grime and grunge people carried on the bottom of their shoes, and between it all, there were little sparkling particles of granite.

One of Lamar's bullets had severed Russ's spine. He would never walk again.

When he was discharged from the hospital, Shanay was waiting. She wheeled him home. It was good to be alive.

He went back to Shanay's place and held his son. It was the end of August and the weather was beginning to turn, so Shanay put a blanket over their laps and they watched TV and he felt warm.

The next day, Russ headed to work.

In Russ's absence, Bumpy supervised Russ's corner. He was a tall, skinny kid with a loud voice. Russ didn't know his real name. It was something Islamic and Bumpy didn't want people thinking he was about that Al-Qaeda life, so he went by Bumpy.

"What up, Russ," Bumpy said. "Heard you was getting out."

"What up, Bumps."

Before Russ got shot, Bumpy worked for him, but now Russ was sensing a change in the dynamics. Bumpy stood tall, looking down at Russ. Acting like he was the alpha.

"What'chu doing here?" Bumpy said.

"Fuck you think? This my corner."

Boogie shrugged. "You ain't been 'round the way in some time."

"I got shot."

"True dat, true dat. But see, dawg, this ain't your corner no more. You feel me?"

"Say who?"

"Who the fuck you think?"

Lucy spent most of her life alone in a dark basement at the end of a short, heavy chain, which hung from her neck. She would exercise on a treadmill for hours each day and was fed well, but she was completely unsocialized to everyone.

Everyone except AK. He loved Lucy like she was his own daughter.

Lucy had fought twelve opponents. And she had killed them all. Tonight, it was Hugo. Also undefeated. But by the look of things, not for long.

Lucy dug her teeth into his neck. His warm, metallic blood gushed over her tongue. Fangs and claws. Chunks of fur and flesh.

Lucy was a Dogo Argentino. Hugo was a pit bull. At least, he had been when he'd entered the fight pit. The fight was over and now he was a corpse.

AK cheered. 13-0, baby.

"Hey, yo, AK. Can I talk to you?" a voice said behind him.

AK turned around and saw Russ looking up at him from his wheelchair.

"Bumpy say he running my corner now," Russ said.

AK shrugged. "Bumpy got the youngbloods' respect."

"What about me?"

AK scoffed. "Look at you."

Russ shook his head. "So, that's it?"

"What, I gotta spell it out for you?"

AK turned back to the ring. A Rottweiler was brought into the ring. It was to fight an adolescent terrier. There was something about the terrier. Russ looked closely at it.

"Yo. Ain't that D'Andre's puppy?" Russ asked.

"Ain't a puppy no more," AK said.

The terrier had scars on its body from past battles.

Russ averted his eyes as the fight began.

It was unseasonably cold that night and the wind didn't help. Russ was underdressed for the weather, but he didn't mind. He felt he deserved punishment. He wheeled around for hours with no particular destination. He ended up in downtown Chicago—the Loop—and watched people with more comfortable lives eat at nice restaurants.

He wondered how he could feel so alone when he was among so many people. That was the funny thing about cities. If he closed his eyes and died right now, he wondered how long it would take for anyone to notice.

Russ ended up at Checkers and ordered a bacon barbecue cheeseburger, seasoned fries and a strawberry milkshake.

He remembered how D'Andre used to dip his French fries in his shake. Russ always thought that shit was nasty. D'Andre told him not to talk bullshit 'til he tried it, but he never did.

Russ wheeled his tray of food to a table and set it down. He picked up a fry and scooped up a globule of his frozen strawberry dairy drink and dunked it into his mouth.

The second it hit his tongue, he began to cry.

That night, he lay in bed with Shanay, unable to sleep, thinking about D'Andre's dog.

25

R yan was arrested for attempting to import illegal firearms. During the execution of a search warrant on Sheehan Ranch, authorities were able to link one of his Colt 1911s to the murder of local auto shop owner Arturo Maciel. When questioned, Ryan made no denials. He not only admitted to killing Arturo, but he wore the murder as a badge of honor.

"Arturo was a drug trafficking illegal and a direct threat to national security. I was protecting my country. Given another chance, I wouldn't do a thing differently."

Ryan was going away for a long time. But it didn't have to be a life sentence. Not if he cooperated.

"Tell me where you got the AR-15," Miranda pressed him in the police interview room.

Ryan refused to cooperate. He did not recognize the illegitimate authority of the Feds, particularly the ATF. These agencies violated the Constitution, specifically the Second Amendment.

Ryan would not do life in prison. He had faith that The Lord's Predators were still out there. Soon there would be a revolution. A second Civil War. And Ryan would be free.

But then a couple months went by and there was still no sign of the Lord's Predators or the revolution. Ryan held onto hope as best he could, but prison can be a hopeless place. He became closer to God. Praying every day for a sign.

Then one day, he got one.

NBC was doing a story on the unsolved shooting that killed Arianna Barros and twelve other people and Pastors Zach and Kelly were among those interviewed. Ryan saw the pastors on the TV in the prison rec room and it was like God was speaking to him.

The pastors said how Arianna was a valued member of their community and how they couldn't imagine why anyone would ever want to hurt her. They claimed to have never made the connection that Senator Marco Barros was her father. They talked about how they prayed every day for her and her family and even for her killer. They prayed that he be caught, so that he could have a chance to repent for his sins. The gates to God's kingdom were closed to no one until the final judgment.

They invited the NBC viewership to download their Valorous app and join them for one of their livestreamed online services this Sunday at 9 AM, 11 AM, 1 PM, 5 PM, 7 PM or 9 PM.

Ryan immediately requested computer and internet privileges. With little else to do to pass the time, he focused on Arianna and her church.

It became an obsession. He watched every sermon. Every Sunday. 9 AM, 11 AM, 1 PM, 5 PM, 7 PM *and* 9 PM. Any money in his commissary went directly to pay his tithes.

Ryan knew that he had possessed the rifle that killed Arianna. He felt connected to her. He felt God was speaking to him through the rifle, driving him to the Pastors.

One day, Ryan wrote a letter.

It was straight up war: Heaven's angels and Hell's demons going at it, day and night. And amidst them were men and women of God, fighting for His cause. I was leading one of those armies. As I looked ahead, I could see Hell's gates. So, I regrouped with the army God placed before me and we stormed down the gates of Hell. I've always felt like I was born to protect the Kingdom of Heaven and all that inhabit it, both here on Earth and there in Heaven. I always felt like I'd be one to wield a sword in His name and protect His people. One day, I will be leading that army. And in the name of Jesus, we will bring down Hell's gates.

He folded the letter and placed it in an envelope, which was addressed to: "PASTOR ZACH. VALOROUS CHURCH. 423 West 8th Street, Los Angeles, CA 90014."

Miranda knew it wasn't uncommon for people to find religion in prison. For most, it was about dealing with guilt and gaining discipline to better themselves. Ryan seemed to use it to justify his actions and deepen his fanaticism.

Miranda had requested to read all of Ryan's incoming and outgoing mail. She read his letter to Pastor Zach, then she read dozens more like it.

Ryan didn't understand. Letter after letter, but no response. He had to get the Pastor's attention. So, he kept his next letter short and sweet.

My name is Ryan Sheehan.

Inmate ID # 04682957, FCI Victorville.

I was arrested by ATF Special Agent Miranda Lopez.

I know who killed Arianna Barros.

We need to talk.

26

D'Andre was only seventeen, but because of the seriousness of his crime, he was being held at MCC Chicago. Big boy jail.

Russ wheeled himself into the visitation room for high security inmates. There was a long row of stalls that reminded him of a shooting range.

He climbed from his wheelchair onto a metal stool and sat in front of an empty partition of bulletproof glass. A guard escorted D'Andre in. At first, Russ didn't recognize him. He was wearing a do-rag and the orange prisoner uniform with his pants sagging down on his ass.

Russ had never known D'Andre to dress like this. But it wasn't just the clothes. It was the way he carried himself. He didn't walk. He strutted. A stiff, erect, "don't-fuck-with-me" gait. D'Andre had never had swagger like that.

D'Andre sat on the other side of the glass. Chin up. Jaw tight. Eyes glacial.

They put their receivers to their ears and Russ forced himself to smile. "How the food in there? Bad as they say?"

D'Andre gave only a cold stare.

Russ paused, considered how to begin. "I came here to let you know that this ain't on you."

D'Andre flinched. "Fuck that."

"Nah, dawg. I should have stopped it."

"You ain't never been hard," D'Andre said.

"It's on me, homie. Not you. You a good person."

"You soft. Pussy-ass bitch."

"You think you hard?" Russ punched the glass. A prison guard shouted for him to knock it off. "You wanna be hard? You think you hard, nigga?"

"Fuck you," D'Andre said, then he slammed down the receiver and walked away.

"It ain't on you!" Russ beat the glass. Eyes welling. "It's on me!"

That same day, AK called Russ to the garage.

"'Sup, Hot Wheels?" AK said with a cruel grin as Russ wheeled himself into AK's office.

"What up? You wanted to see me?" Russ said.

"You remember Chinaman Yu?"

Russ remembered posting election signs around the neighborhood with D'Andre.

"Yeah," Russ said.

"The man made certain promises that he ain't been keeping," AK said. "Now that we got him elected, he think he can forget all about us, just 'cause we street niggas." AK paused. "Sometimes I think prison would be better than these streets."

Russ didn't understand what any of this had to do with him. AK had given away his corner. As far as Russ knew, he was out.

"Need you to hit him," AK said.

"Me?"

AK opened one of the crates he'd gotten from Indonesia. "This here's that military shit," he said, raising a MAC-10 machine pistol. "Can clear out a whole room of muthafuckas like that. All you gotta do is get close enough, point and squeeze. Chinaman won't know what hit him."

AK reached the weapon out to Russ. Russ shook his head.

"I ain't gonna shoot no alderman."

"Why not? Ain't no one gonna give the death penalty to a cripple."

"Nah, man."

AK frowned. He turned the MAC-10 around in his hand and leveled the barrel at Russ.

"You know, you lucky," AK said.

"Why's that?"

"Every nigga get his day. He either go inside or get killed on these streets. That's the only way it ever ends. Today is your day."

"So, what the fuck make me so lucky?"

"Most niggas don't get to choose."

Russ stared down the barrel.

"Aight. I'll do it. Shit."

AK grinned and Russ took the MAC-10.

"My nigga," AK said.

27

D'Andre scanned the bookshelves. He'd heard the prison library had a collection of comics and graphic novels, so he'd created a syllabus for himself. He'd always worked his ass off learning what school taught him. Reading old white authors and learning about old white presidents. How Abraham Lincoln freed all black people.

Yeah, black people were really free.

On some real shit, Lincoln could suck a dick.

D'Andre had spent his whole life learning what school told him he should know and look where that got him. From now on, he was educating himself. Fuck what they say.

They didn't have any Black Panther or Miles Morales, so he went with his third choice, Batman. Bruce Wayne may have been another rich white dude, but at least he was down with the streets, fucking up gangsters and shit, so D'Andre could still kind of relate.

He wanted to start with the classics. A Google search recommended *Batman: Year One* and *The Dark Knight Returns* by Frank Miller. *The Killing Joke* by Alan Moore also came highly recommended.

In the meantime, he requested Luke Cage, Blade, and Black Lightning.

Two thousand miles away, Ryan was also spending a lot of time in the library. Although the only thing he ever read was his Bible. Ryan had been a loner in prison thus far and he probably wouldn't have survived this long if he hadn't been deemed high priority.

The prison brass knew that the Feds still had a vested interest in Ryan and they knew if he were, say, gang-raped or shivved, it would reflect poorly on them. So the guards had been paying extra attention to him. Although in recent weeks, they'd started to let up. All Ryan ever did was watch church sermons or read his Bible in the library. After a couple months, it seemed the other prisoners lost interest and forgot all about him.

He was sitting alone, reading his Bible like always when CJ and Shifty entered. They'd been patiently waiting from the day Ryan arrived for the chance to get at the white boy. They sat at a nearby table and watched him out of the corners of their eyes.

After the only other prisoner in the library left—some old-timer with a braided ponytail—it was just CJ and Shifty and Ryan and that's when Shifty made his move. He snuck up behind Ryan and put a shiv to his throat.

"Hey, sweetie. Don't fight back."

CJ stayed sitting at the table and unzipped his fly. He liked to watch.

With the blade to his neck, Ryan calmly stood and faced Shifty. Unafraid.

"Now take down them drawers," Shifty said.

Ryan said, "Leviticus 18:22. 'Do not practice homosexuality, having sex with another man as with a woman. It is a detestable sin.'"

"I said drop them—"

In a flash of movement, Ryan slashed Shifty with a shank of

his own. Shifty looked stunned. He raised his arm. The severed arteries in his forearm gushed blood.

"Even when I walk through the darkest valley, I will not be afraid, for you are close beside me. Your rod and your staff protect and comfort me." Ryan said as he repeatedly stabbed Shifty to death.

Blood sprayed like a burst pipe.

CJ attempted to turn and flee, but Ryan drove the blade into his spine. CJ's body twitched as it dropped to the floor.

Ryan casually unzipped CJ's throat with the shank. CJ gasped as he bled out from the wound.

A few minutes later, the prison guard that had been watching Ryan returned from the bathroom and found Ryan sitting at one of the tables, covered in blood and calmly reading from his Bible. Two dead bodies on the floor.

Ryan looked up at the prison guard and, answering a question that had not been asked, said, "God told me to do it."

Word spread quickly. By the time the guards were walking Ryan through the cell block in shackles, he could feel the eyes of every prisoner and guard on him.

He was marched to the solitary confinement unit and placed in an eight-by-ten-foot cell with a cement bed and no windows. The guards left him alone in the silent and claustrophobic space. But he was smiling. Because by now, everyone in the prison knew his name.

28

A t around 10:30 PM, AK's phone rang. "Holla."
　　　"Hey," Shanay said.
"'Sup, girl."
"Where you at?"
AK tilted his head. "Thought you was Russ's shorty?"
"You mad?"
"I ain't mad."
"Uh-huh."
"Can't do it for you like he used to, huh?"
Shanay paused. "Why don't you come by the crib?"
AK felt his body heat rising.
"Aight."
Thirty minutes later, AK was outside of Shanay's house. A bounce in his step. He approached the front door, then he heard someone down the side of the house. He squinted in the darkness.
"Hey, yo. Who dat?"
The answer came in a barrage of machine pistol fire. It sprayed his body and threw him down onto the sidewalk. He was dead before he hit the ground.
Russ wheeled himself out of the shadows, holding the

MAC-10.

Really was some military shit.

Shanay came out of the house and stood by Russ's side. "Let's go, baby," she said and wheeled Russ away.

Shanay parked Russ across the street from AK's garage.

"I should go in with you," Russ said.

"Baby. Ain't nobody gonna mess with me," she said.

She crossed the street and disappeared into the garage.

After a moment, she reemerged, carrying D'Andre's dog.

The next morning, Miss Evelyn rose with the sun. She put on the coffee and walked toward the porch to get the newspaper. When she unlocked and opened the door, there was a dog leashed to her doorstep. It took her a moment to recognize the dog, but when she did, she crouched down, ran her fingers over the scars on his body and was overwhelmed with tears. She embraced the creature and welcomed him home.

"You gave him back?" D'Andre said.

Russ was sitting across from him in the visitation room.

"She an old lady. All alone and shit," Russ said.

"AK had him fighting?" D'Andre said, his eyes flinty.

"Uh-huh."

D'Andre shook his head. "He okay?"

"He got scars, but he aight. We all got scars, right?"

D'Andre lowered his eyes and wrinkled his brow. "Niggas gon' be gunnin' for you."

Russ shrugged. "Everybody be gunnin'."

"True dat."

The two sat there. Russ watched the tension ease from D'Andre's frame.

"So, what's good?" Russ said.

"Food in here be shit. I'd kill for some Lay's."

"Now, you ain't mean that literally, right?"

D'Andre smirked.

"I mean, now that you all hard and shit."

"Fuck you," D'Andre said.

They both laughed.

"Hey, yo. You remember Cheese from grade school?" D'Andre said.

"Nigga never washed his clothes, always smelled like bad cheese?"

D'Andre nodded. "There someone in here that look just like him, yo!"

"Shut up."

"I swear, man."

"He smell better than the food?" Russ asked.

They laughed and bantered until the guard announced visiting hours were over and Russ promise he'd come back and see him next week.

"'We find the gun, we find the killer.' Isn't that what you said?" McClean had to be firm because Marco was in the room, standing at his office window. A silent, decaying gargoyle.

"The gun arrived in Arizona through a private sale. No names. No background checks. But still, legal," Miranda said.

"We know what a private sale is, thank you," McClean said.

"This is the only country in the world where any person can get a gun without a single record being kept," Miranda said.

"Don't make this political."

"Life is political," Miranda replied.

Finally, Marco broke his silence. "Who the fuck killed my daughter?"

Miranda shrugged. "It could've been anyone. For any reason."

PART VI

PRO DEO ET PATRIA

29

R eligion affects the same parts of the brain as drugs. Or love. Or sex. Or gambling. Or music.

Solitary didn't bother Ryan. He was high.

He refused food. He would not leave his cell. He would allow his captors no power over him.

He lived in a portrait he'd painted in his head. Of Sheehan Ranch, restored to its glory days. Fresh paint and fat cattle and green grass. He was married to Becky Brock from down the street and documented workers labored beneath the American flag.

Then one day, the angry ginger prison guard told Ryan that he'd rot alone in solitary confinement for the rest of his life and that everyone had already forgotten all about him.

Ryan had trouble living in his portrait after that.

Ryan knew he was a prophet of God. He needed God to show him the way. He prayed and prayed and prayed.

Then that bitch who arrested him interrupted his prayers.

The cell was fetid. Miranda wondered if they were even allowing Ryan showers. He looked feral. Covered in his own waste. The maggots had moved in.

Miranda glared at the red-haired prison guard. "How do you explain this?"

The guard just shrugged. "It ain't my job to wipe his ass for him."

They moved Ryan into an interview room. She gave him a moment to adjust to his new surroundings. "How are you doing, Ryan?" Miranda asked.

Ryan squinted. He looked like one of those abused dogs Sarah McLachlan sang about.

"Is there anything on your mind?" she said. For a moment, Miranda wondered if he'd lost the power of language. "I heard about what happened in the library," she said. "I'm going to talk to prison officials about getting you moved back into gen pop."

Ryan sat up in his chair. His interest piqued.

"But I can't do that if you don't help me," she said. "Who sold you the gun?"

Ryan scowled. "Why am I in here?"

Miranda tilted her head. "Did you forget why you're in here, Ryan?"

Ryan shook his head. "I am in here for protecting American freedom. Protecting it from terrorists, drug traffickers... and you."

"Ryan. I'm trying to solve the murder of an innocent young woman. That's all."

"You think I'm stupid? When UN troops drop from the night sky in black helicopters and the gun-grabbing, black-clad thugs of the ATF threaten our constitutional rights, there will always be men like me to stand up to you."

It was clear to Miranda that Ryan was too far gone to reason with. She moved on to Plan B.

"I understand you've been writing some letters?"

Ryan set his jaw. "What about them?"

"I'm here to ask you about something you wrote in one letter in particular."

Ryan sat back in his chair and crossed his arms.

"'I know who killed Arianna Barros. We need to talk.'" Pastor Zach folded Ryan's letter and slid it into his breast pocket.

"My repeated requests to speak to Ryan Sheehan have been denied. He is being kept segregated in solitary confinement and he is not being allowed visitation with anyone. It makes me wonder, who doesn't want Ryan Sheehan talking and what are they afraid he might say?"

The pastor peddled his conspiracy theories in each one of his sermons, which were live-streamed across the country. Eventually, local news affiliates corroborated that the ATF had arrested and were questioning a man named Ryan Sheehan in connection with the Arianna Barros shooting. Then it went national. CNN. Fox News. MSNBC.

For Pastors Zach and Kelly, it was a gold mine. Tithes were up seven hundred percent. Pastor Zach felt his fate was finally being fulfilled.

Ever since he was young, he had dreamed of having his own megachurch. Other boys idolized action stars and baseball players. His heroes were men like Billy Graham and Jerry Falwell. And his father. Pastor Billy Beck. Who in the 1950s, took his daddy's tiny Texas revival church, then known as the Tree of Life Ministry, and turned it into WorldMovers Church Inc. One of the largest megachurches on the planet.

Pastor Zach was proud that his little Los Angeles parish was part of the WorldMovers family, but he had bigger plans. He knew he wasn't the Messiah. He often had to remind himself that it was sacrilegious to think that way. But he was at least a prophet. An important one. And now God was finally giving him the means to get his message out to the world.

It was Pastor Zach's divine destiny to save the world.

Pastor Zach was at a car dealership, finalizing the deal on his new mother-of-pearl Rolls Royce Phantom Serenity when Miranda called.

"This is Special Agent Miranda Lopez of the ATF."

A thin smile spread across the pastor's face."How can I help you, Agent Lopez?"

"Your presence has been requested by an individual of interest to my investigation."

The prison had cleaned Ryan up for the pastor's visit. Ryan insisted that they be able to speak alone. Suddenly, this fanatical little shit was calling the shots. Miranda had to take it on the chin.

Ryan and the pastor spoke for nearly four hours. Afterward, Miranda attempted to interview Ryan, but he was a brick wall. "All shall be revealed," was all the smug little psycho would say to her.

A prison guard escorted Ryan out of the interview room and back to solitary.

After he left, Miranda removed the audio recorder she had taped beneath the table. There was no legal basis for Ryan's conversation with the pastor to be privileged, so it wasn't against the law for her to record it.

All shall be revealed. Fuckin' A right.

As it turned out, Miranda would learn the gist of what Ryan and the pastor had talked about before she even pressed Play on her recorder.

In the early days of the investigation, Miranda had joined the Valorous Church's email list. She returned home and checked her account and found a new mass email from the Valorous Church. The subject line read: *All Shall Be Revealed.*

She clicked open the email and among various hipster, pseudo-Christian graphics a single sentence stood out like a tumor:

This Sunday during our 1 PM sermon, Ryan Sheehan will reveal who killed Arianna Barros live from Victorville penitentiary. Reserve your spot now and bear witness!

Jesus. They were going to livestream Ryan to the world. They were selling fucking seats.

Miranda shook her head in disbelief. She sat down with a pen and legal pad. Took out the recorder and got to work.

The recording began with a lot of Ryan talking about how he felt connected to the pastor's work. How he believed God had a bigger plan for him. That he was one of God's chosen warriors. Typical delusions of grandeur bullshit.

These two have a lot in common, Miranda thought.

About an hour in, they got to the relevant stuff. The pastor asked him if he really knew who killed Arianna.

Ryan said, "Yes."

"Who?"

"Me," Ryan said. "I shot her. I shot them all. I did it with a Colt AR-15 A4 that had its serial number removed."

"Why, Ryan?"

"The devil made me do it."

"Will you repent?"

"Yes."

She paused the recording. She needed a moment to breathe. To process.

Of course, she didn't buy it. She knew Ryan was lying. The question was, why? Had someone put him up to it or was it just a case of simple attention-seeking? More of his delusions of grandeur?

She called Lance and asked if he could account for Ryan's whereabouts on the night of Arianna Barros's murder. Lance could not. Ryan came and went as he pleased, even before he joined the militia.

Ryan had been in possession of the murder weapon and it seemed like everyone just wanted this case closed. If he confessed to the crime and she couldn't disprove that it was him, then her investigation would be over.

She called McClean and told him the situation. McClean said he would call her back after he spoke to Marco.

For a moment, Miranda wondered if it would be such a bad thing if Ryan confessed. She could say she'd gotten justice for Arianna. She could win Camilla back.

Only she would know it was a lie. She would know that the real killer was still out there and that she had helped them get away with it.

Could she live with that?

When McClean called back, it wasn't what Miranda was expecting.

"Do not interfere."

"What?"

"Let the church go ahead."

"Do you know what that means?"

"It's what the Senator wants."

Miranda rolled her eyes. "As always, I appreciate your support."

"Look. You've been investigating Arianna's death for months and you're nowhere nearer to a suspect. You don't know what it's doing to Marco. At least this way, he can try to move forward."

"But it's a lie."

"No. It's mercy."

Miranda called Cal to give him an update. He said he was in Los Angeles and that they should meet. He gave her the address of a restaurant.

It was the type of place where a burger costs eighteen dollars and the fries were sold separately. *What a racket*, Miranda thought, as she looked over the menu. Contemporary décor and hip music meant they could upcharge three hundred percent for what was essentially glorified McDonald's. Criminal.

Their waitress was a baby-faced round girl with a nose ring

and sleeve of skulls and roses and thorns and daggers. She began by pitching their all-new Boundless burger, a plant-based burger that not only tasted exactly like beef, but was lower in calories and better for the environment because the methane released from beef cattle accounts for over forty percent of greenhouse gas emissions. Join the fight against cow farts today!

She said she would be right back with some waters.

"When did hamburgers become so political?" Cal said.

Tack test-tube born meatless meat onto any menu and gain hipster bonus points. She looked around at young people using their phones to take pictures of their burgers. They weren't paying for food. They were paying for posts and likes. All for the 'gram.

"Why the hell did you want to meet in a place like this?" she asked. They were sitting in a booth near the entrance.

"You haven't been paying attention," he said.

"What?"

"This is where she worked."

Arianna's bio came flooding back to Miranda's brain. She took the place in anew. Her eyes moved to the hostess stand. *That was where she stood,* Miranda thought. A young woman, trying to pay her rent. To get by.

The young man behind the bar kept eying Cal for some reason. He had cartoonish muscles and his body was a confused patchwork of clashing, colorful ink that stood out like gaudy neon signs. His skin glowed spray-tan orange and his teeth were blinding spotlights of white.

He might as well have been holding a bullhorn and screaming, "Look at me!"

Fucking L.A. Everyone was the star of a reality show that only played in their heads.

Of course, this phenomenon wasn't only limited to Los Angeles. The city was merely the epicenter. It was a national disease, disproportionately affecting anyone under thirty.

But then there was Arianna. She hadn't been like other

people her age. She didn't have the "celebrity syndrome," the need to be the center of attention.

She hadn't sought fame or attention or notoriety. It seemed to Miranda that those things wouldn't have vindicated her. She'd had no ego. She'd just wanted to live a quiet, unassuming life. What was she hoping to find in L.A.? What was she running from?

Miranda knew how it felt to be scared of the world. In order to cope, she built a tough shell. Arianna had joined a church.

Camilla was right. How could she let her personal biases get in the way of seeing Arianna for what she was? A human being. An innocent young woman murdered. She couldn't let the pastors do this. She couldn't let them turn the girl's death into a sideshow.

Why would Marco go along with it?

Why would he protect the real killers?

Maybe it was like McClean said. Maybe it really was just delirium brought on by a desperate, grieving father's need for closure by any means. Or maybe it was something else.

Miranda had to entertain all possibilities.

Arianna was a political liability.

Marco was a notoriously ambitious man. He was losing an election, but since her death, his popularity had soared. His reelection was all but guaranteed.

She still felt like she was missing something.

Miranda had trouble believing that Barros could have his own daughter killed just to keep a Senate seat. And his grief seemed so real.

But then again, politicians are sociopaths.

When Miranda was young, her mother had kept a tomato plant. Miranda's job was to always be on the lookout for pests. Snails, worms, insects and the like. Every time she discovered a creature that she'd never seen before, she would trap it and show her mother. One day, she found a green caterpillar. She had never seen one like it before, so she caught it in a clear Dixie cup and put a lid on it. The caterpillar explored the cup, but then after a while, all it did was circle around the bottom. Head chasing its tail. Going nowhere fast.

Then it began to eat itself.

At first, Miranda thought the bug had just accidentally bit itself and learned its lesson. But it didn't stop. It kept blindly chomping away at its own tail, consuming its own flesh. Its viscous green blood filling the bottom of the cup. Eventually, it drowned.

Right now, Miranda felt like that caterpillar. Chasing her own tail. Losing Camilla, who was everything. Drowning.

It was time to escape the Dixie cup.

Sales were up. The Valorous webstore could hardly keep up with demand and the Valorous band's debut album was getting millions of streams every month.

Pastor Zach wasn't just saving the world. He was taking it over.

He always loved the heat of stage lights. Broadcast lighting felt no different. He was sitting next to his wife and opposite Diana Jessa on her nationally syndicated news show, *Diana Jessa Live*.

"Ryan Sheehan wrote me a letter two weeks ago from prison. Since then, I have been corresponding with him on a daily basis," Pastor Zach said.

"Why do you think he reached out to you, but has refused to cooperate with the authorities?" Diana Jessa asked.

"The police cannot offer salvation."

"But you can?"

"Only Jesus can. But I can help him open his heart and find the way. Ryan Sheehan wants redemption. The first step on the journey is absolute honesty. He has been holding a secret that has been eating away at his soul. The identity of the person or persons responsible for the shooting that claimed the life of our Arianna and twelve others."

"But wouldn't it be more appropriate for Ryan Sheehan to cooperate with authorities?" Diana asked. "One could argue that by allowing Ryan Sheehan to publicly name who he claims killed Arianna Barros and the others, you are making it harder for the authorities to do their job and, ultimately, get justice for Arianna."

"God is the ultimate judge, the ultimate administrator of justice and there is no greater courtroom than the church," Pastor Zach said. "Through Ryan's public revelation, the world may join together in praying not only for Arianna, but for her killer. That they receive swift justice and seek redemption for the evil they have done."

"What do you say to people who argue that you and your wife are simply capitalizing off of Arianna Barros's death?"

Pastor Zach's eyes widened and his voice quaked with passion. "I say I am unmasking Satan! Casting him out! I say I am doing God's work—"

"Shut it down," Miranda said as she and a half dozen uniformed cops invaded the set. She knew the backup was overkill, but the cameras were rolling and she wanted to put on a show.

She marched up to Pastor Zach. "On your feet."

Pastor Zach looked around, confused. He didn't seem to process that she was speaking to him.

"I won't say it again."

He hesitantly rose from the chair. Miranda took out her handcuffs.

"Zachary Beck, you have the right to remain silent—"

"What?" Pastor Zach said.

"Anything you say can and will be used against you in a court of law." She forced his hands behind his back and locked his wrists. "You have the right to an attorney. If you cannot afford an attorney, one will be provided for you."

Pastor Zach stammered. Shock turning to fear.

"Do you understand the rights I have just read to you?" He looked at her, doe-eyed and scared. She almost felt bad for him. She ushered him toward the door like a lamb to the slaughter.

In the hallway outside of the soundstage, the pastor finally managed to ask what he was being arrested for.

"Fraud," Miranda said.

Miranda needed to stop the Ryan Sheehan show and she had a nagging hunch that the church's financial records would turn up something scandalous, but a judge wouldn't sign off on a warrant without cause. For years, Pastor Zach had been promising to build a permanent church, so they wouldn't have to rent out nightclubs for their Sunday services. Miranda made the argument that using religious tithes to rent a mansion in Huntington Beach and pay for vacations to Hawaii instead of fulfilling his promise of a permanent church constituted fraud.

It was a dubious charge at best and Miranda knew it would never stick. Countless megachurch preachers had done similar and worse with their parishioners' money. It was their *modus operandi*.

But the arrest charge granted Miranda the access to the church's financial records she needed.

She knew the pastors were getting the shaft and she was the one giving it to them, but ends and means, right? Besides, they got rich off of the backs of vulnerable, brainwashed slave laborers, whom they labeled volunteers. They were hardly innocent.

She had to admit that it felt gratifying locking the pastor up on a Saturday night. He wouldn't get to see a judge until Monday.

When Miranda got the warrant to go through the church's books, the last thing she expected was to see Marco Barros's name all over them.

30

"The most powerful person in America is a religious white man."

Cal was on an operation in North Africa, when one of his team members made the comment.

"Just look at the presidents. Ninety percent fit the pattern. Obama was black. Lincoln and Jefferson had no religious affiliation. All the rest. Christian, white men."

The most powerful person in America is a religious white man.

Cal wondered if Warren Buffett, Jeff Bezos or Jamie Dimon were religious.

Miranda drove with Cal through downtown Houston. Pastor Billy Beck had arranged to meet them at the WorldMovers Church's main campus— a refurbished sports stadium just south of the city.

Miranda's review of Valorous's financials had turned up something fruitful. But the fruit was poisoned. She had to be careful how she bit into it.

She discovered that Marco Barros had been donating large sums of money to Valorous for years.

To Miranda's knowledge, Marco had no affiliation with Pastor Zach's church. So, she did a little digging and learned that he had had dealings with Pastor Zach's father's church going back decades.

Today, the megachurch known as WorldMovers was one of the richest on the planet. It was Valorous's parent church and Marco had been a generous, silent donor since he was in his twenties. He'd pretty much built it.

It was an affiliation Marco had been conspicuously mute about.

In the wake of Arianna's death, Marco was polling well again. Money was pouring into Valorous and, by extension, WorldMovers. But to Miranda, his grief seemed so legitimate. Could it have been regret? Had something gotten out of control?

Either way, the facts were the facts. Arianna's death had benefited Marco. Motive, means and opportunity. And if Marco were somehow involved in his daughter's death, it would explain why he was so eager to let Ryan Sheehan take the blame.

Before confronting Marco, Miranda thought it better to question the WorldMovers Church's president.

She brought Cal along, but kept him in the dark. He was Marco's man and she knew she couldn't trust him. She wanted to gauge how much he knew. Keep your friends close, but your enemies closer. She was still figuring how close Cal needed to be.

The president of WorldMovers Church's name was Billy Beck. He was Pastor Zach's father. This man, in his seventies, still had the vitality and charisma to energize stadiums of tens of thousands of people. Cameras swinging around on arms all around him. His image beamed into the homes of over ten million American viewers on any given Sunday.

But off-stage, Billy Beck was William. Billy Beck had a Southern drawl, but William used non-regional diction.

Billy Beck was charismatic and extroverted. A man of the people. William was reserved and superior.

Billy Beck was a showman. William was a CEO.

You didn't become a multimillionaire without having a mind for business.

"You have questions," William said, with about as much charm as a desk calculator. They were sitting across from him in his office.

"Yes."

He stared at her blankly.

"Do you know Marco Barros?" she asked.

"Yes."

"How?"

"He is a parishioner."

"When did you first meet?"

"Approximately forty years ago."

"And how did that meeting happen?"

"He introduced himself to me after one of our Sunday services. Our congregation was much smaller back then."

"Did you know he was in politics?"

"I believe he mentioned it."

"He's given a lot of money to your church over the years." She waited for him to say something.

"Was there a question?"

"Why did he give you so much money?"

"You'd have to ask him that."

"Did he ask for anything in return?"

"No."

"Your congregation really supported Marco Barros. It could be argued that WorldMovers is the reason he is where he is today, and vice versa."

He looked at her blankly. She sighed.

"Did Marco Barros pay you to endorse him?"

"No," he answered flatly.

"Did you know his daughter?"

"I'd never met the girl. As I understand it, she was more involved with my son's parish."

"And you're okay with your son turning her death into a publicity stunt?"

"That question is inflammatory." He checked his Rolex.

"Why a tree?" Cal said.

Miranda and Billy Beck both looked at him. It was the first time he'd spoken the entire meeting. Cal was talking about a banner that hung behind Billy Beck's desk with the image of a tree on it. Its branches reaching wide and skyward.

"In the early days, we were called the Tree of Life Ministry. That was our logo."

Miranda looked at Cal. He sat there, pokerfaced. She turned back to Billy Beck.

"Thank you for your time, Pastor Beck," she said, then she rose and walked with Cal toward the door.

"You've fucked with the wrong people."

Miranda stopped and looked back at him. "Excuse me?"

His Southern drawl slowly crept in. Emotion rose in his voice and his eyes darkened.

"You arrested my son on a charge that we both know is nonsense. You attacked my faith and my family. People often overlook the Old Testament. They forget that God can be vengeful and truly violent. Tread lightly, Agent Lopez."

This was a far cry from the fluffy spiritual McDonald's the man served up every Sunday.

"Is that a threat, Pastor?"

"No, ma'am. Just a sermon from an old preacher."

Back in Los Angeles, SAC Scarpelli was livid.

"Are you out of your fucking mind? What has WorldMovers got to do with Arianna Barros's murder?"

"I'm still working that out, sir," Miranda said, standing stiffly in front of his desk.

"How does arresting the girl's pastor fit into this grand theory of yours?"

"As I said, I'm still working on it."

"No. You're not."

"Sir?"

"The Senator wants you off the case."

"I didn't realize we answered to him."

"No. You answer to me and, frankly, I agree with him."

"This is bullshit."

Scarpelli's nostrils flared. "I'm sorry. Could you repeat that?"

"There's something hinky going on between Marco Barros and Billy Beck."

"Agent Cooley is taking over the investigation. Get him up to speed." He waved her out of his office.

Miranda gritted her teeth.

Special Agent Chad Cooley.

Kiss-ass. Yes man. Office politician. And utterly incompetent.

If she were a rich and powerful person trying to get away with murder, he'd be the guy she'd want investigating.

She glared across the office bullpen at him.

Big, beaver teeth and a chipmunk face she just wanted to punch.

RIP Arianna.

Cal contemplated the Tree of Life that hung behind Billy Beck's desk.

Deformed it in his memory.

Its sharp and defined upward-reaching branches sagged and blurred into hazy blotches.

Like something cruciferous.

Why would a fat man have a broccoli tattoo? Cal wondered again.

He was waiting for Pat Roti on a park bench in Maguire Gardens outside of the Los Angeles Public Library. It was just after midnight and the tweakers and lunatics were out. He watched a grown man wearing a trash bag for pants take a shit in the park fountain.

Cal hated Downtown L.A. Everything about the place felt empty and hollow. It reminded him of a poem he'd read somewhere. Shape without form, shade without color. But for some reason, he chose to live here.

He felt a cold and spiteful attachment to the place. A poisonous commonality. It wasn't a real city. More like an alien lifeform trying to mimic a city.

And himself? An AI trying to imitate a human?

A Mercedes pulled up and idled by the curb. Pat Roti stepped out and sat next to Cal on the bench.

"Who was Kilo?"

"Who?"

"The fat man I killed out in the desert?" Cal asked.

"You know it's not your job to ask questions."

"I just need to know."

Pat's eyes darted to Cal. This wasn't like him. He considered and then finally said, "Trafficker. He ran girls from Mexico. Trust me, that bastard deserved what he got."

"Kilo had a tattoo on his forearm," Cal said. "It was old and stretched-out, but it looked like this Tree of Life symbol that was once used by the church that I've linked to Arianna Barros. Kilo went into hiding only a few weeks before Arianna's death. Why?"

"That's not important."

"It might be."

"It's not," Pat said. "Look. I'm walking a tightrope here. It's my job to maintain my clients' confidentiality, but it is also my responsibility to protect you. The less you know the better. Your only task is to find the person who pulled the trigger on Arianna Barros, and kill them, so stop asking so many damn questions." Pat rose from the bench. "You've been ordered to do a thing, so get it done. It's never been a problem for you before."

Pat Roti walked back toward the Mercedes.

So, Kilo was a sex trafficker, Cal thought. It was the first time he had ever asked about someone he had killed. Yeah, the guy was a scumbag, but knowing who he was somehow made it more real. Something inanimate animate. And him more culpable.

Maybe Pat was right. The less he knew the better.

Cal wasn't sure why he told Miranda about Kilo.

Maybe Kilo reminded him of Pat.

Running whores.

Maybe he was tired of being treated like a whore.

He'd worked for Pat Roti for years and Pat still only viewed him as a lackey. A minion. Kill, and don't ask why.

Miranda looked into Victor "Kilo" Cortes. He was a Minister at WorldMovers Church until he went AWOL a few weeks before Arianna got killed. She asked Cal if she should even bother trying to find him. Cal didn't answer.

Of course, there was no way to connect any of this new information to Arianna's murder. Not yet, at least. So, they sat on it. Another puzzle piece.

Meanwhile, Cal was getting restless. He read once that the great white shark is what's known as an obligate ram ventilator. They lack the ability to use their buccal, or cheek, muscles to pull water into the mouth and over the gills like other fish. Instead, they must "ram" water over their gills by swimming. They must be constantly moving in order to breathe. If they stop swimming, they drown.

Cal was a great white shark. He could feel the case turning cold. Could feel himself losing oxygen. So, he decided to drive back out to Arizona and take another run at Lance.

He was surprised. The old-timer was more welcoming than he expected. Cal guessed that it was because he missed his grandson and he would take any company he could get. Even loners get lonely.

Lance handed him a beer and they sat on his porch. He asked if Cal had any updates on Ryan and Cal said no, but they both knew it wasn't looking good.

Lance shook his head, his eyes distant. "Do you have any kids?" he asked.

"No, sir."

"I don't see how anyone can raise a child in today's world."

Cal shrugged. "People feel like it's what they're supposed to do." 'Cause that's what their parents did and their grandparents did. *The earth is overpopulated with people doing what they're supposed to do,* Cal thought.

Fucking like bunnies. Polluting and deforesting. Making more bunnies. Who pollute and deforest. Causing climate change and pandemics.

Or so it's said. Cal wasn't a scientist, just a believer in science.

Fires and hurricanes and disease. Natural disasters. And that was how Cal saw himself.

A force of nature, a natural disaster. Culling the fuck-bunny herd.

When a tsunami kills a thousand people, you don't call it evil.

Cal didn't know what his body count was, but it was definitely less than a thousand.

"I know it makes me sound like an old man—hell, I am an old man—but..." Lance trailed off, his eyes distant. "Hell, I remember we used to bring our rifles to school with us. Leave them in our cars and go hunting after class. Now, it seems there's a mass shooting every other day. We got goddamn militias itching to hunt other human beings. It's like a damn horror movie that won't end." He shook his head. "When did it all change? When did everybody in this country get so damned crazy?"

He was speaking more to the universe now than Cal, which was fine with Cal, because he sure as shit didn't have an answer.

"I just don't recognize this world," Lance said. "I suppose

that's why I failed him. Ryan. I never knew how to relate to him."

His gaze was focused now as he turned and looked at Cal. "The boy frightens me," he said with pain in his eyes.

Cal knew how dangerous people like Ryan were. Knew the type.

Ryan was promised the American dream by virtue of who he was. Call it male entitlement. Call it white entitlement. Call it Christian entitlement. Cal didn't fucking know.

What he did know was that few things were more dangerous than a spurned man with a gun.

He'd seen it with dictators and mass murderers. They'd do anything, hurt anyone, to ensure their fantasies of power and control became reality.

But Cal's concern wasn't saving the world from people like Ryan. His only objective was getting the information he needed out of the narcissistic little asshole and the way he saw it, Lance was the best way to do it.

"Ryan claims to know who killed Arianna Barros, but he won't cooperate," Cal said. "Do you think you can help?"

Lance shrugged. "I'm not sure what I can do."

"He's doing twenty-five to life. If he doesn't help us, you can be sure that it'll be life."

The old-timer saw a chance to right what he believed was his wrong. To fix what he saw as his deficiencies as a grandfather. "I'll talk to him. That doesn't mean he'll listen, but I'll talk to him," he said.

After Pastor Zach's arrest, he decided to "postpone" Ryan's livestream event and encouraged Ryan to work with the authorities. At first, Ryan was depressed and angry at the pastor for caving to the Feds, but the Lord works in mysterious ways.

Ryan was moved back into gen pop and he discovered that

while he was locked away in solitary, he'd become something of a celebrity.

Valorous had painted him as a sinner seeking redemption, comparing him to the Penitent Thief.

Alt-right groups had heard about how he murdered "Cartel member" Arturo Maciel and then bravely fought in a gun battle on the border with the Lord's Predators militia. They saw him as an outlaw patriot.

He'd even heard that people were taking pilgrimages to Sheehan Ranch, just to see where he was from.

And Ryan's murder of two black inmates in the library had gotten him all kinds of love from the Aryans.

Ryan didn't kill them because they were black. He killed them because they were sodomites. But he let the Aryans believe what they wanted to believe.

See, Ryan only ever really had a problem with the Muslims and the Mexicans. But prison broadened his horizons.

He learned all about other races and cultures and why he should hate them, too.

His new cellmate was a thirty-three-year-old man from Arkansas named Tom Wiggles. The first thing Ryan noticed about him was how smooth his skin was. Not even by prison standards. It was smooth like a woman's. His front tooth was chipped and black from a "run-in with the darkies" and it made him look ugly whenever he smiled. Ryan was slightly disturbed by his Nazi tattoos, but other than that, he seemed alright.

"It ain't your fault," Tom Wiggles told him. "You've been misinformed and conditioned by society to be ashamed of who you are. To feel inferior."

Tom taught Ryan about white genocide and how the Holocaust never really happened and that the swastika is really an ancient symbol of good luck. How slavery was a blessing to black people.

"If it weren't for white people, they'd all still be shitting in huts, getting AIDS or hacking each other's limbs off back in

Africa. And how do they repay us?" Tom said. "White people are the only race in the world made to feel guilty for their achievements. If everyone else had their way, they'd erase our culture off of the face of the earth. Why should 'white pride' be a bad thing? Why can't we be proud of who we are? It's bullshit."

Tom Wiggles made Ryan feel good about himself. Built his confidence. Made him feel safe.

Ryan didn't know it, but he was falling in love.

Cal had offered to pay for Lance's trip to Los Angeles, but the old man had refused. This was something he had to do himself. Lance landed in LAX, got his rental car and took the 210 East to the 15 North toward Victorville. The fresh air, sunny sky and picturesque mountains felt like an affront to his depression.

He arrived at FCI Victorville. The building was grey and the land was barren.

The sun was not bright here, it was oppressive. The air was dusty and dry and everything was either dead or dying.

Lance found the place comforting. A companion to his misery.

He sat in the prison visitor's room. He thought he would feel anxious, but he didn't. He was just so fucking tired. Like a fighter who had lost the fight three rounds ago, but refused to go down.

Ryan bounced into the room and sat across from him behind the reinforced glass window. He picked up the receiver.

"Hey, grandpa," Ryan said, smiling. "How's the Bronc?"

Lance cleared his throat. "They, uh… they took it as evidence."

"If it ain't one thing, it's another." Ryan sat back, relaxed. "You know what I was thinking about this morning? How in seventh grade I used to get picked on by these two older kids. Bobby Walker and Chucky Malone. You remember them? Big, brick shithouse motherfuckers. I didn't like to let on, but I was scared of them. That's when my dad taught me how to shoot. He taught me, just like you taught him. The S&W .38. The AR-15. Man, oh man, did I love that Colt 1911. Turned out I had an eye like a peregrine. Once those boys saw that, they didn't mess with me anymore. 'God created man, but Sam Colt made them equal.'"

Lance wrinkled his brow and fought against the pressure behind his eyes. "Arturo didn't deserve what you did to him."

Ryan looked bewildered. "Grandpa. Of course, he did. Of all people, I would have thought you would understand. This is war."

"The ATF has some questions for you. Just answer them."

Ryan shook his head and crossed his arms. "You're on the wrong side of this, Grandpa."

"It's the right thing," Lance said. "If you help them, maybe one day, many, many years from now, you'll be allowed to come home."

"I am home. We are home."

"Ryan. If you don't help them, you'll spend the rest of your life in prison."

"The Lord is our home. It was a long road, but I did not turn back. And I've arrived. All praise be to Him. Do you not see what he has done?"

"What has he done?"

"They know our name again. The Sheehans are kings again."

A tear streaked down Lance's cheek. "Please, tell me you're sorry for what you've done."

Ryan was silent.

"I didn't know how to be there for you," Lance said. "I didn't know how to face what I didn't understand. I told myself you were okay, but deep down, I knew it was a lie. I was scared. I was a coward. Please, tell me you're sorry for what you did to Arturo."

Ryan leaned forward and looked Lance in the eye. "I'm proud of what I did." He slammed down the receiver.

"I'm sorry, Ryan," Lance said. "I love you."

But Ryan was gone.

Lance took the next flight home. The pain came with him. He considered going on a tear, but he figured, Why waste the whiskey? Drink wouldn't do it. Not for pain like this.

He walked out to the broken-down, old horse barn. The place was the nightmare of a once beautiful memory. He remembered the time when it was alive.

After Vietnam and the mental hospital. Twenty years old and trying to restart his life. The horses were his support group. He cared for them and they cared for him.

And then he met Maddy.

Hiding up in the hayloft and dropping from the ceiling through the hay bale trap doors, scaring the wits out of her. She'd scream and then they'd laugh so hard that they couldn't breathe.

Two years before their marriage and forty-three before the cancer diagnosis that would take her away from him.

They suffocated on laughter together.

Lance walked through the dark stalls. They quartered only shadows now. But the ghosts were still there.

Splash and Magic and White Christmas.

And they both cared for the horses. He and Maddy together. He was no longer alone. And the war was quiet for a time.

Apollo, Guinness, Connery.

And then Michael was born and he held his tiny body and he thanked God he survived the war to create this life.

And then Michael grew and he went to war and he came home and Lance thanked God again because no father should outlive his son...

The nights were getting cold now. The chill embraced him. He could see his breath. But he wasn't ready to leave. Not yet. Just a few more minutes with the horses.

Lucky Line, Debutante, Silver Rain.

And Toby. Beautiful brown thoroughbred.

His first date with Maddy. He took her out on Toby.

When he let her ride alone, Toby ran away with her and she panicked and fell and landed in a thick patch of mud. He was petrified. He ran to her and he reached out and she grabbed his wrists and pulled and he splashed into the mud with her and they asphyxiated on laughter again and that was where they had their first kiss. Dolled up in mud in a time before cell phones.

It was the happiest moment of his life.

He slid a single bullet into the chamber of his revolver and put the barrel to his head.

The gunshot echoed through the empty stalls.

31

W hen Ryan heard about Lance's suicide on the news, Lance wasn't even the story. "Grandfather of Ryan Sheehan dies of self-inflicted gunshot wound."

The news used it as an excuse to spout off firearm suicide statistics and advocate for more gun control.

Fucking liberal media. Puppets of the ZOG. Ryan knew that his grandfather had been assassinated.

But why? What was he getting too close to?

There were so many questions whirling around Ryan's head that it hurt. The ATF had sent Lance to find out about the AR-15. Had they killed him because he failed? Or had his grandfather come on his own? Hoping to get Ryan to talk, so that he could make a deal with the ATF? And that scared them.

Of course. It was all an act. The investigation, everything. They didn't want the truth to come out. And they killed Lance because he was asking about the gun.

But who exactly were they? The Federal gun-grabbers, or maybe the United Nations? And what did they not want Lance to find out?

It all came back to the AR-15.

The pastors were in custody and Ryan's big event was indefinitely postponed. Someone didn't want him talking. That was the only explanation.

Ryan thought about his grandfather, dying alone. Agonized over what his final thoughts might have been.

He had to do something. Fight back. Honor his grandfather.

But he didn't trust that Fed cunt.

So he called Cal.

"You're not a Fed," Ryan said. "And I need answers." He was sitting across the prison glass from Cal. "I want to get the people that murdered my grandfather. I want them to suffer. To remember my name."

Murdered?, Cal thought. Jesus, the kid was batshit. But he played along. "Tell me what you want me to do," Cal said.

"They don't want me talking about the gun. They don't want the truth to come out."

Cal didn't bother asking who exactly Ryan believed "they" were. "If we find the man who sold you the gun, we can get to the truth," he said.

Ryan nodded. "I was only meeting him to buy a couple of rifles and handguns. He threw in the Bronco for a grand. It was like he was trying to get rid of it."

"Was this one of the rifles he sold you?" Cal showed him an evidence photo of the AR-15 used on Arianna. Ryan nodded.

"You're sure?" Cal asked.

"AR-15 A4. Iron sight. Custom grip. I never forget a gun."

"What can you tell me about him?"

"White. Mid-thirties. I think he was a veteran."

"What makes you say that?"

"Just the way he talked. How he carried himself. He used military time, and he had this sort of calm about him. My dad was the same way. My grandfather, too. It's not a peaceful calm. More like the calm in the eye of a storm. Do you know what I mean?"

Cal knew exactly what he meant.

"And then there was his face. It was all fucked-up," Ryan said. "Looked like a bullet scar. He was missing his right eye."

Cal called Pat Roti and asked him to search the VA's records for Caucasian men in their thirties with high-caliber bullet wounds to the right sides of their faces.

The next day, he was back in the visitor's room. He held his iPhone up to the glass partition and scrolled through patient headshots. A slideshow of faces, freshly-stitched and red and swollen.

After a few minutes of this, Ryan sat up in his seat. "That's him," he said.

"You're sure?"

"Hundred percent. That's the guy."

The man that Ryan identified was Wyatt Lemieux. He was an ex-marine, wounded in Iraq. A sniper had taken off half his face.

After coming home, the VA noted "psychological instability characterized by stark anti-government sentiment." He declared himself a sovereign citizen and disappeared. No current address or way to contact him, just a P.O. Box in Oregon where he had his disability benefit checks sent.

Disgruntled, homeless vet. Could have targeted Arianna because of who her father was, Cal thought.

Cal didn't tell Miranda. He was working on a kill order. There would be no arrest, no trial. Just a fucking execution.

He drove through the night, stopping only for a bottle of water and bag of beef jerky at a gas station outside Salem.

Lemieux's post office was situated in a quiet, old logging town near Mount Hood National Forest. VA benefit checks arrived on the fifth and twenty-first of each month. Cal arrived on the morning of the twenty-third.

He spent the day casing the place. Maybe he would get lucky and Wyatt hadn't picked up his check yet.

Afternoon became early evening and Cal's hope of catching Wyatt at the post office faded with the daylight. Just before closing, Cal entered the post office building and asked the very friendly Asian woman behind the counter if he could please speak to the manager.

The manager, a tall, spindly man, asked Cal how he could help him.

Cal explained that he was a private investigator attempting to track down a person of interest. "This man," he said, laying down the VA photo of Wyatt Lemieux.

The manager's body stiffened. "You need to be careful," he said, his eyes fearful.

"You know him?"

The manager nodded slowly.

"You know where I can find him?"

"You need to be careful," he said again, more clearly this time. "People don't go there."

"Go where?"

"Head up the road and make a right on Mayapple. Follow it until you see the sign."

"Thanks." Cal said, turning to leave.

"If you go in, you're on your own. No one will rescue you."

Cal nodded and walked out the door.

He drove down Main Street, made the right on Mayapple Road and cruised through a thick blanket of firs. Visibility was virtually zero. Only the road ahead of him and behind him. The deeper he went, the more secluded it became. There were no houses here. No addresses. The gravel road gave way to a dirt road, which dead-ended at a large sign, spray-painted on rusty sheet metal.

SOVEREIGN LAND
KEEP OUT

The sign obviously had no legal standing. Wyatt had claimed squatter's rights on public land and the locals had decided to just leave the crazy bastard alone.

Cal opened the back of his Range Rover and equipped his FN SCAR. He scanned the perimeter of the forest. It was a strategic nightmare. The bramble was thick and the terrain sloped upward through dense trees and jagged boulders. There were countless hidden vantage points for the enemy to hide, observe and orchestrate an ambush.

The threat was invisible and, therefore, everywhere.

Cal was not a religious man, but there was a line from the Bible that always seemed to come to his mind in these rare moments where he was compelled to feel powerless.

If I perish, I perish, he thought.

Then he stepped across the border, a dark tourist in this so-called sovereign land.

He trod lightly, noting the places where Wyatt had hid bear traps beneath the fallen foliage.

Wyatt had chosen an ideal location. The geography was designed to keep people out. It was a treacherous and unfriendly uphill hike over rock-strewn turf and through heavy thickets. Progress was further impeded by felled trees and well-placed rockslides, blasted from the faces of boulders.

And, of course, Cal had to constantly be on the lookout for any other booby traps Wyatt might have left.

It was a slow and frustrating adventure, to say the least. But once Cal penetrated the perimeter defenses, both natural and manmade, the forest opened onto a mirror-blue lake, which reflected the trees and mountains and heavens above with the theatrically of 35-millimeter film.

The beauty was simply surreal.

Cal was seduced by the lake. He stood on its bank and

though he knew it was foolish, he set down his rifle and sat on a felled log.

The wind off of the water massaged his face and scalp with cool fingers and the warm fragrance of pine needles in the sun seemed to embrace him. The calm cooing of a distant loon slowed his pulse rate like a metronome, sending him into a peaceful state of quasi-hypnosis.

Sovereign land.

He thought about the old-timer shooting himself in his own barn.

He felt both sad and happy for him. His war was over. That's the only way it ever really ends.

But here. He could see himself living in a place like this. At least for a time.

The noise was quieter here. The nightmares soft-focused.

He wondered why he hadn't yet taken the same way out as the old-timer.

Cal believed that most human beings were really at least two people. There was the one that wanted to live and the one that wanted to die. They were constantly wrestling one another. In most people, the one that wanted to live dominated.

They strengthened it with various nutrients: possessions, work, status, antidepressants, meditation, exercise, family, love, religion.

To Cal, all of that was Novocain. Safety and security were what sent you sleepwalking to the grave.

He needed an even match between his two selves. Life against death. God and the Reaper.

Homeostasis was a synonym for comatose. War was life.

The sun was high in the sky and soon it would be setting. Cal tore himself from his lakeside meditation, picked up his rifle and resumed his mission. He figured Wyatt's camp would be somewhere near the water.

He scanned the wooded horizon. His gaze landed on a cliff

perched like a limestone fortress over the clean, calm lake. He set off in that direction.

By the time he arrived at the cliff's base, the sun was setting. He was on unfamiliar terrain and the path ahead was likely to be rigged. Darkness was not his ally. Not to mention that by now, it was highly likely that Wyatt had spotted him, wherever he was.

If I perish, I perish. Cal began the ascent.

The path upward was hazardous. Wyatt had hidden a half dozen grenade tripwires, which Cal managed to spot and avoid.

The summit was dark. He scanned the area with his thermal scope.

No signs of life. Which didn't mean anything. If Wyatt were a trained soldier, he would know how to hide his body's infrared signature.

Cal pushed through pines into a clearing where the soil was soft. Tomatoes, beetroot, onions, black beans, potatoes and cabbage sprung from the earth in neat rows.

Up ahead in the piney bramble, Cal discerned a well-camou-flaged bivouac constructed from moss-covered sticks and branches. He raised his rifle, squared up to the target and, leaning forward into his gun, crept toward the shelter.

Just outside the entrance, he pulled the rifle into his shoulder and firmly grasped the gun's fore end, locking his elbows close to his body and holding the muzzle in position.

The rifle was under tension. His sights were slightly shaky, but that was okay. He was prepared for rapid shots at close range.

One last time:

If I perish, I perish.

And he dashed into the bivouac.

His body recognized the feel of the tripwire and reacted before his brain had a chance to process that the bivouac was bait and he had walked into a trap.

He was controlled by reflex, not logic when he leapt blindly and the bivouac exploded in a fireball.

He fell twenty-five feet into a rocky gorge. His ribs cracked and his left forearm splintered. The jagged midsection of his ulna bone leered at him through red flesh.

It took him twenty minutes to get his shirt and belt off. Another thirty to find a rigid stick and fashion the splint.

He surveyed his surroundings. He was at the bottom of a vase. The only way out was up, but the cliff walls protruded outward. He wished he had broken one of his legs instead because it was physically impossible to climb out with only one arm.

It was the third time he'd walked into an ambush. First the kid in South Central, then the old-timer in Arizona and now this. Was he losing his edge? Or did part of him want this? He wasn't suicidal. But being suicidal wasn't the same as having a death wish. Maybe part of him believed he belonged down here.

Beaten, broken, dying.

It was over. He would be discovered and killed by Wyatt or, more likely, left to die alone down there. He figured dehydration would kill him before infection. Eternal rest atop the cliffs of sovereign land.

He laid his battered body down in the dirt and laughed because he was remembering the Parable of the Ass.

"I tried. I really did. They took me off the case. Everything is so fucked. Please..." Miranda's voice cracked. "I need you." She ended the call.

Miranda paced around the loft. She thought about smoking a joint, but this was a form of anxiety that drugs couldn't anesthetize. It was existential anxiety. She felt like she was suffocating. She had to get out.

She took the elevator down to the lobby and held the building door open for a UPS delivery man. If she hadn't been so upset, she might have realized that nine o'clock was awfully late for a delivery or that the sun was down and there was no reason for the delivery man to be wearing his brown UPS hat.

Well, maybe one reason. The scar.

A hideous deformation on the right side of the delivery man's face, which she tried not to stare at.

She lowered her eyes and nodded politely as Wyatt thanked her for holding the door, then she continued on her way.

32

M iranda didn't have a destination in mind, but she ended up in East L.A. The neighborhood she'd grown up in. Although it was mere miles from where she now lived, she hadn't been back in many, many years. Aside from some of the old madre y padre shops being turned into Dominos or T-Mobiles, the area was essentially the same.

She stood across the street from the house she had lived in with her mother and sisters. She wondered how many times it had changed hands after they left. Rusty chain-link guarded the yellowed lawn. A stolen shopping cart was parked on the cracked ribbon driveway leading to a carless garage overflowing with detritus. The austere, neglected grey stucco face of the home stared at her like an old man with Alzheimer's. Had the lights in the windows not been on, she'd have thought the place abandoned.

She decided it better not to idle. People could get the wrong idea around here.

As she walked through her old neighborhood, the memories came flooding back. First kiss, first joint, first fight, first run-in with the cops. The place was like a portal to her younger self. She thought of all the things she wanted to tell that girl. But most of all she wanted to assure her that everything would work out. That angry, frightened, confused girl, trying to be tough. She wanted to hold her the way she wished her mother would have if she hadn't been constantly working for their survival. She wanted to tell her that it would all be okay.

But would it? Because, if she was being honest, she was still angry, still frightened, still confused.

Who killed Arianna? And why was this church so intent on covering it up?

It didn't matter. They were too rich and too powerful. She'd fooled herself into believing she'd gotten out of East L.A. The expensive loft, the gun, the badge, the *respeto*. It was all just a wonderful delusion. The reality was, you only rise as high as they let you. The powerful do not give away their power willingly. They may have dressed her up real nice but she still was and always had been one of the voiceless.

Wyatt had no problem picking the lock to Miranda's apartment. Once inside, he quietly slid on a pair of nitrile gloves, pulled out his Beretta M9 and cleared each room.

Once he confirmed the place was empty, he holstered his handgun and got to work. He opened her MacBook and pressed a plastic slide onto the Touch ID. He was in.

He plugged a flash drive into the USB port and searched the Mac's hard drive for anything related to "Arianna Barros." He dragged and dropped the search results to his flash drive.

Next, he unscrewed the bottom of the WiFi router. He was about halfway through installing the bug when he heard someone unlocking the apartment door.

He placed the router down. There was no time to put it back together. He barely made it into the closet as the apartment door opened and Camilla entered.

"Miranda?" she said.

He peeked through a crack in the closet door. Watched her place her purse and keys down.

Camilla was directly between him and the exit.

Camilla looked at her iPhone and tilted her head. She punched her fingers against the screen, then released a heavy sigh. She moved to the WiFi router and checked the wires.

Wyatt spotted a fire escape by the back window. His way out.

As Camilla examined the router, its bottom fell out.

"What the hell?"

Camilla shrugged off the router, placed down her cell phone and unraveled her hijab. It felt good to let her hair down. She moved toward the closet. Wyatt crouched like an animal ready to pounce.

Camilla opened the closet door and Wyatt sprung forward and wrapped his hands around her neck.

He hadn't planned on killing anyone. So he'd cut off air flow long enough for her to lose consciousness, then make his escape.

He never would have guessed the 5'5" Muslim woman could have driven her knee so hard into his balls.

He gasped for air, lost his grip and keeled forward. She drove a low kick into the meaty sweet spot just above his knee, then drove a straight fist into his nose.

Cardio kickboxing three times a week at Equinox. Better stress reliever than Xanax.

Blood trailed down his face and his eyes teared. Through fuzzy vision, he watched Camilla sprint for the door.

Fuck. This was supposed to be clean.

As Camilla opened the door and stepped out, Wyatt raised his Beretta M9 and fired three shots into her back. Her body toppled into the hallway.

Wyatt grabbed Camilla's cell phone, then rushed out the back window and down the fire escape.

Union Station was just over one mile from Miranda's apartment. He legged it. Bought tickets on the first train to Chicago.

· · ·

He came into her home. Her fucking home. Now this was personal.

Camilla was in surgery and Miranda was on the warpath.

CCTV outside of Miranda's building had caught the battered, scar-faced man in the UPS uniform fleeing the scene. They also had his blood, taken from Camilla's knuckles.

It didn't take long for them to ID him.

Naturally, Miranda wanted to crucify the prick, but Scarpelli wouldn't let her anywhere near it. Conflict of interest.

"This is my investigation," Miranda protested.

"No. Arianna Barros is your investigation," Scarpelli said. "We don't know that this is that."

"What the fuck else would it be?"

"Plenty of people have grudges against ATF agents. There's no evidence linking this break-in to your case."

No evidence, she thought.

She drove out to Victorville and used her ATF credentials to get an emergency interview with Ryan. It was just after two AM. The guards dragged a sleepy Ryan into the interview room, where Miranda simmered.

"I'm going to show you a series of photos." Miranda spread a half-dozen headshots across the table. Wyatt's was among them. She asked Ryan if he saw the man that sold him the AR-15.

Ryan smirked. "He didn't tell you."

"What?"

"Cal came to see me. I told him who I bought the gun from. And here you are, asking the same question. I was right to trust him."

Miranda gritted her teeth. "Do you see that man in any of these photos?"

"Go fuck yourself."

It took every bit of willpower she had to keep herself from knocking his teeth out.

Before she left the prison, Miranda checked the visitation log and saw that Cal had visited Ryan.

As she sped south down I-15, she tried Cal's cell. The number was disconnected.

Shady fucker.

No positive ID from Ryan meant she couldn't link Lemieux to her case. Which meant she'd be left on the sidelines as far as he was concerned.

She was frustrated. Not just because in her gut she was sure that this Wyatt fucker was connected to the conspiracy. Whether it was through the church or Marco Barros or both of them or neither, she didn't yet know.

But there was something else.

She couldn't quite put her finger on when or where, but she was sure of it. She'd seen his face somewhere before.

Miranda got back to Los Angeles in time to sit-in on Scarpelli's briefing.

Wyatt Lemieux. Afghan War vet. PTSD. Drifter. Regular on the gun show circuit. Considered armed and dangerous.

"After the assault, the suspect fled to Union Station and boarded a train to Chicago. The suspect also stole the victim's cell phone. GPS places him on the train."

"It's too obvious," Miranda said. "He's trying to throw you off the scent."

"Miranda—"

"I know, I know. It's not my investigation. But, come on. Who doesn't know that cell phones can be tracked?"

"He's spooked. We are not dealing with a stable mind here."

"What about the PO Box in Oregon?"

"Doesn't it make more sense for him to run than to go back to where he could be recognized?"

Scarpelli had a point. After the briefing, Miranda spoke privately with him in his office.

"Look, let's say he is just some gun nut with an axe to grind against the ATF," she said. "How did he get my home address?

What about the slide with my thumb print he used to access my computer? This guy is a homeless vet and he's trying to install a bug on my router? Someone is helping him."

"That's certainly a possibility," Scarpelli said. "But we won't know until we catch him." He put a comforting hand on her shoulder. "I appreciate that you want this man brought to justice, but you're too close to this. Take some time off. Let us do our job."

Oh, she'd take some time off, alright.

She'd have to sit this one out, there was nothing she could do about that, but it was still a free country. If she wanted to take a vacation up to Oregon, her boss couldn't stop her.

Of course, because she'd be going in a non-official capacity, it meant she wouldn't have back-up should things go tits up, but the way she saw it, that motherfucker had come into her home.

Now she was going to come into his.

33

C al dreamt that he was slipping down one of those tube water slides and it kept getting smaller and smaller around him until his arms were pinned by his side and his nose pressed against the fiberglass, and as he approached the end of the slide, the slide didn't spit him out, but just dead-ended and he was stuck down at the bottom unable to move with the water pooling and he couldn't breathe.

The rain woke Cal and he was surprised to find that he was still alive.

It was dark and the heater breathed warm air into the car. The wipers swiped cold pellets of rain as they clacked against the windshield. Miranda followed the road that the post office manager mentioned. He said that a private investigator had been around, asking the same questions. He said he'd tell her what he'd told him. "Be careful."

Up ahead, the road dead-ended and her headlights illuminated the Sovereign Land sign.

She pulled over and parked next to Cal's Range Rover.

She got out of her car and shone her flashlight through the Range Rover's windows. Once she was satisfied that the vehicle was empty, she checked her weapon—a Glock 22—and marched past the sign and into the dark woods.

The rain was heavy and cold and it soaked the leaf-littered ground, revealing the bear traps. Seeing them, Miranda tensed and gripped her Glock and her flashlight.

Be careful.

There is no past. There is no future. Only the present.

Cal was caught between two worlds. His broken body was lying in the rainy chasm, but his soul was drowning in a claustrophobic, dead-end slide at the bottom of the world.

What if this was life after death? An eternity of cold, dark suffocation. Paralyzed. His muscles and mind in a state of perpetual atrophy.

No one to hear his screams. Not even able to scream. Was this his punishment? For his arrogance. His superiority. In believing that he was god of his own universe.

Had he been wrong all along? Was morality, in fact, real?

If it was, then that meant...Cal was evil.

He'd never seriously entertained the concept before, always so sure, so certain of his infallibility, but now the thought rippled through his mind and his chest like exploding planets.

I am evil. And now I am drowning. Someplace cold and dark.

And he prayed for someone to fish him out.

Then he saw the figure on the cliff above, looking down at him.

When the Four-train arrived at Chicago Union Station, Scarpelli was waiting with a team of ATF agents. They promptly boarded, surrounded Wyatt's cabinette and announced themselves. When they kicked in the door, they found the room empty.

Camilla's cell phone was left on the untouched bed.

Scarpelli released a heavy sigh. "He was never on this train. He played us."

Wyatt descended the rocky ravine on a rope. A scoped M16 rifle was slung across his shoulder. He approached Cal and stood over him, eyeing him like dinner.

Without a word, Wyatt bound Cal's hands and tied the rope around his chest. Then he grabbed Cal's FN SCAR, climbed back up the cliff and yanked Cal up after him. The pressure of the rope against his cracked ribs was agonizing. Cal fought his body's urge to pass out from the pain. Once he had been lifted out of the ravine, Wyatt led Cal at riflepoint through the cold and rainy woods.

Fifteen minutes later, they arrived at the foot of a large, moss-covered boulder. Wyatt tore away some bramble at its base, revealing the mouth of a cave.

Wyatt ushered Cal inside with his rifle barrel and sat him on the cool, hard ground. There was a tent and manmade fire pit. A clothesline and electric lantern and books and marble notebooks. Lots and lots of marble notebooks, which Wyatt began to gather.

"I had to come back. I couldn't leave without my writings," he said as he stacked the notebooks. "My work is not yet done."

He piled the notebooks into a tattered military duffle, then he turned to Cal. "Who sent you?"

Cal said nothing. So Wyatt stomped his shattered forearm. Cal shrieked.

"He did, didn't he?"

Cal gritted his teeth.

Wyatt examined Cal's FN SCAR rifle with a knowing grin. He aimed down the rifle's sightline.

"Special Ops assholes with your fancy Belgian guns," Wyatt said. He tossed the rifle aside. "Gimme the M16 any day. That's a real American soldier's gun."

He gripped his carbine and glared at Cal. "I assume you've been trained on how to resist enhanced interrogation? I could waterboard you until you're brain-damaged and I still wouldn't get anything, would I?"

Wyatt slung his M16 over his shoulder and slowly unsheathed a KA-BAR knife. "Men tend to get more cooperative when they see parts of themselves being removed."

Wyatt front-kicked Cal onto his back. "What did you give for your country? For what?" He dangled the knife. "This is what they do. They take you apart, piece by piece, until there is nothing left."

He brought the knife to Cal's nose.

"We should both know better, but we never learn, do we? He sent you. He betrayed me," Wyatt said, looking Cal dead in the eyes. "You can never trust a politician."

Cal writhed as Wyatt pressed the blade into his nose.

The bang was loud. Even at their distance.

A grenade going off somewhere. A tripwire.

The weather had saved her.

She'd noticed the first tripwire when wet leaves downed by the heavy rain caught on the line, exposing the trap. After that, she was meticulous about every step she took.

As she approached the base of the cliff leading up to Wyatt's camp, a mudslide dislodged another one of Wyatt's tripwires and caused it to detonate.

Fuck, Miranda thought.

That was bound to get somebody's attention.

Wyatt grew up on Westerns. Gunslingers and lawmen and savages.

He threw a noose over a tree bow and strung one end around

Cal's neck. Then he piled three stones at Cal's feet. He yanked the other end of the rope, lifting Cal by his neck. Cal stepped up onto the wobbly tower of stone and struggled to balance himself and avoid hanging to death.

Wyatt tied off the other end of the rope. Then he placed his electric lantern nearby and left Cal like that.

Wyatt hiked to the top of a wooded ridge and found a clear vantage point with lots of cover. *Just like deer baiting,* he thought.

He knelt down and aimed through his M16's scope at the first stone in the pile beneath Cal's feet. It was about a hundred-yard shot.

He inhaled and held his breath and squeezed the trigger.

The first stone flew off of the pile and Cal pointed his toes to balance himself on the next one.

Still got it, Wyatt thought.

Miranda heard the rifle shot and jogged in that direction. She took long, high strides and stayed on the lookout for more tripwires.

She crouched in the brush. There was a light up ahead. She slowly crept forward and saw Cal strung up and out in the open.

The veins in his neck bulged and blood spots were forming in his eyes.

He looked at her, dying.

She stared back at him from the bramble.

Another gunshot.

The next stone flew from Cal's feet.

Miranda localized the sound. Approximated the shooter's location and distance.

Cal's toes were barely grazing the final stone now. His face was blue. But still, she stood there. Unmoved. Watching him suffer.

Cal's wide, bloodshot eyes pleaded. *Help me. Help.*

Wyatt scanned the area with his crosshairs. No one coming to help.

He aimed his rifle at the final stone and pulled the trigger.

The stone flew from beneath Cal's feet in a small explosion of dirt, leaving him completely suspended by his neck. Miranda watched the life drain from his face and grimaced. She raised her Glock and shot out the electric lantern.

Wyatt switched his M16 to full auto, squeezed the trigger and fired blindly into the dark valley. 5.56x45mm rounds shredded the landscape like paper. His muzzle flashes like signal flares on the dark ridge.

Wyatt reached the end of his clip, slung the rifle over his shoulder, pulled out his Beretta M9 and marched toward the clearing.

He found Cal's body lying in the dirt. Whoever had shot out the lantern had also cut him down, but they were too late from the looks of it.

"Federal agent." The voice came from behind him. "Drop your weapon and slowly turn towards me."

Miranda trained her Glock on Wyatt's back. Wyatt stood there, frozen.

"I won't tell you again."

Wyatt dropped his handgun and turned to face her.

Miranda glared for a moment in disgust at the gruesome face staring back at him. The same face she'd seen beneath the UPS cap. Her finger tensed on her trigger.

But then she remembered Arianna. Camilla would have wanted her to arrest him.

"Drop to your knees and place your hands on your head."

Wyatt complied.

She circled behind Wyatt, pulled zip cuffs from her pocket and reached for his wrist. Wyatt quickly reached back, grabbed her forearm and flung her over his shoulder. Her body slammed onto the ground in front of him. He swiftly pulled his KA-BAR knife and drove it toward her chest as—

Gunshots tore into Wyatt's back.

He fell forward onto Miranda. Dead.

Miranda heaved Wyatt's heavy body off of her and looked at Cal, lying in the dirt, holding Wyatt's M9 handgun. He had emptied the clip.

"I needed him alive," she said.

34

I *don't know who I am.* The thought cycled through Cal's head like a bullet in a cylinder. He had never asked questions. Always followed orders. Always been the good soldier. And now he was lying in a hospital bed and he had no idea why.

I don't know who I am. I don't know anything.

That motherfucker knows something, Miranda thought. She was sitting by Cal's bedside. *That motherfucker knows something that he's not saying.*

"Why didn't you tell me about Wyatt Lemieux?" she asked, her eyes narrow. "Why did you kill him?"

She wanted to grind his face into asphalt until it looked like ground beef and he screamed everything he knew.

Look at her looking at me, Cal thought. *There's a sadist behind those eyes.*

She was thinking about letting me die in those woods. She watched as I hung from that tree. Even after she knew where the shots were coming from. She waited. Watched me suffer. Enjoyed it.

"I saved your life," he said, his voice hoarse and his throat rope-burned.

"And I saved yours," she replied.

Camilla was in a coma because of this motherfucker. Miranda had held the door for that scar-faced lunatic, looked him in the eye and let him into the building, so he could break into her apartment and shoot Camilla. Cal had known then. He had known about Wyatt and said nothing.

Cal had heard about how Wyatt broke into Miranda's apartment and put her lover in the hospital.

Heard about how the woman was Muslim and her family, who didn't know she was gay, now had a lot of questions.

"You killed Wyatt. Now we'll never be able to prove who was really behind this," Miranda said.

Cal had seen the other side. The darkness, the confinement, the despair. He knew he was responsible for the pain that Miranda was feeling right now. Knew it was because of him that the woman she loved was in critical condition. And he wanted to help.

"Wyatt said he'd been betrayed," Cal said. "He seemed to think that he and I were working for the same person."

Miranda stared at him, unsure.

"He said, 'You can never trust a politician.'"

In nature, when food is scarce, an animal will sometimes eat their own young. The runt. The one with the least chance of survival in a predatory world.

There is no such thing as a pacifist wolf. Eat the weak, so that the strong can survive. Is it natural or pathological?

Marco Barros was polling well. Gun stocks were up. The church's influence was growing. In six years, Marco would have a real shot at the presidency. Means, motive, and opportunity.

Camilla died at around two AM in her hospital bed. Miranda didn't have the strength to be angry. She didn't have the strength to be anything anymore. She had nothing left. And nothing to lose.

Eat the weak.

Eat the strong.

Eat them all.

Marco Barros hadn't been seen in DC for three days and nobody had been able to get hold of him. It had been eight months since Arianna's funeral, but it just didn't seem to end. It was constantly on his mind and the anxiety was taking its toll.

What if somehow the truth came out? His life would be over.

He was at his breaking point, so on Friday afternoon, he told his people he would be out of town and out of contact for the weekend, then he got in his Mercedes and drove eight hours to the Adirondack Mountains. He was still in his suit when he walked into the general store. He bought everything he needed. Hiking pack, boots, clothing, tent, freeze-dried food, water. Then he rented a canoe and took off into the wild.

He didn't cry at Arianna's funeral and the media had noticed. Some of the sleazier tabloids and conspiracy theory websites even had the audacity to suggest he didn't grieve the passing of his only daughter. Or even that he was involved in her murder.

But no one took those claims seriously. So, at least there was that.

Everything he remembered about that day was filtered through a cocktail of booze, benzos, and insomnia.

How had it come to this?, he remembered thinking at the funeral. How had he lost sight of himself so much that he was burying his own little girl?

Jimmy McClean was there for him through it all. Comforting

him. Doing anything he could to ease Marco's suffering. He'd always looked up to him like a father.

He didn't know Marco's secret. That made him feel guilty. This kid who idolized him, but didn't know what he really was.

He wondered what McClean would feel if he knew the truth.

Disgust? Disillusionment? Hate?

McClean was a good kid, close with Arianna. He kept a strong face for Marco's sake, but Marco was sure that he took her death hard. He made a mental note to go easier on him.

On Marco's first night, he made friends with a family of ducks on Long Lake. A mother and two ducklings. He sat outside his tent and tossed them chunks of freeze-dried lasagna.

The next day, he canoed up the Raquette River through firs and pines and tall grass. Every now and then he'd pass another canoe or kayak and wave to its passengers. It felt good not to be recognized. Like he was someone else.

Anyone but himself.

He made Raquette Pond by sunset. A vibrant orange glow reached across the crystal blue pond. There was so much beauty in the world. Why had he squandered his chance to be a part of it? For what?

Power? Money? Comfort?

He could stay here, unknown, living in the wild for the rest of his days. Like the ducks. Never set foot in DC again.

That night by his campfire, he remembered being back in Edinburg, Texas. He couldn't have been older than ten. He and some other boys were camping in the desert just outside of town, cooking marshmallows on metal skewers.

A boy named Roberto found a desert toad and kicked it into the fire. The toad tried to leap out, but Roberto kept kicking it back in.

Marco and the other boys just watched. Eventually, the toad's skin was charred and black, but its throat pouch still bulged with air. Burnt black and crispy, but still alive.

Then Roberto impaled the animal with a skewer and roasted it like a marshmallow.

Marco didn't stop him.

As he watched the toad burn with the other boys, he didn't feel much of anything.

What was wrong with him?

He came from a hard place full of hard people with hard lives. A place of wolves. Of suffering.

To be soft was to be a *maricón*. A faggot.

The church saved him. Plucked him out. Wealth and comfort, or maybe age, had softened him. Because looking back now, he pitied the toad. But he also knew that he was no longer that ten-year-old boy.

The boy could watch the animal burn and feel nothing, but that boy was also incapable of holding the toad to the flame himself.

Adult Marco could burn a village down, while mourning the inhabitants.

The next morning, he canoed back to Long Lake and looked for the family of ducks, but couldn't find them, so he didn't get to say goodbye.

When he got back to his Mercedes and checked his cell phone, he had dozens of missed calls and voicemails. He ignored them.

He called Arianna's mother. After their divorce, she insisted that he call her by her full name, Cecilia, and not his pet name for her, Ceci.

But in his heart, she remained Ceci.

They hadn't spoken at the funeral. Or after. They still hadn't spoken about Arianna.

"Marco?"

"Hi."

"Where the fuck are you?"

He loved her like a sister.

"The Secret Service has been harassing me," she said. "Elián is freaking out."

"I'm sorry about that."

After Arianna's murder, DHS had assigned him protection, which he'd rebuffed. His going AWOL for three days must have ruffled them.

"I'm fine," he said.

"Good for you."

He wondered if she knew who the man she married and divorced really was. He wanted to tell her he loved her. He just couldn't love her in the way he should have. The way she deserved. He wasn't capable.

He wanted to cry. But he couldn't.

They came from the same place. She never left. And he knew what he would sound like to her.

A *maricón*.

He wanted to talk about Arianna.

"I don't know why you're calling me," she said. "Arianna's gone. There's no reason for us to speak anymore."

She hung up.

He called everyone he needed to call to let them know he was okay and continued to refuse Secret Service protection. He could handle a firearm better than any agent and he kept plenty around. By the time he arrived back at his house in Georgetown, it was almost five o'clock, so he poured himself a scotch.

His mood had changed on the drive back from the Adirondacks. He had tried to see the glass as half full. Ceci was right. Arianna was gone now. There was nothing left tying him to his old life. The final traces of the dirt-poor beaner from an immigrant border town were gone for good.

He was Marco fucking Barros and in six years he'd be president.

ve now is the future, he told himself. *I can be happy again.*
le.

Delusions are like pills we take to get us through the day. He poured himself another scotch.

Then Miranda walked into his study with a gun in her hand.

35

M iranda had anticipated some kind of security presence. If he had Secret Service, she knew she'd be fucked.

She'd cased the house all weekend with no sign of Barros. Then she heard the Senator had gone missing. On the third day, just when she was about to give up, Marco pulled his Mercedes into his driveway.

He was alone. He didn't even lock the front door. This was a man who either thought he was bulletproof, or didn't care if he died.

She stood in the entrance to his study with her Glock in her hand.

Marco glanced around the room, looking for answers that weren't there. She was alone.

"Wyatt Lemieux is dead," she said.

"Who?"

"The man that shot your daughter. He was killed four days ago. Just before you went AWOL."

"I had no idea."

"Sure you didn't."

"Are you insinuating something?" He glanced at the Glock in her hand and swallowed hard. "I'm sorry. What are you doing here? I thought you were taken off this case." He reached for his cell phone.

"Don't fucking move," she said. "Don't even breathe."

Gun in hand, she walked further into the study and sat in the chair across from his desk. Marco remained standing with his palms raised in front of him.

"Wyatt pulled the trigger, but we still don't know why," she said, keeping her Glock trained on Marco. "The truth died with him."

"Agent Lopez. I have no idea what the hell is going on. This is the first I'm hearing about any of this."

She tossed a file onto his desk. "Read it."

Wyatt opened the file, perused it and ruffled his brow.

"Donations to WorldMovers going back forty years. First five grand a month, then ten, then twenty. Forty years. That's around the time you entered politics. One can argue that it was your religious base that won you your first election. You got rich together. The church built you and, in return, you built it."

Marco was indignant. "What does my faith have to do with any of this?"

Now she placed a photograph of Kilo on his desk. The color drained from Marco's face.

"Do you know this man?"

He looked at her, his eyes wide. "No."

"Are you sure?"

"Yes."

"He was a minister at your church. A member from the very beginning."

"I don't know him." Marco's gaze was cloudy and distant. He had to sit down. "I mean, I've seen him before, yes, but I don't know him."

"What is his name?"

"Victor." He cleared his throat. "Victor Cortes."

"And what did he do?"

"What do you mean? You just said he was a minister."

"You know what I mean. What did he do?"

Marco lowered his head.

"Victor Cortes was a pimp," Miranda said. "He trafficked underage girls from Mexico."

Marco closed his eyes and exhaled.

"Some church," Miranda said.

She leaned back in her chair, keeping her Glock trained on Marco. "There's one thing that's still bugging me. Would anyone really stage a mass shooting, kill their own daughter, just to gain support?"

Marco's eyes shot open. "What?"

"I mean, that shit's one step below Hitler-level crazy. Not to mention, risky. 'Pro-gun Senator's daughter killed in mass shooting.' Couldn't that backfire?" She leaned forward. "But you had that handled, didn't you? 'Senator Barros Reaffirms Support for Gun Rights in Wake of Daughter's Shooting.' You came out both the victim and the hero. Your poll numbers went through the roof. It really was a brilliant piece of political maneuvering.

"The one thing I can't figure out. What was she running from? The two of you weren't speaking. She moved across the country to get away from you."

"It wasn't like that."

"What did she know? Why did she have to go?"

He shook his head. "I have no idea what you're talking about."

"What were you afraid might come out? You're gearing up for a presidential run in a few years. You can't have any skeletons in your closet. So, you're cleaning house. First, Kilo, then Arianna—"

"I don't have time for this," he said, rising from his seat.

"Then me."

"What?"

"Sit down."

"You're not going to shoot me."

She fired a shot over his right shoulder, blasting out the bay window behind his desk. He flinched and ducked back into his chair.

"You sent Wyatt Lemieux to bug my apartment—"

"I don't even know Wyatt Le—"

"Shut up."

Marco bowed his head like a scolded schoolboy.

"You sent Wyatt Lemieux to bug my apartment," she continued. "He messed up, and he killed someone very close to me. So yes, Senator Barros. I am going to shoot you. But first I'd like you to tell me why you had these people killed. We'll start with Kilo."

"I didn't even know he was dead."

"Did he have something on you, Senator?"

"No."

"Do you like them young?"

"Never! I would never! For Christ's sake, I have a daughter!" Tears began to stream down Marco's face.

Miranda froze for a moment. She wasn't expecting this. Then she hardened and raised the gun. "Last chance to make peace with your maker."

Marco only cried more.

Miranda sighed. "Goodbye, Senator."

"I was only twenty-three. Running my first campaign for city council. Church every Sunday. I was a goddamn virgin, saving myself for marriage… I didn't… I would never…"

He paused and caught his breath and said, "There was no woman." And then he swallowed hard and said, "His name was Raul."

Miranda flinched.

"I met him at the church. We became friends," he said. "I didn't know he was working for Victor."

"And you and Raul…"

Marco cringed. "Victor filmed it. Me with him. I didn't know until after."

"The church blackmailed you? For forty years?"

"That's not what they called it. Pastor Beck called it 'repentance.' I paid my monthly tithes and he kept my sin in confidence, he said, to help me stay on the path of righteousness. For a while, I even believed it.

"But then, Arianna started getting mixed up with the church. She had no idea, of course. She met the church in Texas and thought they were legit. Their youth wing was run by Pastor Zach."

"Valorous."

Marco nodded. "I tried to protect Arianna. I didn't want her involved with the church, but she took it all wrong. Her mother and I had recently divorced. I'd moved to DC and I wasn't around much. I think she thought I didn't want her to be a part of my life and that's why I was pushing her away from the church. So, she moved to Los Angeles to work for Valorous. Now they didn't just have me, they had my daughter. The tithes got higher.

"I didn't want to say those things. That I was pro-gun just after my daughter had been shot. I was under pressure from the NRA. I was down in the polls and Billy Beck wasn't ready to lose his proxy in the Senate. If I lost the NRA's support, it would have been over for me. It was play ball or else…"

"Or else what? Why not come clean?"

Marco shook his head.

"It would ruin me. People see a thing like that, they assume it's what you are."

"Isn't it?"

"It's not who I am. It's just something I did."

Delusions are like pills we take to get us through the day.

"Did you and the church have any sort of falling out? Can you think of any reason that they would hurt your daughter?"

He shook his head. "Face it, Agent Lopez. It was just a random shooting. There is no grand conspiracy. These things happen every day in America."

"If you really believe that, then why did you hire the private investigator?"

Marco drew his eyebrows together. He looked genuinely confounded. "What private investigator?"

Cal sat on the park bench in Maguire Gardens. The sun was down and the usual miscreants were out, but they didn't bother him.

Animals can sense a predator.

It was a warm night and if it weren't for the stench and soullessness of the city, this might have been a nice place. There was no denying that Maguire Gardens was aesthetically pleasing with its fountains and manicured lawns and cypress trees.

It was a place where people literally pissed on culture.

They'd filmed the famous scene from the film *Heat* around here, where Robert DeNiro, Val Kilmer and Tom Sizemore shot it out in the streets with M16s in broad daylight.

Cal always thought it was funny how people viewed DeNiro in that film. Like there were two heroes. Pacino, the cop, and DeNiro, the criminal. Two sides of the same coin.

Cal doubted Michael Mann saw DeNiro's character as a hero when he wrote and directed the film.

Not the same coin, not even the same wallet.

Cal scanned 5th Street. Remembered DeNiro haphazardly unloading his M16, not giving a fuck.

Why do we worship sociopaths? Wish fulfillment, Cal thought.

People are always so preoccupied with right and wrong. Reward and punishment. They are all guilt-filled pimples on the ass of an imaginary God, ready to burst.

What shrinks called sociopathy, Cal called freedom. His lack of conscience was his superpower. But that was all before he saw the end of the slide.

Prison hadn't done it, mindfulness meditation hadn't done it, flipping burgers hadn't done it.

Only death could. That dead-end fucking waterslide at the bottom of the world.

Cal could feel himself growing a conscience. Like an open nerve he couldn't protect. It worried him.

The black Mercedes pulled up. Pat Roti got out of the back and sat next to Cal on the bench.

"It's done," Cal said. "The man who killed Arianna Barros was a mentally unstable vet named Wyatt Lemieux. I tracked him to Oregon. He's dead now."

"Our client will be pleased."

"Lemieux pulled the trigger, but he wasn't working alone. You need to tell Marco Barros."

"Why would I do that?"

"The Senator hired us to get justice for his daughter. He should know that there may be others out there that were involved."

Pat Roti shook his head. "What did I tell you about asking questions?" He looked Cal in the eye. "Who said we were working for Marco Barros?"

Pastor Zach had been spending a lot of time at the beach since he made bail. Praying morning, noon, and night. Praying on Arianna. Praying for the continued prosperity of himself, his family, and his church. And also praying for the Federal Agent that was trying to destroy him.

Special Agent Miranda Lopez.

"Forgive her, Lord. She knows not what she does."

But part of him wanted to punish her for her arrogance. This nonbeliever, this sullied Philistine, challenging him. God's chosen.

I have an army of young people who would follow me off a cliff, he thought. *What does she have?*

He was pretty sure she was gay. And for whatever reason, that made him feel more secure.

She doesn't deserve my wrath, he told himself. *She deserves my pity.*

If only he could get her to accept Jesus as her personal lord and savior.

This was one of the ways his church was different from his father's. The gay thing. His father preached that being gay was a sin. But Pastor Zach accepted homosexuals (although sex before marriage was a sin and marriage was, of course, only between a man and a woman).

Pastor Zach believed in the inclusion of marginalized peoples.

If only he could make Miranda see that he wasn't the enemy. Because he did know something. Something about Arianna. Something he hadn't told anyone. Arianna had shared the information with him in confidence and he felt duty-bound to keep her secret.

He was sitting on the beach. The sun was warming him like God's love. He remembered going to the beach as a boy. Standing in the sand and feeling so small before the vast and endless ocean. He didn't feel so small anymore. He always knew he was destined for great things and he was on his way. He knew God was testing him with the lesbian Fed. And he knew he would triumph.

His cell phone rang. "Hi, Dad," he said.

Billy Beck was in his Houston office. "I just spoke to the lawyers. All charges have been dropped."

"Praise Him," Pastor Zach said.

"I also met this federal agent."

"Well, thankfully, we don't have to worry about her anymore."

"Don't be a fool, son. That woman is like a dog with a bone. I saw it in her eyes. She is heathenish," Billy Beck said. "I need you to make her go away."

"How?"

"There's got to be something you can give her."

"Dad. She's just one woman. We have the Lord on our side."

"She's not worth our time."

"But we haven't done anything wrong."

"That doesn't matter. It's the appearance of impropriety. Valorous is a WordMovers Church. What hurts you, hurts us all. Your little MTV parish is quickly becoming a stain on our brand."

Pastor Zach thought of Arianna's secret. He couldn't betray her. "I can't do it, Dad."

"Then I can't have your church associated with WorldMovers."

"Are you kicking me out?"

"That's up to you. When a limb is infected, you heal it or you chop it off. Your church is infected, son. Pray on it. Show me how to treat you."

Billy Beck hung up.

It would mean betraying Arianna's confidence, but if it meant finding Arianna's killer, who could still be out there, a danger to society, wasn't that the greater good?

That night, Arianna visited him in a dream and told him to cooperate because she didn't want to see his church suffering the way it was.

The next day, he called Miranda.

Jimmy McClean had some fucking explaining to do.

Miranda had called him after her little meeting with Marco Barros and demanded to know why the Senator had no idea that Cal was working on his daughter's case.

"Frankly, I didn't have faith in you," McClean said. "After the way our first meeting went, can you blame me? I didn't want to upset Marco, so I hired Cal to supplement the investigation behind his back."

"Supplement, my ass," Miranda said. "You hired a hitman."

"Wyatt Lemieux killed Arianna, and twelve other people,"

McClean said, his voice choked with emotion. "He got what he deserved."

There was a moment of silence on the line as McClean composed himself. "I need you in DC to debrief, so we can finally close the book on this thing," McClean said.

"I can be there the day after tomorrow."

"You have something more important than this?"

"Yes," she said. "I do." She hung up the phone.

Miranda was on her way to Reagan National. She had to be in Los Angeles by morning.

Pastor Zach had called. Said he had information relevant to the Arianna Barros investigation that he would only give to her in person. He wanted to meet at the beach.

Miranda wasn't in the habit of letting persons of interest call the shots, but the way she saw it, Huntington Beach beat some sweaty interrogation room. Besides, Miranda was dying to gauge how much Pastor Zach knew about his father's dirty little secrets regarding Marco Barros. So, she let the egomaniacal little shitbird have it his way and met him on Humboldt Beach just after midday.

He wore his hair up in a man-bun. Distressed denim cutoffs, a black bleach tie-dyed sleeveless shirt and a wooden crucifix around his neck.

Christianity sponsored by Urban Outfitters, Miranda thought.

He smiled at her. "Thank you for coming."

"I'm on a very tight schedule, so go ahead and tell me what you need to tell me."

Pastor Zach pursed his lips. "I want you to promise to stop attacking my church—"

Fine," Miranda said. "Now, let's hear it."

"But not just that." Pastor Zach said. "I want to show you. Before I tell you what you've come to hear, I need you to feel the Holy Spirit."

"What the hell are you talking about?"

"Agent Lopez." He looked at her, all wide-eyed and stupid,

and he gestured to the ocean. "Will you allow me to baptize you today?"

You gotta be fucking kidding me, Miranda thought. *I took the redeye for this shit?* "If you're withholding information relevant to this case, I'll get you on obstruction."

The pastor smirked. "You think that all religious people are crazy, don't you?" he asked. "You think that I'm crazy?"

"Pastor." Miranda gazed at him with steely eyes. "I think you just made me even more determined to fuck your shit up."

She turned and stormed back toward her car.

"My father has threatened to kick me out of his church if I don't make you go away," Pastor Zach said.

Miranda stopped and looked back at him.

"But that's not why I'm doing this," he said.

"Then why are you?"

"Because it's what Arianna would want." He gestured again to the ocean. "It will only take a moment, and then I will tell you Arianna's secret."

Fuck this preacher. She marched back to her car and unlocked it, pulled her gun and holster off of her belt and sealed them in the glovebox. Then she locked the car and went back to Pastor Zach.

"Let's get this over with," she said.

He smiled and took her hand. They waded out into the ocean until the water was waist-deep. Pastor Zach gently placed his left hand on her upper back.

"Miranda Lopez. In the name of the Father, the Son, and the Holy Spirit," he said, putting the palm of his right hand on her chest. "I baptize you." He shoved her backward.

The water warbled in her ears like muted ghosts. It tasted like the salty earth. It stung her eyes. She saw the murky figure of the pastor standing over her. The gravity of his hand pushing her down, down, down. She suddenly felt like she was at her own funeral.

We were buried therefore with him by baptism into death...

Her Catholic childhood came flooding back into her mind. The mystery of faith, which Miranda always figured as the man upstairs passing the buck on all the bad shit that happens to people who don't deserve it.

God never took responsibility, not for the bad shit, so either God was a deadbeat or he didn't exist.

Miranda was a pious child, so she chose to believe the latter.

She saw Camilla's face, dancing, ethereal and aqueous, and she gasped for air and tried to call out to her. Tried to rise, but Pastor Zach forced her down hard with all of his strength.

She would not escape. She would not escape this. She was drowning. Drowning in Camilla.

She screamed and fought and waves and bubbles splashed upon the surface, but still Pastor Zach held her down.

Her lungs were raw and she felt the ocean on her skin, particles and molecules that existed before the beginning and would persist long after she was gone, and she was suddenly aware of how small she was not just in this immense ocean, but in a universe of black holes and dark matter and so, so much she didn't understand and somewhere out there was—

Camilla.

Arianna.

She never knew them, never understood them, only assumed she did. *Who was I to look down on them for wanting to feel connected to something greater?*, she asked herself. For seeking comfort in something spiritual in this cruel and unsolvable Rubik's cube of life?

Pastor Zach pulled her up just before she passed out. She choked on air and shoved him…and wanted to hug him until his ribs broke and his guts spewed out his mouth.

I know nothing, she now knew.

The mystery of faith.

· · ·

Miranda sat in the sand with the pastor, still wringing the salt water out of her hair.

"She had only just begun talking about it to my wife and me," Pastor Zach said. "But there was a reason Arianna joined my church. A reason why she came out to L.A.

"She had been sexually abused. It started when she was very young. Eight years old. And it continued for years. That is why she gave her life to Christ."

"Who?" Miranda asked. "Who was abusing her?"

"I'm afraid we didn't get that far."

"What makes you think this has something to do with her murder?"

"I don't know that it does, but when I heard the news about her death, it was the first thing that came to my mind," the pastor said. "Whoever this person was, she seemed very afraid of them. So much so that she wouldn't give us any hint as to who they were."

It didn't matter because the second Pastor Zach told her why Arianna came to L.A, it clicked and Miranda knew.

Miranda knew who had Arianna killed and why.

36

M iranda walked across the beach toward her car.

She decided that Pastor Zach didn't have anything to do with Arianna's death or the blackmail of Marco Barros.

She got behind the wheel of her car. Beyond her windshield, the sky was painted in deep reds and purples and oranges as the sun set into the ocean.

Her thoughts returned to Camilla. And through Camilla, back to Arianna.

Poor Arianna. A young girl. Taken advantage of and abused. Seeking comfort and relief wherever she could.

"Why did this happen to you? Why?"

It was no longer just a material question; it was an existential one. Because she now knew who Arianna's true killer was.

Miranda thought about Arianna before the church. The wild child. Pot, alcohol. All before the age of fifteen. It all fit with someone trying to block out trauma. Her mother, with her drinking problem. A long streak of one sleazy boyfriend after another. Could have been any of them.

So, how was she so sure that it was Elián Killington that molested Arianna and then had her killed?

It wasn't the porn. Although that was certainly an indicator.

It was the American flag that hung over his bed with the blue stars and the red-and-white stripes running vertically. It was the handmade "EXEMPT" license plate on his beat-up Honda.

Elián Killington considered himself a sovereign citizen. Just like Wyatt Lemieux.

Arianna flew the coop. The statute of limitations wasn't up on rape or child molestation and Elián got nervous. She left home, and he could no longer control her, and if there is one thing that pedophiles are obsessed with, it's control.

So he reached out to Wyatt, whom he knew from the movement, and had her taken care of. The extra bodies were, what? Camouflage? Make it look like another mass shooting, rather than a hit?

Right now, all of the evidence was circumstantial. Not enough to prosecute.

So she decided right then and there that she would get the details of why he did this, even if she had to beat it out of him.

Maybe McClean was right. These people didn't deserve to be arrested.

She sat in her car for thirty minutes, watching the sun go down.

Crying an ocean.

She didn't sleep on the plane ride back to DC. All she could think about was bringing down Elián. Her meeting with McClean was at nine AM. He'd want to be debriefed about Lemieux and he'd probably also want to try and smooth over his hiring Cal without the Senator's knowledge, but Miranda was over it. Hell, she was with him.

McClean was just making sure Arianna got justice. By any means.

Which was why she was sure he would help. Now that Lemieux was dead, Scarpelli and the powers that be would try to close the investigation. She needed McClean to convince them to keep it open. She needed him to advocate sending her down to Texas, so she could nail the sovereign citizen pedophile prick.

She had to establish a definite link between Elián and Wyatt. She was sure she could find it, all she had to do was dig.

It was going to take resources. Federal law enforcement viewed the sovereign citizen movement as the most immediate domestic terrorist threat. Worse than fundamentalist Islam, worse than white supremacy. Sovereign citizens interpreted the Constitution selectively, as best suited their needs. They made their own laws. She couldn't believe she hadn't seen it earlier. She was too dead set on nailing the church and Marco Barros. A sovereign citizen was just the type of person who would have an entire apartment complex shot up because a girl ran away from him.

Miranda sat across from McClean in his office with all of its framed photos. She still thought the room was ridiculous, but somehow viewed him as less of a douchebag.

Jesus fucking Christ. There was that sensation again. Liking him. Not in a romantic way. Camilla was still way too fresh. It was more of a maybe-in-another-life type of feeling.

"His name was Wyatt Lemieux. He was a drifter," Miranda said. "A regular on the gun show circuit. Bought and sold firearms out of his Bronco."

"The Bronco he sold to the Sheehan boy?" McClean asked.

"That's correct."

"I wonder why he sold it?"

Miranda shrugged. "He was a disturbed individual."

"I suppose people that carry out mass shootings don't think in logical ways that you or I could comprehend," McClean said.

Miranda was just about to bring up motive and the possibility that he had been hired by Elián when McClean's pretty, young secretary peeked her head in and said something about so-and-so needing five minutes of his time.

McClean apologized to Miranda and asked if she wouldn't mind waiting.

"No problem," Miranda said.

McClean followed his secretary out of the office.

Alone now, Miranda took in the plethora of photographs. Oprah Winfrey, Barack O'Bama, Steven Spielberg, Elon Musk, Lebron James, the Pope who'd resigned and the current one.

Before, she saw these photos as a monument to his vanity. Now she realized it was something else. Something she could understand. Jimmy was an orphan. They'd both had tough childhoods and they'd both beaten the odds. They were both young, rising stars in their fields. They both knew the feeling of having to overcompensate for their lack of breeding and experience, so she could forgive the showy photographs. It wasn't arrogance. It was insecurity. After all, everyone said Jimmy McClean was the future. It is a lot of pressure having so many expectations cast upon you. Colleagues secretly rooting for you to fail.

Miranda's phone rang. "Hello?"

"Agent Lopez. This is Pastor Kelly from Valorous Church."

Pastor Zach's wife? Miranda cringed.

"I heard you spoke to my husband about Arianna?"

Miranda wasn't sure how to answer. Where was this going? Her eyes scanned the shelf of photos as she thought of how to respond.

"How can I help you, Pastor Kelly?" she said.

"We never knew the name of Arianna's abuser."

"Yes. Your husband said as much."

"But Arianna did tell me something about him. A nickname."

Her gaze landed on the photo of McClean and his soldier buddies posing with their M-27s in Iraq. What Miranda thought of as "the Dick Pic."

"He had a nickname?"

"No. She did. Her abuser had a nickname for her."

Miranda's eyes focused. Then widened. She picked up "the Dick Pic." Squinted at it. There was a ginger soldier with a red mustache, a burly black soldier with a Travis-Bickle-style mohawk, a rat-faced soldier with beady eyes.

"What was it?" Miranda said.

Miranda knew she had seen the face before. At the time, she couldn't place where and it had bugged the shit out of her.

"Angel Eyes," Pastor Kelly said.

Posing just over McClean's right shoulder in the photo, his face not yet scarred, was Wyatt Lemieux.

"Her abuser called her Angel Eyes."

37

"'**A**ngel Eyes,'" Marco had said. "That's what Jimmy used to call her. 'Angel Eyes.'"

Miranda was remembering her first meeting with Marco. Those were the only words he said before Jimmy ushered them out.

Her palms were sweaty and she felt dizzy. She threw down "the Dick Pic" and rushed out of the office. She had to get someplace safe. Someplace she could think.

"No rest for the wicked," McClean said with a grin as he sauntered back into his office moments later. He stopped when he saw that Miranda was gone.

"Agent Lopez?" He scanned the room. "Huh."

Then he noticed one of the pictures on his bookshelf was lying face down. When he picked it up, his heart stopped.

How could he have forgotten about it? He knew the devil was in the details. So he had planned every angle. Every conceivable outcome. At least he thought he had.

His old buddy Wyatt Lemieux gazed back at him from the photograph.

Miranda had seen it. She knew what he had done.

McClean's face curled into a scowl.

Plain sight. The best place to hide.

Point, the devil.

Miranda double-bolted the door to her loft, paced the room with her sidearm in her hand and tried to work it all out in her head.

It was McClean all along. He'd killed her not just because she was a political liability, but also because she'd spurned him. She'd moved to L.A. to get away from him.

She remembered the disdain in McClean's voice when he talked about "that cult" that took Arianna away from him.

McClean killed her not only because he was afraid of what she might say, but also because he couldn't have her. Control her.

Few things are more dangerous than a spurned man with a gun.

But then what about WorldMovers? Billy Beck? Why was this church so intent on covering it up?

Sometimes the right answer is the most obvious one. The church was never trying to protect Arianna's killer. It just wanted the publicity from Ryan's confession.

The powerful only want one thing. More publicity = More followers = More money = More influence = More power. Power was what it was all about.

The one thing she couldn't figure out was how Cal fit into all of it. Why would McClean send his buddy Lemieux to kill Arianna, then hire an outside contractor to kill Lemieux?

Either way, Lemieux was right about one thing. He should have known. You can never trust a politician.

Her cell phone rang. It was McClean. She tried to sound casual.

"Special Agent Miranda Lopez."

"We didn't get to finish our meeting. I hope everything is okay?" There was no edge to his voice. It was friendly.

"Sorry about that. Something came up."

"Do you hunt?" The question was abrupt. It threw her off balance.

"I'm going quail hunting tomorrow. I'd love for you to join me."

Her mind raced. She had been so dazed in his office, so taken off-guard. She'd just set the picture down and fled. Her only thought was getting the hell out of there and getting someplace she could think. Shit. Why couldn't she have just stayed cool?

She cleared her throat. "I've never been hunting before."

"Oh, you'll love it. I have a shotgun you can borrow." He paused. "Shall we say noon? I'll email you the address." He paused again. "It's a private preserve. Very private." He paused one last time and then said, "The perfect place for a private conversation."

Loaded shotguns in the middle of nowhere with a sociopathic killer who wanted her dead. What could go wrong?

She'd figured out the who and why, but she still had one problem, and it was a big one. She couldn't prove any of it. The pastor wouldn't go on record, so she couldn't even prove the abuse and even if she could, McClean sexually abusing Arianna didn't mean he'd killed her.

By now, McClean would have destroyed the photograph. She could probably link him to Lemieux through military records, but there were over two hundred Marines in a company and no one was going to talk against a brother in arms. The military loved McClean.

The case was circumstantial. She'd need a hell of a lot more to bring down someone like McClean. She'd need a confession.

She knew it was risky, but this fucker was responsible for Arianna. For Camilla.

What did she have left?

She put it at fifty/fifty that McClean was planning to kill her. It was either that or he'd try to buy her off and, if she refused, *then* he'd kill her.

The wire was left over from the Mexico gunrunning operation. She'd never gotten around to returning it.

She drove down a remote Virginia road. Tall firs and thick woodland walled her in on either side. She wondered if this would be the last trip she ever took.

The road tapered off into a dirt path. Miranda eased her car around a bend and the woods opened up onto a large field of tall grass bordering a cornfield. She pulled into a dirt clearing next to McClean's gleaming gray Mercedes-Benz pickup.

McClean was waiting with one shotgun hanging by his side and another slung over his shoulder. Miranda stepped out of her car and he grinned at her.

"Glad you could make it," he said. "You won't need that." He was talking about her service weapon.

Miranda glanced at the shotguns, then turned her back and placed her sidearm in the glovebox of her car. She turned back and faced McClean.

He raised one of the shotguns. "I assume you know how to use one of these?"

Miranda took the gun and examined it. Mossberg 500 Classic pump-action. She checked the chamber. It was loaded.

McClean watched her with a thin smirk. Once Miranda was satisfied with her weapon, he said, "The quails are waiting."

Miranda followed McClean through the tall grass. The wind rustled the grass like ghosts.

McClean led her to a brushy shelterbelt, which lined an old, chipped fence at the edge of the cornfield.

"Upland birds love linear cover," McClean said, as he walked the fence line. "I'm going to flush them out."

Suddenly, a chaotic flurry of feathers and beaks burst from the shelterbelt. McClean raised his shotgun and took aim at the pair of quails in flight. He fired a volley and one of the quails fell to the earth. The other escaped.

"You didn't shoot," he said, turning to Miranda.

Her shotgun was levelled at his chest. "I didn't come here to shoot birds."

McClean lowered his head, turned and calmly trekked over to the felled bird. Miranda kept her gun on him the entire time. He picked up and examined his kill.

"Do you believe that people are animals?" He placed the dead quail in his hunting bag. "End of the day, we all do what we need to do to survive, right?"

He turned and stared down the barrel of her shotgun.

"So, how much?" he said.

Miranda paused. *Get him talking*, she thought. *Get him on the wire.*

"Before we discuss numbers, I need you to tell me everything. Leaving that picture out in your office was sloppy. I need to make sure there's nothing else you overlooked."

McClean studied her. He seemed unfazed by the shotgun leveled at his heart. He turned away and looked at the horizon.

"I don't think we are animals," he said. "I think we have souls. Animals aren't capable of love."

"Not all people are, either."

"Maybe." He smiled, but he wasn't happy. "I told you before, I've only ever been in love with one person my entire life. And now she's dead."

McClean turned back to her and met her gaze. His eyes shimmered. "I'll give you one million dollars," he said.

She knew that if she took the money, she would be implicating herself in the crime. They'd be in it together.

Miranda lowered her shotgun. "Start at the beginning. If we're going to do this, I need to be sure that I can protect myself. I need to know everything."

McClean took a deep breath. "It started with the church. WorldMovers or Valorous or whatever the fuck you want to call it. Marco recommended that I get close with them. He told me that their support could make or break me. Billy Beck had this man, Victor Cortes."

Kilo, Miranda thought.

"They told me he was a minister, but he was no minister," McClean said. "There was a girl. He introduced me to her." He paused. "I didn't know she was underage."

"Cortes recorded you. With her. And then the church tried to blackmail you," Miranda said.

McClean nodded.

Billy Beck tried to do the same thing to McClean that he had done to Marco forty years earlier.

"So I sent Wyatt to get the tape back." McClean cleared his throat. "By any means necessary."

McClean paused. "Wyatt told me that he 'talked' to Cortes and got the tape back. He told me Cortes didn't survive the 'talking to.' I was led to believe that the tape had been destroyed and Cortes was dead."

"But Wyatt lied," Miranda said. "He botched the hit and Cortes went into hiding."

McClean nodded. "His fucking pride. I think that's why he overreacted so much on the next job."

"Arianna," Miranda said.

McClean looked at the ground.

"You sent Wyatt Lemieux to kill Arianna," she said.

"I panicked. After the Cortes incident, I worried that if the church found out about Arianna, they'd use her against me, too. Wyatt was supposed to make it quick and painless. It wasn't supposed to happen the way it did. Those twelve other people. Wyatt did that all on his own."

"Why?"

"He was always a crazy son of a bitch. After he was injured in Iraq, he only got worse. He just fucking lost it. He killed all those people, then he sold the Bronco and the murder weapon and went off the grid. He knew you'd find him. He was looking for a fight. He didn't want the war to end.

"Then I found out Wyatt had lied and Victor Cortes was still alive and I realized I needed professional help. I had plenty of friends in the military and the CIA. They hooked me up with Cal."

"Cal cleaned up Victor Cortes and Wyatt Lemieux for you," Miranda said. "But if you knew it was Wyatt who killed Arianna all along, why didn't you just tell Cal right away? Why send him along to supplement my investigation?"

"I didn't know him, or this Pat Roti fella he works for. He's a shady bastard. Half a gangster, if you ask me. I didn't want them to know the details. The last thing I needed was to be black-mailed by those two on top of everything else. Find the person that shot Arianna and kill him. That was the extent of their knowledge of it."

"What about my apartment?"

"That was all Wyatt. Like I said, he was waging a one-man war."

"Bullshit. The guy's shitting in the woods, then suddenly he's lifting fingerprints and installing bugs on routers?"

"Wyatt lived the way he lived out of choice, not necessity. In the Marines, he specialized in communications and he'd been in the mercenary business for a while. Despite the way he lived, he had the know-how and the tech to bug your place."

Miranda wasn't sure if she believed him, but it didn't matter because in five minutes, she'd have the prick in bracelets.

"So you hired Cal because you didn't want us to capture Wyatt and risk having him talk. You didn't want to be connected to him in any way. You wanted him dead."

McClean looked back at the horizon. He wouldn't meet her eyes.

"And Lemieux was only supposed to kill Arianna. For you."

"Yes."

"Why? Arianna hadn't talked. What made you think she would?"

"That church was changing her." He was begging her to understand. "She wasn't the same person. The girl I loved was already dead and gone."

You mean the person you could control was gone, Miranda thought.

Miranda paused for a moment. Then she said, "Okay. I'll take your money."

McClean nodded, still unable to meet her eyes and they walked back to their vehicles.

Miranda handed the shotgun back to McClean.

"I'll wire the money this afternoon," he said.

Miranda turned to her car.

"I've answered all your questions," he said. "Will you answer just one for me?"

Miranda turned back to him.

"Did you really think you were going to get out of here with that fucking recording?"

Miranda thought she would be scared, but she wasn't.

She was pissed.

She turned and jolted the few steps to her car, swung open the door, dove across the console, whipped open the glove box, and reached for her gun. But it wasn't there.

She looked back and McClean hadn't moved. He was looking at her, grinning. Then he whistled.

Three men emerged from the cornfield behind McClean.

Miranda recognized their faces. She'd never forget them now.

The ginger had grown his facial hair. What was once a mustache was now a full mountain-man beard. The muscular black guy still had his *Taxi Driver* mohawk. And the rat-faced one had gained a little weight.

It was the rest of McClean's "Dick Pic." In the flesh. Armed with AR-15-style rifles.

The men surrounded the car. Miranda stepped out of the vehicle and faced McClean. "People know where I am," she said.

"I doubt that," McClean said. "The Barros case is closed. Scarpelli told you to stay away. Aside from your office, who else is there for you to tell? You don't have anyone left."

Miranda clenched her jaw and squeezed her fists.

"But even if you did tell someone where you were going, who's to say you ever arrived? No cell towers to place you out here. And I've got three witnesses that say you never made it."

Miranda looked at the scary men that surrounded her.

"You recognize my friends? We were a unit. Wyatt was one of us. And you killed him."

"What? No, I didn't," she said.

The Dick Pic Unit glared at her.

"I didn't kill Wyatt!" she said. "He did."

McClean tilted his head. The statement didn't seem directed at him.

That's when the bullet tore open Red Beard's throat.

After McClean's phone call, Miranda immediately went to see Cal in the hospital. She now knew that Cal had no idea he was working for McClean, but she still had no inkling of who this man was. What he believed or where his loyalties lay.

It seemed the more she learned about Cal, the less she knew. He was what he had always been. Dark matter. A mystery.

He was lying in his hospital bed, still all fucked up, when Miranda told him about McClean and the abuse Arianna had suffered and that by killing Lemieux, he wasn't getting justice for Arianna, but rather, allowing his true killer to get away with it.

Cal gave her nothing.

She didn't know the chill her words gave him. The dark memory of that dead-end waterslide.

She wouldn't know that Cal now understood the truth in Pat Roti's dogma. *The less you know the better.*

Because now that Cal knew, he was going to do something very fucking stupid.

Cal was hiding in a copse beneath camo netting, crouched behind an oak tree, with his eye to his rifle's scope, watching the pink mist spritz from Red Beard's neck from the bullet's impact.

Even with his arm in a cast and a couple Vicodin for his cracked ribs, Cal was a hell of a shot.

First one's free, he thought.

Now that he'd lost the element of surprise, the others wouldn't go down so easily. These guys were ex-soldiers. Trained and experienced. Cal really wished he was at a hundred percent.

Before Red Beard's body even hit the dirt, the Dick Pic Unit's training kicked in. They pounced behind McClean's pickup. 5.56×45mm bullets tore through the vehicle's frame like a can opener.

Miranda used the brief window to flee into the tall grass. Cal's gunshots kept cracking out. Laying down cover fire.

Behind her, the Dick Pic Unit fanned out and returned potshots into the copse. Their immediate objective was now to flush out the shooter.

Meanwhile, McClean watched Miranda crouch and scramble through the tall grass, hop the chipped fence, and disappear into the cornfield.

The shooting stopped as Mohawk and Ratface converged on the copse. The shooter was in there somewhere and they had him covered from either side.

The prick's an amateur, Ratface thought.

He was hidden beneath camo netting, but he hadn't used a camo-stock barrel. Average person would have missed it, but not a pair of guys who have been in the suck. They spotted it right away, sticking out from the camo netting like a boner at a high school dance.

Mohawk hand-signaled Ratface and they flanked either side and when they were in position, they opened fire and blew the sniper away.

Ratface tore off the camo netting and had a split second to realize the prick in fact was not an amateur before he burst into flames.

The camo netting was connected to incendiary grenades.

The sniper was elsewhere, but Mohawk would never find out where. One of Cal's sniper bullets split his head open.

McClean arrived at the edge of the cornfield and followed a trail of snapped and disturbed stalks.

The path became more obscure. Miranda must have seen that she was leaving a trail and become more careful.

He'd been led into the maze, then abandoned. He looked around and tried to pick up her trail again and that was when he thought he saw Father Balliston moving through the corn stalks.

He knew that was impossible.

Father Balliston was in hell now, but before that he was a priest at the boy's home.

He'd had a funny little game he'd play with all the children during Bible study. "Silly Thumbs." Father would chase the children around the yard. Oh, how they'd frolic and giggle. And when he caught one of them, "Silly Thumbs!"

Right in the seat of the pants. Right up the bum.

. . .

He couldn't track her anymore. The path was gone. He looked around, surrounded by dry corn husks. Dizzy and lost. He smelt the smell of burning nature. Raising his eyes to the sky, he saw black smoke.

The fire was coming.

McClean fled, snapping stalks, scratching through stickeljack. He knew that Father Balliston wasn't chasing him, but it felt like he was.

He was just a child. He was told it was just a game. That it was fun. His young mind was confused because it didn't feel fun. But a grownup said it was, so he laughed and played like the rest of the kids.

He'd always wanted to be a priest.

But then one night, Father Balliston took him into his bedroom and he didn't want to be a priest anymore.

He wanted power, so that he would never have to feel powerless again.

It was an easy transition to politics. The duplicitousness, the manipulation and hypocrisy were inbred in him.

The powerful took what they wanted. They took him.

Just like Father Balliston, Marco Barros saw in McClean something he could use. A Republican that could bring in the young vote.

Marco never knew that McClean was aware of his secret. His great big lie.

Every figure of authority McClean had ever known was a liar in one way or another. So what did that say about the highest authority, God Almighty?

The fire reached the cornfield and McClean was still lost. He squinted through itchy tears and choked on black smoke. Sticky weed clung to him like parasites.

. . .

He'd just wanted something pure in his life. He'd never known joy or warmth or compassion until he met Arianna. He was attracted to her innocence. Something he felt he never had. He took it from her, just like Father Balliston took it from him.

Dry yellow corn stalks quivered to ash around him. He couldn't see anymore. Flames cackled like this was the punchline to his life.

But despite Father Balliston. And despite all of McClean's personal misdeeds. He'd never given up on his Catholic faith.

He hadn't had the strength to go to confession. To speak aloud to God what he had done to Arianna.

He wandered blindly through the burning cornfield.

Praying.

He just wanted to get out and go to confession. To finally face up to God what he had done. And then, he would accept whatever fate was in store for him.

It took two days for firefighters to extinguish the blaze. The wildfire had scorched nearly a hundred acres and they'd recovered four bodies so far. Miranda didn't know if one of those was Cal's.

McClean survived the fire and was treated for smoke inhalation. He checked himself out of GW hospital before the warrant for his arrest was issued. He went straight to Saint Stephen Martyr Church on Pennsylvania Avenue, where he received confession. At around twelve-thirty in the afternoon, he returned to his home. The autopsy placed his time of death at approximately one PM.

The gunshot was ruled self-inflicted.

The weapon used was an antique Colt Peacemaker. It was the same gun Marco Barros had on display in his office.

Barros had retired from politics, placed his house in Georgetown on the market and disappeared into the Adirondacks or Finger Lakes or wherever the fuck somewhere.

D'Andre would get out of prison after serving 717 days.

Turns out a long-term federal investigation led to the arrest of gun control advocate and Democratic Chicago alderman Charlie Yu. The indictment charged Yu with trafficking arms from Muslim extremist groups in Indonesia to Chicago street gangs.

Star witness at his trial was this cat D'Andre.

He snitched and got out. On the streets, snitching usually gets a TOS (Terminate On Sight) put out on you. But D'Andre had an in with the guy that was running shit now.

They called him "Thrown," or "King," or "King Thrown." D'Andre knew him as Russ. After Russ gunned down AK, he earned control of both AK's and Spooky's turfs.

And of course, he protected his friend.

For his part, D'Andre wanted no part of the life.

There was a black Captain America now. D'Andre put his energy into writing. Comics, stories, screenplays. His only refuge. However finite. However temporary.

But isn't everything, D'Andre would tell himself.

Ryan wouldn't get parole. But it was all good.

He had Tom Wiggles. And a Ph.D. in Hate.

Even after everyone on the outside forgot all about him and the ranch went into foreclosure, it was okay.

Ryan would continue to believe in his Holy War. God would free him one day. The revolution was coming.

The evidence locker in the ATF's Los Angeles Field Office was like a firearms library, which housed anything from homemade single-shot weapons to anti-aircraft guns and everything in between.

Miranda pondered these creations.

She'd heard it said that the difference between a tool and a weapon is that a weapon's sole purpose is to incapacitate or kill other living things. Whereas, say, a knife could kill, but also cut a steak.

It was all in the intention.

The Colt Peacemaker that killed McClean was tagged and sealed in an evidence bag. She placed it on the assigned rack. Just a few feet away from the AR-15 that killed Arianna Barros.

She looked at the rifle and thought of D'Andre and Ryan and Lance and Lemieux.

Who else had the rifle met?

She scanned the racks and racks of guns. Witnesses all to the intentions of man. If only they had voices. The stories and secrets they could tell.

She remembered when McClean asked her if she thought humans were animals.

She didn't. But she didn't know if they were necessarily better.

Miranda went home to her empty loft. Camilla's hijab rested on a chairback. It still had the scent of her and even though each whiff brought more tears, she kept breathing her in.

She held onto the aroma and dreaded the day it faded away.

Then she laid her head on her pillow and though she would always ache for her, she was finally able to get some rest.

EPILOGUE

B randan hadn't seen the burger guy in a while.

He was more pissed than usual because he'd flunked out of the police academy for the second time after his uncle, who was a Captain with the L.A. County Sheriff's Department, pulled strings to get him another chance.

He had to wear long sleeves and put makeup on his badass hand and neck tattoos to hide them, which he wasn't too happy about. Then the other cadets razzed him because of his shaved legs, even though he explained it was for bodybuilding competitions. The final straw came when he couldn't finish the mile run warmup and a smaller cadet snickered behind his back, so he tried to fight him.

It was the first time anyone had almost gotten arrested their first day at the Academy.

So he wouldn't be a cop. Whatever.

He had finally gotten his Kimber 1911, the one like John Wick had, and he liked to show it off. He told people he did drive-bys and shit and tried to build a rep that would get him laid, but he'd also tried to get a date once by saying his mother died of cancer, so no one ever really believed anything he said anymore.

Fuck 'em. Fuck 'em all.

He knew he was wasting his life working in this restaurant. He was meant for great things. They'd all see.

He didn't know it then, but this was the moment the seed was planted for him to go out and shoot cops.

When the burger guy came in for his obnoxiously large order, Brandan was ruder than usual. He just pointed to the take-out trays and walked away.

Cal hadn't spoken to anyone since the fire. Not Miranda. Not Pat Roti. He hadn't let anyone know he was still alive.

He walked the aluminum catering trays of burgers out to his Range Rover and drove to Skid Row. A lone warrior on a lost battlefield.

He fed the wounded, and saved the last burger, but he could not find the Marine. He asked around and learned the Marine had OD'ed the week before.

Addiction is like Russian Roulette. A game to be played, but never won.

The Marine had finally lost.

Cal sat on the Marine's vacated milk crate. He thought about death and exorcism and demons.

He was No One. From No Where. Living only in the present.

But in this moment, sitting in the dead Marine's spot, he thought about his past. Paved in dead bodies.

Then he thought about the future. And that was when Pat Roti called.

"I don't want to kill people anymore," Cal said,

"You think you can just walk away? After what you did?" Pat Roti said. "There is pain in your future."

Cal hung up the phone.

Pat Roti would send men to hurt him. To try to kill him.

But that was okay.

Let them try.

Pain is inevitable. But he could choose to live.

The war would always be there.

Thanks for reading! If you loved my book and have a moment to spare, I would really appreciate a short review as this helps new readers find my work.

Cal will return in *The Padre*.
COMING SOON

For updates, visit:
Alex-Davidson.net

ACKNOWLEDGMENTS

I would like to thank my family, both immediate and extended, for always supporting me, even though I tend to ghost. Mark Schorr for his guidance. John Glenn for being a great creative ally and teacher. Bob Teitel for showing me that you can be successful in Hollywood and still be a stand-up guy. Russell Hollander for always believing in the idea for this novel. My brilliant cover artist, Slobodan Cedic. All the talented folks I had the privilege of knowing and working with at NYU.

And finally, you, the readers who took a chance on my novel.

ABOUT THE AUTHOR

Alex Davidson is a multi-award-winning screenwriter, play-wright, and author. He earned his MFA in Dramatic Writing from NYU's Tisch School of the Arts in 2009. He lives in Boston.

Learn more about Alex and his work at: Alex-Davidson.net

Made in the USA
Monee, IL
17 February 2021

60712601R00166